A **LAWSON RAINES** NOVEL

SHOOTING STAR

ALSO BY BRADLEY WRIGHT

A LAWSON RAINES NOVEL

SHOOTING STAR

Copyright © 2019 by **Bradley Wright**

All rights reserved. No part of this publication may be reproduced, distributed or transmitted in any form or by any means, without prior written permission.

Bradley Wright/King's Ransom Books
www.bradleywrightauthor.com

Cover Design by DDD, Deranged Doctor Designs
Shooting Star/Bradley Wright. -- 1st ed.
ISBN - 978-0-9973926-6-1

For Frank and Norma Wright
For Earl and Carol Holcomb
Thank you for the most wonderful parents a man could ask for.
And so much more.

Truth is stranger than fiction, but it is because fiction is obliged to stick to possibilities; Truth isn't.

— MARK TWAIN

Monsters will always exist. There's one inside each of us. But an angel lives there, too. There is no more important agenda than figuring out how to slay one and nurture the other.

— JACQUELINE NOVOGRATZ

A **LAWSON RAINES** NOVEL

SHOOTING STAR

1

"Who was he?"

It was not an easy question to answer. If it sounded as though his men were completely blindsided by one man, Clint would look weak in the eyes of his new employer. Not an option. If he acted as if it wasn't a big deal at all and it would be easy to handle, Marty Sloan might not trust him, might see through Clint's thin veil. Dangerous. Clint Hues had been doing this a long time, making people bend to his employer's will, but he had never been embarrassed on the job like he had been in that bar. The man who had interrupted his important conversation with an extraordinary amount of violence a day ago seemed like a ghost.

"Was he really just there having a drink and then he intervened?" Sloan asked, filling Clint's silence.

"I'm not sure. But I will find out."

Clint didn't usually tread so carefully, but Marty Sloan wasn't just the head of one of the fastest-growing movie production companies here in Los Angeles; he was the head of a crime family boasting decades of power in the city.

Sloan stroked his salt-and-pepper beard. He wasn't a

large man, but his posture suggested power. So too did the mansion they were sitting in. "I brought you in because of your reputation, Hues. You're known for results, and for your ability to get things done quietly. Have I made a mistake?"

"No, Mr. Sloan. I will make Victoria Marshall understand that the movie she's producing will be made by your studio. And whoever this man was who interrupted the meeting will not be a problem again."

"Look, Hues, I don't really care about the man who kicked your ass. I saw the bar's surveillance tape, your face is just as visible as his." Sloan stood from his chair behind his desk. His tone became more serious. "I care about the cops and the FBI that are most certainly looking at that same video right now, trying to figure out who he is but also, more disturbing to me, who the hell you are. I care about the person who hired the man who kept you from making Victoria hand the project over to me. And I care about all of it blowing back on me. Do you understand?"

Clint did understand. And he had already thought through all of these things. He'd been through pressure situations like this before. Right now all he could do was own up to the fact that he had jeopardized everything for Sloan. And assure him, through his actions, that it was all going to get cleaned up. It's what he did. He had danced around the police and the FBI on many occasions. They didn't worry him at all. He was far more worried about the man in the bar. He'd never seen someone fight like that. And the way in which he showed no mercy meant he was capable of a lot worse. Besides, if someone had hired him, finding out who the man at the bar was and making him talk would be the quickest way to that information. No one embarrassed Clint like that and got away with it. This business with Marty Sloan was important to him. But making sure everyone knew how hard Clint hit back when he got embarrassed meant even more for the longevity of his career.

"I understand, Mr. Sloan. And I assure you, none of this will blow back on you."

Sloan walked over and opened the door to his office. His seven-year-old son burst into the room.

"Are you done with your meeting yet, Dad? Dinner's ready!" The boy threw his arms around his father.

Sloan's wife hurried into the room, taking their son by the arm and pulling him back out of the office. "Sorry, Marty. Dinner is ready."

Sloan nodded, then spoke to his son. "I'm coming right now, little man. Go ahead and fix me a plate."

His wife and son rounded the corner back to the kitchen.

Sloan gave Clint a cold look. "You'd better be sure this doesn't blow back on me. If my family is affected by this, I'm sure I don't need to tell you what happens after that. However embarrassed you are by what this man did to you at the bar, you'll be begging me to take it that easy on you."

Clint wasn't used to someone talking to him like that. It wasn't easy, but he swallowed his pride. You didn't want to get on Sloan's bad side if you wanted to work in Hollywood again. On camera or behind the scenes. Ever since he was a teenager, Clint had made a living, not at all legally, in this underground criminal Hollywood world. It had taken him a lifetime to move this high up the food chain. One man in a bar wasn't going to be the thing that brought him down.

"I'll update you tomorrow," Clint said.

"Show yourself out."

Clint walked out of the multimillion-dollar mansion

with his tail between his legs. A feeling he wasn't used to, and one he wouldn't soon forget. His cell phone began to ring. It was Jenny, his longtime partner in crime. She was a computer genius, and Clint was hoping that after giving her the video from the bar she would be able to find something out about the stranger who'd caused all of his current troubles.

"Talk to me," Clint answered.

"How'd the meeting go?" Jenny asked.

"Embarrassing."

"Shit. Well, I think I have something that will make you feel better."

"Yeah? What is it?"

Clint could hear typing in the background.

"I ran facial recognition on the guy that kicked your ass," Jenny said, taking a jab at her longtime partner.

"Easy," Clint warned.

Jenny laughed. "You know I saw the video. It was pretty brutal—"

"Will you just get to it already?" Clint was fed up with the entire situation.

"Right, well, I found him."

No sweeter words could have been spoken.

"Good work," Clint said as he got in his car. "And what is this dead man's name?"

"Lawson Raines."

2
——————

"Lawson Raines?" FBI Agent Frank Shaw attempted to clarify.

Claudia looked up from her computer and eyeballed her partner. "Yeah. Why, you know him?"

Frank got up and walked over for a better look. "That's him?" Frank pointed to the video of the bar fight they had been called to investigate. Most bar fights were handled by the police. But when a high-profile filmmaker, a notorious Hollywood fixer, and some unknown man who wipes the floor with all of them, and then escorts said filmmaker out of the bar, the FBI often gets a call.

"He's a lot bigger than I remember, but yeah, that's Raines all right. I was in the Las Vegas division with him for a year over a decade ago. You didn't hear what happened in Vegas last summer?"

Claudia paused the video, right at the part when Lawson Raines grabs Clint Hues by the throat and throws him against the wall like a rag doll. "This isn't the guy who took down the De Luca family, is it? After serving ten years for the murder of his wife? That Lawson Raines? I knew the name sounded familiar."

"Yeah, same guy. He was a real stickler for the rules, real prick too. But I knew he didn't do it. The thing with his wife. All you had to do was see him with her one time to know he would never hurt her. But what the hell is he doing in a bar with a scumbag like Hues a year later? In LA?"

Claudia shook her head. "I don't know, but he sure isn't afraid to make enemies."

Frank sat down, removed the lid off his coffee, and took a sip. He was built like a stone wall. His short dark hair matched his dark eyes, and the lines on his face told stories of a never-ending war with crime.

"So what do we know?" Frank said.

Claudia tucked her medium-length brown hair behind her ear, closed the laptop computer, and gave him a shrug. "All we really know is that your friend Lawson interrupted one of the seediest guys in LA while he was clearly talking business with Victoria Marshall."

"Friend? Hardly. Do we know who Hues is working for?"

"He's a job-by-job man, as far as we know. No real long-time employment with anyone. I can look into who Victoria Marshall's been working with and see if there's any sort of connection. But right now I've got to get home and feed Molly."

Frank scoffed. "You act like that dog is your child. Maybe you should consider getting a life."

"You mean like you, Frank? Mr. Socialite himself? When is the last time you had adult interaction that wasn't with me or someone else here at the department? And hookers and bartenders don't count."

"They don't?" Frank stood. "Then it's been a long damn time for you too. That Tinder app doesn't count either."

Claudia smiled and flipped him the bird. "Go kill yourself with another one of your cancer sticks."

"That's not a bad idea . . . Listen, let's keep this thing with Raines between you and me right now, okay?"

"Okay, Frankie. Want me to try and run him down?"

"See what you can find about what he's been up to for the past year. If anything."

"Copy."

"Tell Molly I said hello."

Frank grabbed his pack of Marlboro reds from the desk and walked down the hall out the back door. Claudia grabbed her keys and followed. The sun had just set in LA and the temperature was around a perfect seventy-five degrees. Frank lit a cigarette.

"You following me?"

"Just needed some air." Claudia smiled.

Frank took a puff. "Strange that Raines is here. He's a Kentucky boy. He thought Vegas was too big, not sure how he landed in LA. He hates criminals too. So I'm really not sure why the hell he's making enemies with one of Hollywood's most infamous fixers."

"No idea, but the weather's nice."

Frank took another puff.

"Where's this guy been the past year?" Claudia said.

"Well, ever since news made it around the law enforcement community about what he'd done in Vegas last year, as far as I know, he hasn't popped up on anyone's radar."

"This is a hell of a way to make an entrance," Claudia said. "I'm assuming he doesn't have the same phone number as a decade ago. Verizon probably doesn't have a 'wait ten years to pay' plan."

"I suppose not. Might have his old partner's. She might

know where he is, but eleven years is a long time to keep the same number. Not sure I even have hers."

"I've had my number for longer than that. You should give it a shot."

Frank looked through the contacts on his phone. "Cassie Murdoch LVFBI. Still got it. Let's see if she'll answer."

Frank pressed call as he flicked some ashes to the ground. He put it on speaker so they both could hear.

"This is Cassie," she answered on the third ring.

"Cassie Murdoch?" Frank confirmed.

"Ding ding! Bob, tell him what he's won! Who the hell is this?"

Frank smiled. "You haven't changed a bit, still as fiery and sarcastic as ever. Just the opposite of Raines. Frank Shaw. Las Vegas FBI. Oh, about a decade ago."

"Holy shit. Frank Shaw? Haven't heard that name in a while. You still stealing other people's evidence and taking credit for your fellow agents' accomplishments?"

Frank's smile faltered. "And you're still jealous of us agents that actually get results, I see. Good, we'll skip the pleasantries."

"Sounds good to me, Frank. You called me, what the hell do you want? I'm late for dinner."

"When is the last time you spoke with your old partner?"

Frank dropped his cigarette and stepped on it, then walked over to his old Ford Crown Victoria. Claudia lingered behind him.

"Who, Jim Nash?" Cassie said.

"No, your *old* partner. The one you had before he went to jail."

"Lawson? I haven't spoken to him at all. What's it to you?"

Frank opened the door to his car. "This what we're doing? Fine. I read the papers. I know you helped him in Vegas with the De Lucas. He's in trouble here in Los Angeles and I want to help him."

"You called the wrong person, Frank. I haven't seen him since he took his daughter back to Kentucky. Good catching up with you, though. Hope you find what you're looking for."

Cassie ended the call.

"Well, sounds like you two were the best of friends," Claudia joked.

"Same old Cassie. She knows where he is."

"I'll see if I can find her then. At least we have a number to work off of."

Frank nodded. "Don't go stepping on that little dog now. You'll lose your only friend."

Claudia walked away. "Don't go dying of lung cancer. You won't be able to continue reveling in your own misery."

3

"No, Dad, you're saying it wrong!" Lexi Raines walked over to Lawson, who was sitting on the couch, grabbed his hand, and pulled him to his feet. Lexi was tall for her age, but her dad towered over her. "Maybe if you act it out, it will seem more real." Lexi moved him in a half circle in front of the fire. Lawson played along. "There, now . . . be sad."

"I'm not an actor, Lexi."

Lexi's shoulders slumped. "Dad, just try, would you?"

Lawson, though he thought his daughter was adorable, was growing tired of trying to help her run lines. He just wasn't good at it. His effort showed. He pouted his face to try to please her. He deepened a frown as far as he could make it go.

"What are you doing?"

"Being sad."

"You look like a clown."

"I feel like a clown."

Lexi tossed her script onto the coffee table and let out a deep sigh. "Forget it. I'll wait till Cassie gets here. Thanks for trying, Dad."

Lawson couldn't help but feel relieved. Even though he had moved to LA, bought this house in the hills with the money they found in the walls of De Luca's office, and tried to make a home in Hollywood so his thirteen-year-old daughter could chase her dream of becoming an actress, he didn't know he would be expected to be an actor too. The past year he'd been doing nothing but playing catch-up, learning how to be a dad, a friend, and even just getting used to being a civilian again. The ten years in prison changed him. And no matter how hard he tried, he'd never be the man he was before he lost everything.

The doorbell rang.

Lexi bolted for the door. "Make Cassie that drink she likes. You know she'll want one as soon as she walks in."

Lawson smiled. He had often thanked the gods that Lexi was 99 percent her mother. But every once in a while he could see that one percent of himself come through. Lexi could read people. She studied them. Much like Lawson. It made him a good detective and agent, and he figured it would go a long way in helping Lexi get into character as an actress. He was glad he could help her in at least one positive way.

Lexi opened the door and Cassie hurried through. She looked just like an FBI agent. The black pantsuit, her long blonde hair pulled into a ponytail, and the ever-present bulge of her sidearm jutting out from her hip. Though she was no longer with the FBI, the private investigation firm she had opened let her be exactly who she was. A fiercely tough, smart-as-a-whip woman, and one hell of a detective.

"Hey guys," Cassie said in a huff. "What a day. Lawson, make me one of those bourbon lemonades, would you?"

Lexi leaned out from behind Cassie and gave her dad a

smile. Lawson gave her a wink from the kitchen. She'd read Cassie like a book.

"Already got it started." Lawson poured the honey and the lemonade into a shaker and gave it a few tosses. "What's got you all frazzled today?"

Lawson took a sip of his Blanton's bourbon. Neat. He didn't need all the sweeteners.

Cassie looked between Lexi and Lawson as she took a seat on the stool at the kitchen's center island. "Well, *you* actually."

Lexi took a sip of her honey lemonade. No bourbon. "What'd you do now, Dad?"

Lawson pushed Cassie's drink over to her, and she downed it in one slug. "Good thing I made a couple." Then to Lexi. "Honey, can you go—"

"I know, I know. Go do something somewhere else so you two can talk about something."

Lawson smiled. She was her mother through and through. And far too mature for a thirteen-year-old. "We'll only need a minute."

Lexi held up her palm—*talk to the hand*—and walked to her upstairs bedroom.

Cassie jumped right in. "What the hell are you doing, Lawson? You'll do a job for someone, but you won't come and work with me?"

"I don't know what you're talking about."

"Save it, big guy." Cassie pointed at the wounds on Lawson's knuckles. "I know you haven't just been doing push-ups and running the Hollywood Hills until the soles of your shoes are worn out. I saw the video. Do you realize who you tuned up in that bar?"

"Tuned up?" Lawson took a drink. "What is this, 1954?"

"Don't." Cassie shook her head emphatically as she grabbed the shaker and poured her second drink.

"Don't what?" Lawson was going to play dumb until Cassie's head exploded.

"Don't do this thing where you play dumb just to frustrate me. It never kept you from telling me when we were partners, and it sure as hell won't get you out of telling me what happened now."

Lawson thought he could see smoke starting to billow from her ears.

"Okay, Cass. Who did I 'tune up'? And why does it matter?"

"Oh, no one really. Just Hollywood's finest fixer. You really enjoy having the worst criminals on your bad side, don't you?"

Lawson knew by "worst criminals" that she was referring to the swath of crooked officials and organized crime members that he battled in Vegas.

"I didn't know."

Cassie called him out. "Bullshit, Raines. You always know. But you did it anyway. Why?"

About a month ago Lawson took Lexi to her first real audition. She'd been working with an acting coach, a voice coach, and seemingly every other kind of coach since they arrived in LA six months ago. The part was the lead in a new Disney movie. An ambitious first role. Lawson cautiously encouraged her and went along to offer support. It felt good to be her dad again.

While they were there, one of the producers—and unbeknownst to Lawson an A-list filmmaker—Victoria Marshall—commented on Lawson's size. Told him *he* should be in movies. When he introduced himself, bypassing the comment, she recognized his name. Nero De Luca, the crime boss Lawson had taken out a year before, apparently had invested in one of her movies. So when he died, she read the story and heard about the former FBI agent who had hacked his way through De Luca's entire crew, almost single-handedly.

Lawson thought nothing of it. As he did whenever that story came up, he downplayed it until the person who brought it up stopped talking. But later that night, Victoria called him. She started by saying that she was extremely impressed by Lexi, but the call was to hire him. Long story short, she was getting pressured by some Hollywood power-houses to bring a coveted script to a certain production company, and she was nervous about a meeting they were forcing her to take. Lawson said twice that he wasn't inter-ested—even though he needed the money, what with the house in the hills and all of Lexi's coaches—but the promise of Lexi going to the top of the list for this big role ultimately was too much for him to turn down. Ten years without being able to be a father to his daughter made him eager to make up for it.

But even then he knew he shouldn't get involved at Victoria's meeting. And from the sound of it, Cassie was letting him know that his instinct to stay away had been a good one. But he didn't listen to it. And he knew that he was about to hear exactly why he should have.

Unfortunately, the situation was a lot worse than he and Cassie would have ever guessed.

4

LAWSON WALKED CASSIE OUT, GAVE HER A HUG, AND IGNORED the concerned look on her face as he shut the front door. He turned back to the all-open room, a kitchen, dining, and family room combo. Tall ceilings, modern aesthetics, and a TV over the fireplace that Lawson only watched when Lexi made him. He cared about none of it. Lexi and Cassie picked out the house. He could have lived in a two-bedroom apartment. Space didn't matter to him. Living in an eight-by-eight cell for ten years had that affect. Lexi thought it was cool that it used to be some actress's home, but it was someone Lawson had never heard of. She was really famous at one time, and Lexi thought it might rub off on her. Not to mention the stars who apparently were their neighbors. Again, Lawson didn't care. As long as Lexi was happy, he was happy.

Which is why the news of the man he had protected Victoria Marshall from was disturbing. People like Clint Hues retaliate. And by trying to help Lexi get a part in a movie, he had inadvertently put her in danger. A mistake he was regretting as he poured another bourbon. Of course Cassie was right. Lawson had done his homework before Victoria's meeting. All he really wanted to do at the bar was be a fly on the wall, and be there in case Victoria's life was in danger. In fact, he told himself he wouldn't do anything unless he saw a weapon. He really hadn't meant to intervene. Especially in the violent way that he had. But when he saw this Clint guy grab Victoria's wrist so forcefully, something in him snapped. He supposed it was what happened to his wife, Lauren. Even before then, he had never tolerated a man putting his hands on a woman. Ever.

So, he did what any natural protector would do, and he bloodied all three men. With a special message to Clint as he lay bleeding on the floor. *You feel like a big man now?* The words replayed in Lawson's mind. When he said them, he was crouched over Clint on the floor of the bar. *You remember what this feels like. You understand me? Remember it next time you put your hands on a woman.* Then he walked out of the bar. Lawson imagined that this "fixer" *would* remember. And he would try to "fix" Lawson for it too. Even if Lexi gets the part and goes on to fulfill her dreams, it might not be worth what was coming. Men like Clint, when they get embarrassed, word gets around. Their reputation is their livelihood. He would want his revenge.

And as bad as all of that was, it was worse. Cassie's news that the video made its way to the FBI took things to another level. Not because they would question him. He wasn't worried about the police. They didn't really go hard after a man who took down scum. His concern was that if the FBI had the video, and police had the video, whoever helped Clint Hues run his operation would also have a video. Lawson's face wasn't a hard one to track. It had been all over the news on multiple occasions in his life. They would be onto him soon, and he would need to be prepared.

"That's probably enough of that stuff, don't you think, Dad?"

Lawson jumped when he heard his daughter's voice. He gave her the eye. "Aren't you supposed to be in bed?"

Thirty-six years old and his thirteen-year-old daughter already knew better than he did. But he finished the drink anyway. He finished it right before three loud bangs sounded off somewhere outside the house, followed by the screeching of tires as a car went speeding away.

Lawson moved for his Sig Sauer P226 he kept in the top drawer.

"Lexi, get upstairs and lock your door. Now!"

He'd heard gunshots enough in his life to know that is exactly what had gone off outside. He pulled back the slide on his gun, loading a bullet, and walked over to the wall of windows that overlooked the driveway and front lawn. He searched the darkness for any sign of movement, but couldn't find anything. Then the front light came on. He jerked around, Lexi hadn't listened. Instead, she had hit the light and was searching for something through an adjacent window.

"Lexi!"

"Dad! I see someone!"

Lawson ran over and put Lexi behind him. "Where?"

Lexi angled around him and pointed to a dark spot out to the left. "There! Someone's on the ground. You think they're okay?"

It was faint, but Lawson could just make out what looked like a person lying on the ground. He turned to Lexi. "Lock this door behind me. Don't open it for anyone. I'll be back in a minute."

"You want me to call the police?"

The bar fight flashed across Lawson's mind. "No. Just stay put. I'll check it out. Maybe it's nothing."

Lexi nodded. Lawson opened the front door, shut it behind him, and waited until he heard Lexi turn the dead bolt. Beyond the light of the porch was pure darkness. It extended halfway into the front lawn. Where he'd seen a body on the ground a moment ago, he now saw nothing. He tightened his grip on his gun and moved down the steps onto the driveway. He felt exposed. He walked back up, unscrewed the lightbulb in the sconce, and moved back down. He could no longer see in the darkness, but neither could anyone else if they were waiting. He took a few steps forward. All he could hear was the distant sound of traffic from Hollywood Boulevard and a small chorus of insects. As his feet got their first feel of grass, he finally heard something else.

A cat?

He took another step. He heard another low and soft groan.

A woman?

Lawson raised his pistol as he lowered himself to a knee. He squinted into the night, searching for any sign of movement.

A soft call came from a woman not far away. "Help me. Please."

"Who are you?" Lawson finally said, the tip of his gun searching in front of him.

"Please help. They shot me."

Lawson moved forward slowly. Worried it could be a trap, his mind was racing.

"Please, it hurts."

Then came sobs.

Lawson moved forward quickly, and he nearly tripped over her in the darkness. When he reached down to feel for her body, she winced, and he felt something wet.

"Are you alone?"

He could barely see her.

"Yes. Can you help me?" The woman managed through muffled tears.

"Where are you hurt?"

"My left arm . . . it burns."

Lawson felt for her right side, scooped her into his arms, and began walking back to the house. As she cried, his mind ran through the scenario. A woman being shot and wandering onto his property? It was as unlikely of a coincidence as anything he could think of. It was even crazier considering it happened just forty-eight hours after Lawson busted up a notorious criminal. He couldn't see a way the two could be connected, but it was almost as difficult to think of a way it couldn't be. He believed that coincidences do happen. But one so quick on the heels of an extraordinary event like two nights ago didn't seem plausible. Regardless, a woman was bleeding badly, and he needed to get her some help.

Lawson kicked at the bottom of the front door. "Lexi! Let me in!"

Not a second later the front door was flung open. Lexi stepped back. She was seeing what Lawson had felt: the blood on the woman in the cocktail dress.

"Get me some towels, a belt, and the keys to the car."

The woman jerked her head over and looked up at Lawson. She was stunning.

"Car keys?"

"Yeah, I have to get you to a hospital."

"You can't . . . I can't go to the hospital." There was fear on her face.

"Lexi, get what I asked you to get and let's get out of here."

Lexi took two more steps back but didn't leave the room. Her eyes didn't leave the woman's face. She was looking at her as if she recognized her.

"Lexi, what is it? Do you know her?"

The woman shot a look at Lexi, then turned back to Lawson and clutched his arm.

"I can't go to the hospital. Please. Just . . . just help me stop the bleeding and I'll go."

Lawson was confused. In the light he could clearly see she was shot in the arm. No scenario of someone getting shot ended without going to the hospital. Unless . . .

"Are you a criminal?" Lawson said. "That why you don't want to go? 'Cause I can just call the police."

Lawson didn't need this complication. Not now. Not with the battle he knew he was about to have regarding his actions at the bar.

Surprisingly, Lexi spoke before the woman could.

"She's not a criminal, Dad."

Lawson looked at his daughter. "How could you know that?"

"Because literally everyone knows that."

Lawson looked down at the beautiful woman in his arms. Then back at Lexi. "I guess I'm not everyone. So spill it."

"She's an actress, Dad. Probably the most famous one in the world."

5

Lexi finished laying out the towels on the couch. Lawson walked over and laid the woman down. He stood to take inventory of her wound. By no means was he a doctor, but he had been around long enough to know if something serious like an artery had been hit.

"Looks like you got lucky," he said as he removed his shirt.

The woman was clearly taken aback by Lawson's size. The extent of his muscular frame wasn't a sight she saw all that often. She moved her eyes from his body to her arm.

"You call getting shot lucky?" Then she winced again, clearly in a great deal of pain.

Lawson ignored her and tied his shirt tightly around her upper arm, just above the bullet wound. The bleeding had slowed, but he wanted to make sure he gave it the best chance he could to clot.

"Lexi, call an ambulance. And then call the police."

He'd thought it over. It could bring nothing but trouble if he didn't call this in. No matter how bad it looked that he'd been in the bar fight, and then this happened on his property, it would be worse when the police came sniffing around and he hadn't called in an attempted murder.

Once again, the woman clawed at Lawson. There was genuine fear in her eyes.

"You can't!"

She tried to sit up. Lawson took her by the shoulders and coached her back down.

"You can't call the police. Please!"

Lawson didn't understand. If she didn't do anything wrong, why wouldn't she want help? Help getting her wound tended to, and help finding out who did this and why.

"You have to relax. And I have to call this in. There is no reason—"

"You don't understand. No one can find out about this!"

Lawson stood. "You have five seconds to make me understand. Otherwise I'm calling you an ambulance. I'm not putting my daughter in danger by being an accomplice to whatever the hell this is."

The woman nodded. "Like your daughter said, I'm an actress. A very famous one. But I took some bad advice, and the wrong roles, and my last two movies didn't do so well. I am in talks to star in a movie that will put my career back on track, but if word of this gets out right now, they will drop me for sure. I know this doesn't seem like a big deal to you, but I have been through a lot in the last couple years, and I need this." Her eyes began to well up with tears. "I *need* this."

Lawson took a water bottle from the coffee table and handed it to her. "Sorry. But your career isn't worth endangering my daughter."

Lawson pulled his phone from his pocket.

"Wait, Dad—"

Lawson held up his hand. "Lexi, go get her a blanket."

"But, Dad, just listen to her. Please—"

"Lexi."

"Please," the woman said. "Just hear me out."

Lawson knew better than to hear her out. He knew what he should do. But there was something about her that made him listen. Maybe it was his daughter pleading with him that made him put his phone back in his pocket. Lexi had never begged him for anything. He knew it was wrong, but he was at least going to wait for her to say her piece. Then he would call.

"I can't really explain to you what it is like in Hollywood. But if someone like me gets stories like this told about them in the press, it will swirl forever. It will be the only thing people associate with me from now on. Not my acting. I might never work again."

Lawson didn't know this woman, so it was hard for him to care that a spoiled, rich Hollywood actress wouldn't be getting any more starring roles. Especially when she, albeit involuntarily, had involved Lexi in this problem. He also knew that people usually didn't get shot for no reason.

"Why were you shot?"

The woman looked surprised. "I-I don't know."

"Bullshit."

"Dad."

"Lexi, stay quiet or go upstairs. I know you may think you like her . . ." Lawson looked back at the woman. "What is your name anyway?"

"Taylor."

He looked back to Lexi. "I know you may think you like Taylor because you like her movies, but you don't really know her. And she's not really telling the truth. She wants me to put you at risk to save her career, but she doesn't want to be honest with me. That's not how this is going to go down."

Lawson reached for his phone again, and Taylor sat up a little on the couch.

"Okay. Okay, you're right. Please. Just hear me out. I promise I'll be honest with you."

Lawson looked over at his daughter. Her eyes were pleading just as heavily as Taylor's. He let out a sigh. Taylor continued.

"You're right. I know who shot me. And if I go to the police—"

"Let me guess, they'll kill you," Lawson interrupted.

"Worse." Taylor winced in pain as she moved to sit up a little more. Her shimmering sequin dress was covered with blood. The mascara had run down her face among her tears. "They'll kill my sister."

Lawson knew when the words were spoken that he had just been pulled into a tangled web. A mess that wasn't his, but yet now it was. Taylor was crying now, and Lexi came over with some tissues. As she sat beside Taylor, pushing the tangle of hair from the supposed movie star's forehead, she looked back up at Lawson, tears of her own ready to fall at any moment.

Lexi made sure Lawson was looking at her. "Dad, we have to help her. You're really good at this kind of stuff." Then she looked at Taylor. "He's really good at this kind of stuff."

They both looked back up at him.

Shit.

"Lexi, go call Cassie and tell her I need a doctor who can be discreet. Tell her I'll explain later."

Lexi jumped up and threw her arms around Lawson. "Taylor, my dad will fix this. He can fix anything." Lexi bounded off to call Cassie. While those words were good to hear from his daughter's mouth, Lexi also didn't understand what all of this meant. But Lawson did. And it seemed that Taylor did as well.

"I know what this means for you, to not call the police. I'm so sorry I've put you in this position. If there was any other way, I would do it. You have to know that I would."

Lawson didn't respond to her thank-you. His mind was already running.

"Is it drugs?"

Taylor looked away, embarrassed. Then she nodded. "But I promise you, I'm clean now. I have been for six months."

"Then why are they after you?"

Taylor looked away again and began to cry. Lawson walked over to the kitchen to give her a moment.

"Bourbon or vodka?" Lawson asked, looking inside his open liquor cabinet.

Taylor cleared her throat. "Bourbon. Thank you."

Lawson opened his bottle of Blanton's and poured both of them a drink. He had a hunch the trouble this beautiful woman was going to bring him would be immense. He couldn't care less that she was a movie star. But at least she knew how to drink. That made him laugh to himself that maybe she'd be worth helping after all.

6

Lawson handed Taylor the glass of bourbon. She thanked him and took a sip. She let her head fall back against the pillow and closed her eyes for a moment, letting a deep breath escape as she relaxed. Other than his wife, Lauren, he had never seen a more beautiful woman. Even under all the distress, blood, and tears, he could tell why she dazzled on the silver screen. She was tall and fit, and had long tan legs, long dirty blonde hair, high cheek bones, big cat eyes, and lips Angelina Jolie would be jealous of. He tried to give her a moment, but his detective brain had already begun spinning.

"Taylor, why would people be shooting you because of your sister's drug problem?"

Lexi was in the other room getting Lawson a T-shirt, so while she was gone he wanted to try to find out more of the story.

Taylor opened her eyes, an emerald green, and took another sip of bourbon. "Long story short, I paid her debt but they wanted more."

"And you refused?"

"I couldn't just keep giving them money. They would never stop asking for more."

Lawson took a drink. "And for the same reason you won't call the police now, you didn't call the police when they threatened you, right? You just thought they would quit demanding money?"

"I don't know what I thought. I've played some badass roles, but I have no idea how this stuff works in real life. I thought if I paid what my sister owed, they would leave me —us—alone. If I went to the police, the paparazzi would know. The story would be everywhere."

Lawson understood.

"So, who are these people?"

"I honestly don't really know. The dealer I used to buy from is gone. My sister said some cartel or something moved in, raised the prices, and got her hooked on heroin. It was always just coke for me. I was stupid. My fiancé had died and I started to spiral."

Lawson could certainly relate to spiraling after losing your significant other.

"Probably shouldn't have given you that drink."

"No, it's fine. Alcohol has never been a problem for me. Well, no more than anyone else."

Lexi came back downstairs and handed Lawson a shirt. Taylor sat up a little further.

"I'm really sorry I got you into this. And I'm sorry I'm asking so much of you. I just don't really know what to do."

Lexi said, "You're lucky it happened to you here. Where somebody like my dad can help."

Taylor smiled.

"If I'm going to help you, Taylor, I need more to go on. What were you doing in this part of town? Why didn't they make sure you were dead? Cartel members, if that's really

27

what they were, don't usually make a habit of leaving witnesses."

Taylor looked at Lexi. So did Lawson.

"I know, Dad. Go upstairs, Lexi. You're too young for this, Lexi."

"Thank you for your help, Lexi," Taylor said.

Lexi smiled. "I just hope you're okay. Tell my dad what he needs to know. He'll fix it."

Taylor smiled, and Lexi begrudgingly went upstairs.

Taylor said, "They meant to keep me alive. The man in the car told me right before he shot me that if I didn't pay, next time I'd be dead."

Lawson thought about it for a moment. The man who'd had her must have been a professional. To shoot someone with a pistol, even at close range, and know you wouldn't kill them is someone much more skilled than a cartel thug. Red flag number one went up for Lawson.

"So you don't know the man?" Lawson said.

"No."

"What did he look like?"

"They had a bag over my head. It's somewhere in your driveway. It came off when I was running from them."

"Did he have an accent?"

"Not that I could discern."

Just because the man wasn't Mexican didn't mean he wasn't cartel. But it did seem a little off. Her story wasn't really making sense to him yet.

"Where did they pick you up? Do you remember the car they were driving?"

"Dad! I think I saw someone outside!" Lexi shouted from upstairs.

Lawson's hand immediately reached for his gun.

"Can you walk?"

"I-I'm not sure." Taylor started to get up. She winced but made it to a seated position.

"Don't move."

Lawson rushed over to the front door and shut off the lights, then to the kitchen to do the same.

"Lexi, get down here. What did you see?"

Lexi came thundering down the stairs. "I was looking to see if the doctor was here yet, and I saw something move out by the road!"

"Help Taylor to your room, now. Lock your door and don't come out until I come and get you."

"Okay, I won't. Be careful, Dad."

Lawson skulked to the front door as Lexi went to the couch. Lawson heard Taylor wince as Lexi helped her up. There was barely enough light in the room for them to see, but they headed upstairs.

"Don't come out of that room, Lexi."

"We won't."

Lawson moved to his right along the wall until he came to the first window. He peered around it, but the porch light was still off, so there was nothing but darkness. The street light at the top of the driveway that helped Lexi see whoever was there didn't reach down to the house. For the second time that night, Lawson felt completely exposed. These massive windows had been a massive mistake. He reached to his left and flipped on the porch light but forgot he had unscrewed the bulb. He strained to see but as far as he could tell, there was no one there to greet him. He saw no movement at all.

Lawson tuned his ears, listening for something . . . anything.

The floodlight kicked on at the back of the house.

Lexi was right, someone was there.

7

LAWSON MOVED PAST THE KITCHEN TOWARD THE SLIDING glass door that led to the back deck. The floodlight that had come on hung just outside the door. It could pick up motion several feet into the backyard. Lawson sidled up to the wall and gave the deck a look, but saw nothing. He unlocked the door and slowly slid it open. There was almost complete silence. He took a step out on the deck and saw the shadow of an arm of someone walking around the corner of the house. Adrenaline surged as he readied his gun and stepped forward across the deck, down the stairs, and to the edge of the house.

Lawson swung around the corner, gun extended, and he just barely pulled his finger away from the trigger when he found Cassie standing there pointing her gun at him in the light of the moon.

"Jesus, Lawson! I almost shot *you*!"

"Me? I almost shot you!"

They both lowered their guns.

"What the hell are you doing out here snooping around?" Lawson said. "Have you lost your mind?"

"When Lexi called about the doctor, I doubled back to make sure everything was okay. I was just checking the perimeter to make sure the shooter was gone."

"You couldn't call and let someone know?"

"I texted you, Lawson. Let me guess . . . Mr. No Technology doesn't have his phone on him."

"No. Why would I? I was going to bed."

Cassie rolled her eyes. "Can we go inside? The doctor should be here any minute now."

Lawson shook his head and started walking toward the back entrance.

Cassie continued, "Sure, Cass, follow me. Let's have a drink. Thanks for coming back to help. Oh, and thanks for calling a doctor who's willing to risk his medical license to come for a house call on an undocumented attempted murder."

Lawson looked back at Cassie, not appreciating her sarcasm. "You done?"

They walked inside, and Lawson turned on the lights.

"No, I'm not done. Why the hell isn't whoever got shot on the way to the hospital? Why didn't you call the police?"

Cassie blew a tuft of hair off her forehead. She was getting herself worked up. One of Lawson's least favorite, yet also one of his favorite, things about her.

"First of all, calm down."

She hated it when he told her to calm down. He was smiling on the inside.

"Calm down? You're telling me to calm down when you are breaking about six laws and calling me in as an accomplice?"

Her normally pale skin was now a fiery red. Lawson was enjoying this.

Cassie was still spun up. "It's just like you to be ungrateful. So, where is she?"

"Who?"

Cassie rolled her eyes. "You're doing this on purpose. Make me a drink. You know who."

"Everything okay, Dad?"

Lawson spun fast and saw Lexi peeking around the stairs.

"Lexi, I told you to wait in your room."

"I know, but I heard Cassie's voice and figured it was okay."

Lawson shook his head. "How's she doing?"

Before Lexi could answer, Taylor walked around the corner holding a towel to her shoulder.

Cassie's jaw dropped. "Ho-ly shit. You're Taylor freakin' Lockhart." Then to Lawson. "That's Taylor freakin' Lockhart. The biggest movie star on the planet."

"So I've heard." Lawson turned to Taylor. "How you feeling?"

"Tired."

"Oh my God," Cassie kept on. "I *loved* you in *Let Me Go*. Sooo good."

"Cassie," Lawson interjected, trying to stop her.

"No, seriously. I still think about that movie."

"Cassie, Taylor has been through a lot. And since when did you become a fan-girl?"

"Shut it, Lawson. Not everyone is like you and hates entertainment. You've probably never even heard of her."

There was a knock at the door.

"Taylor, that's probably the doctor," Lawson said. "Lexi, take her upstairs. He can take a look at her in your bedroom. Cassie, stay down here with me. We need to talk."

Lawson let the doctor in, and he went upstairs to work

his magic on Taylor. Cassie stayed behind and joined Lawson on the sofa.

"I haven't told Taylor this yet, but I can't help her with this. I've got enough to worry about making sure the repercussions from the bar don't come back on Lexi."

Cassie was quiet for a moment.

"Cassie?"

"I'm thinking. I mean, it's Taylor Lockhart. She's so hot I'd bang her. And I'm strictly into men."

"How's that helpful?"

Cassie smiled. "I forgot, the new Lawson hates jokes . . . All I mean is, I get what you're saying. We've already got a shitstorm brewing with what you did the other night."

Lawson caught the word "we." His old partner was a bulldog, and no matter what happened, he knew when worse came to worst, he could count on her. He was hoping it wouldn't come to worst.

Cassie continued, "And someone like you who's served a long prison sentence should probably stay as far away from whatever this little shooting is. You probably don't have quite as much grace as the rest of us. Even though you were FBI a long time ago and you did pull one of the greatest takedowns in organized crime history. Still. I get it. T-R-O-U-B-L-E is about the last thing you need right now."

"But?" Lawson was patient.

"But it's Taylor Lockhart."

Lawson still wasn't convinced. "You say that like it means something. It doesn't. Not to me."

Cassie finished her drink. "Well, maybe it should. You're already this deep. You're already in trouble, concealing a crime. Might as well see it through."

Lawson could tell there was something else behind

Cassie's motivation. "You going to keep *not* saying it? I mean you're saying everything else, so just spit it out."

"Fine. I could help you with this. It's a big name. Could be good for the new private investigation firm that is currently struggling to get cases."

Lawson stood. "Two things: One, I don't care about the PI firm. Two, I told you, I don't need the trouble. You help her, I'm out."

Cassie joined him standing. "I don't get you, Lawson." Cassie made a sweeping motion with her hand and looking all around the room. "I see this house. I see the coaches Lexi is learning from. I know that ain't cheap. You're going to have to make money at some point. That's why you took that stupid job of going to that bar for that movie producer or whatever she was. The one that's now got you in hot water. But you won't do any work for a PI firm that you have half of your money in, and your old partner to work with? Why? I don't understand."

"I'm tired." Lawson didn't feel like discussing it. "I'll call you in the morning after I talk to Taylor and tell you whether or not she wants your help."

"That's it?"

"That's it."

"You don't want my help with this Hollywood fixer thing you've gotten mixed up in either?"

"I'll handle it."

Cassie hung her head and let out a sigh. Then she nodded her head, defeated. She walked over to the foot of the stairs. "Night, Lexi! Taylor, I hope you feel better!"

"Night, Cassie!" Lexi shouted back.

Cassie lingered for a moment.

"Lawson, I know it's only been a year since you got out of jail. And I know you've got a lot on your plate raising Lexi by yourself. But this isn't prison. You aren't by yourself anymore. You have someone to watch your back. You've got to let people back in—let *me* back in. You don't have to do this alone."

"You a psychologist on the side now too?"

Lawson's effort to deflate the situation with humor fell flat.

Cassie took one last look at Lawson, then walked out the front door.

8

LAWSON JOGGED DOWN THE LAST OF THE HILL AND TURNED right onto his driveway. It was the same six-mile run he'd made every day since they'd moved. He never missed a day. His daily exercise regimen was the only constant he'd been able to salvage from his old life with Lauren. The life before all the pain that changed him entirely. Before the run he pounded out the customary two hundred push-ups. The two hundred squats. And the four hundred sit-ups. All the same as every other day of his life. And it felt better than ever that morning. He figured it was because he was losing control of some of the harmony he had created with Lexi here. The workout, though, he could always control. It always helped center him.

As he looked at the house he'd bought for Lexi, it still felt so foreign. Not necessarily because it wasn't Kentucky. Or because it wasn't Las Vegas where he'd lived for three years before they murdered his wife. But because it wasn't that eight-by-eight cell. He purposely gave Lexi the master bedroom. Not as a kind gesture toward his daughter, but because the guest bedroom was much smaller, even though it was still too damn big. And he hadn't slept one good night since they had moved in. Not since he'd been released from prison actually. Lawson never thought acclimating to being free would be so difficult. But it was.

On the run he was able to organize his thoughts. He had a busy day ahead, one that would need answers to a lot of questions. He needed to have a chat with Victoria Marshall. If she needed security before, it was even more imperative now. Whoever sent in Clint Hues to try to bully her more than likely still wanted what they wanted. But Lawson believed they would be even less civil now in their second attempt. Which led him to the questions that needed to be answered: Who hired Clint Hues, and what did this person want from Victoria Marshall? Victoria should be able to enlighten Lawson on both. If she didn't, he could no longer be of service to her. He had no time to deal with vague details or misinformation.

The next thing he needed to know was what the FBI knew and what they might want from him, just in case they came asking about the video from the bar. When Cassie told him Frank Shaw had called her, his stomach turned. Not only was it bad that Lawson was on the FBI's radar, but Frank Shaw wasn't exactly his best friend back in Vegas. When Cassie and Lawson had moved up the director's chart of go-to agents for the big cases, there were a lot of people in the Vegas division who didn't like it. But Frank Shaw had been the most vocal. And before Lawson was framed for murder and went away, his relationship with Frank had been at an all-time low. Lawson imagined his trouble at the bar the other night would jump straight to the top of Frank's to-do list.

All of that and more needed to be accomplished today. It would be the only way Lawson would feel good about coming home to his daughter. Her safety was all he cared about. The biggest wild card in all of it was Clint Hues and how he was going to retaliate. It wasn't a matter of if he would, but when. Lawson had a mind to think being proactive and reaching out to him first might be the way to go. But right now, he had to handle this situation with Taylor. With all *he* had going on, there was no way he could further bury himself in trouble with what *she* had going on. No matter if it would help Cassie's private investigation firm, no matter how much Lexi looked up to Taylor, and no matter how beautiful she was, he just couldn't take it on.

But wow was she beautiful.

Lawson looked through the large front window and could see Taylor doing something in the kitchen while she was talking to Lexi, who sat at the adjacent dining room table. Lexi's grin was ear to ear. This was trouble. Lexi hadn't made a lot of friends since they'd moved to Los Angeles. And he knew that she was missing some female camaraderie. That was apparent any time Cassie would come over. Lexi stuck to her like glue. Letting Taylor stick around had been a mistake. And letting Lexi think he was going to help her, and that she would be hanging around the house for a while, was an even bigger one. He had to move this along today. Before Lexi got too attached.

He lingered watching for a moment longer. Taylor was in a pair of Lexi's oversized pajama pants. They were a little small so they hugged tight. He could see the patched wound on her shoulder because of the tank top she was wearing. The tank top also showed off her natural curves. Lawson hadn't been with a woman since he lost his wife eleven years ago. And he could feel it making him weak as he stood there watching Taylor interact with his daughter. The way he imagined Lauren would be if she was still with them.

Lexi looked over at the window, saw Lawson standing there and excitedly waved him in. He buried the swirl of his desire for Taylor and the longing for Lauren, and walked inside. Lexi got up and ran over to him.

"Dad, you won't believe what Taylor said she would do. She said because we were nice enough to help her that she would read lines with me and teach me how to be a better actress! Can you believe that?"

His mistake of letting Taylor stay had become a complete disaster. The excitement in his daughter's eyes at that moment was more than he'd ever seen. Granted, he had missed ten years of her life, but right now she was over the moon. Lawson feared he now had no choice in the matter. He could disappoint Taylor, she was just a good-looking stranger. But Lexi? He'd rather die than disappoint her.

"That's good, sweetheart."

It was all the enthusiasm he could work up knowing how hard it was going to make his life having Taylor stay. He walked over to the kitchen and excused himself around Taylor to grab a towel to wipe his sweat. She smelled like a fresh shower. And he noticed that she didn't hurry to take her eyes off him. The feeling she was giving him was something he hadn't felt in a long time. And he didn't like it.

"Good? That's all you've got, Dad? Good?" Lexi walked over to the opposite side of the center island. "Dad, this is like Lebron James offering to teach you how to play basketball. Like Roger Federer teaching you how to play tennis. Like—"

"All right, Lexi. I get it. I agree. It's a big deal." Then to Taylor. "Thank you. That's very kind of you."

"You kidding me?" Taylor said. "It's the least I can do. I'd be on every news station in the country right now if it wasn't for you."

Lawson might have underestimated how well-known Taylor was. Between Cassie's and Lexi's reactions and Taylor's relentless need to keep all of this private, he felt like he had the queen of England at his house. He was going to have to familiarize himself a little better to know what he was dealing with. He knew he was out of touch with pop culture; ten years in a federal penitentiary will do that. But they all were making him think he was from another planet.

Maybe they weren't that far off.

"Well, you and I need to talk, but I've got a few things to do today if you don't mind staying here and watching Lexi."

"Dad, I don't need a babysitter."

"Oh, I'm not a babysitter, Lexi. I'm your new acting coach."

Taylor gave Lexi a wink and a smile. Lexi's face lit up like a Christmas tree. And the only thing Lawson could do was think about the shitstorm the last couple of days had created, and how he had no idea how the hell he was going to come out unscathed.

9

"I need your help."

It was the last thing Lawson wanted to say to Cassie that morning, but there was just no way around it.

"More help? What happened?"

"What hasn't happened?"

"Been a long couple days. Did Eric make it there yet?"

Lawson stepped out into the garage. He didn't want Taylor or Lexi to hear this conversation. He hit the button and the garage door opened. A black Chevy Malibu was sitting on the side of the road just outside his driveway.

"Chevy Malibu?" Lawson said.

"That's him. He won't let anyone in or out."

"Thank you."

Lawson had texted Cassie when he first woke up that he needed someone to watch the house. He didn't even know Taylor, there was no way he was going to leave his most prized possession alone in her care. An off-duty officer made him feel a lot better about going out and running his errands.

Cassie said, "So what do you need? I thought Big Bad

Lawson Raines could do this on his own. What do you need a PI firm for?"

"If you're going to keep harping on this, I'll find someone else to help. You know full well I can't be a private investigator until my record is cleared. So drop it."

"Just get it cleared already. I don't understand what is taking so long. You received a full pardon. Make some calls and get it done."

Lawson had had enough. "I've got to go. Just check on Lexi periodically, would you?"

"Don't be like that. You know I just want you to clear all this up so you can actually do some legitimate work."

"I need more information about Taylor Lockhart."

"Yeah?" Cassie said. Lawson could hear her smiling. "I saw the way Lexi looked at her so I had a feeling you might be asking that. I'll email over what I have."

Lawson was lucky to have Cassie. She was an all-star, and he needed to make use of her. Especially since she was so enthusiastic about Taylor as it was.

"You know I can't pay you," he said.

"I'm also going to get to work on seeing if I have some contacts that can push your paperwork through. We've got to get you cleared so you can actually get paid to work. If you've already blown through the money we found in De Luca's wall—"

"Thank you, Cassie," Lawson interrupted. "I know I'm not the best at this friend thing anymore—"

"Don't worry about it. Just let me know what you need. I'm only working some small-time case right now. I'm mostly free. What are you doing right now?"

"Going to see Victoria Marshall. It's time we had a come-to-Jesus meeting."

"Need me to look up Clint Hues? See if I can find out who he's working for?"

"I've got to get going," Lawson said. He still had trouble asking for help.

"I'll take that as a yes," Cassie said, letting him off the hook. "This would be a lot easier if you would just open up."

"Let me know what you find out. Just be careful when you're digging. Try not to let on that anyone wants to know."

"You're welcome."

Lawson ended the call. It felt like pulling his own teeth to ask for help. He didn't know why it was so hard for him. But it really was. He unlocked the door and got in his Nissan Maxima. He had really wanted to buy a 1967 Shelby Mustang GT 500 with some of the money they took from De Luca's stash. But as he pulled away from the house that he'd spent most of that money on, he was glad he went practical on the car. Because if he didn't have enough problems already, money getting tight wasn't making things easier. The only reason he was dealing with this Victoria Marshall stuff was because he needed to start making some money. He just hoped it wasn't going to be much more trouble than it was worth.

On the way out of his driveway he gave Eric, the officer watching his house, a nod and a wave. As he wound down the hill that led out into West Hollywood, he cracked the window to let in some fresh air. It was another beautiful Southern California day. The rays of sun filtered through the swaying leaves of the palm trees as the breeze blew through. The sky was a bright blue . . . once you looked above the layer of smog, that is. And the traffic had already begun to swell. Lawson didn't really understand the appeal of the big city. But he also wasn't much of an out-and-about kind of guy. And if you weren't an out-and-about kind of guy, a big city was nothing but a colossal inconvenience.

As he turned onto Sunset Boulevard, heading toward Wilshire for Victoria's office, his phone began to ring. He didn't recognize the number. But then again, he didn't really associate with anyone but Cassie anymore, so how would he?

"Hello?"

"Lawson Raines," a man's voice replied, low and gravelly. "It's been a long time."

Lawson had no idea who it was. "Has it?"

He turned right on Wilshire. Traffic was moving pretty well for a work morning.

"About eleven years, I guess."

It clicked. "Frank Shaw. It has been a while. You still sound like you're gargling rocks. Must have never quit smoking."

"And you're still a prick, Raines. Some things never change."

Lawson didn't have time for this. "Well, good catching up with you, Frank. Have a nice life."

"Now, hold on, Raines. I'm calling to help you. From the looks of things, you could use it."

If asking Cassie for help felt like pulling teeth, Frank Shaw even thinking Lawson would need him was like an anvil to the nuts.

"The day I need your help, Frank, is the day the world ends. And why would you want to help me now anyway? You were nowhere to be found when they pinned my wife's murder on me."

"Now, you know I'm real sorry about how all that went down. But there was nothing I could do. You had the DA and most of Las Vegas PD running you down. I tried to—"

"Good-bye, Frank."

Lawson put his phone on the console and turned into Victoria's office parking lot. He couldn't listen to that asshole for one more second. Now all he could hear was Cassie's voice in his head, telling him he should make good with Frank. *Make an ally out of him instead of an enemy, because you need all the friends you can get right now.* He even heard her Tennessee accent too. If Lawson didn't have his own conscience, he certainly didn't want Cassie's. Even though she was probably right. Still, not Frank Shaw. He would go a hundred extra miles to avoid getting "help" from him.

10

Just a couple blocks down the street from Victoria Marshall's office, Marty Sloan was just arriving at his own. There were several upcoming movie projects that needed tending to, but he had a bigger problem brewing in one of his even more profitable businesses. The one he'd inherited from his father, and the one that paved the way for him to be able to make movies in the first place. He had intended to get out of the drug trade once the movies took off, but the money was still too good to pass up. You make one bad movie, it can ruin you. You sell some bad drugs and a couple lowlifes might die from it, but no one cares. You keep feeding your family.

The problem he was having was that a cartel had moved in on some of his territory in Venice Beach. The solution was obvious, at least it would have been from his father's perspective. Kill the men selling in your area, and be ready for war if that's what it takes to run them out of town. But Marty, even though he was now the same age as his father when he started the business—fifty one—was nothing like his father. Their only similarity was they both would do anything for their family. It drove both men's every decision. For his father, he used violence because he believed it kept his family safe. But Marty believed using your brain was a better way in almost every case. And it kept people from snooping around and possibly interfering with his movie business.

He didn't like having these sorts of meetings at his production office, but he would no longer have them at his home. He'd already brought enough scumbags around his son. He didn't want his son inheriting, or even knowing about, this business. There was no pride in it for him. Movies would be his legacy.

He walked into his office, and his two main Southern California underbosses were sitting in front of his desk. This was going to be a short meeting; problems with movie production were Sloan's focus today.

"All right, let's have it. Marcos, you first."

Marcos had been around as long as his father. Marcos was always pushing Sloan to use more force. His old-school mentality clashed with Sloan's most every time. "One of my foxes was shot and killed last night. She was getting close to our new enemies in Venice, and I guess they found out about her. I'm sending four of my best in after this little nuisance."

"No, let's cut off their supply and run them out," Sloan said.

"Don't do this. Not here. One of our own was shot. You know we have to hit back harder. If we don't, we will lose Venice."

Sloan knew Marcos was right. He didn't like it, but killing can only be retaliated with killing. Otherwise, word would get around and they would be run out of Los Angeles entirely.

"Keep it quiet," Sloan said.

"Always."

"Speaking of keeping things quiet," the second under-boss spoke up. He went by the name Gallo. Sloan didn't even know his real name, and he'd known him for almost a decade. He was much younger than Marcos, and even more brazen. Sloan was constantly having to reel him in. But he was loyal and always did whatever he was asked to do. "I found out who interfered with Clint at the bar the other night."

"What's he talking about?" Marcos asked.

Sloan ignored Marcos. "You know where he is?"

"Yes, boss."

"We have someone watching him?"

"I did exactly as you asked."

"You're sure? I need to know who he's working for."

"I have been doing this a long time. If I tell you I'm sure, you can bet on it."

Marcos stood. "What is this? What is he talking about, Sloan?"

"This doesn't concern you, Marcos."

"Everything we do concerns me. If it's a rival gang involved, I need to have men ready for retaliation."

"Calm down. There won't be any retaliation. This isn't related to the business."

Marcos scoffed. He put his hands on his hips, just below his bulging stomach. "I don't know why you insist on this movie business. Sure, it's a great front, but involving my men in whatever the hell you've got going on is dangerous. You don't see how—"

It was Sloan's turn to stand. "That's enough. I said it doesn't concern you. Is that clear?"

Marcos stared for a moment. Sloan could tell a protest

was on the tip of his tongue. "Your father would say the same thing I'm saying. I'm just trying to make sure everything keeps running smooth."

"My father's not here. I am. This is my business. You have enough problems to worry about, Marcos. So go worry about them."

Marcos didn't say another word. He left, and Marty was alone with Gallo.

Marty brought it back to the subject at hand. "So we'll know his every move then?"

"Every move."

"Good. I need to make all of this happen."

"Boss, why not just kill him?"

"I told you, I need to know who he is working for. I'm assuming you have a man on him?"

"Of course," Gallo said.

"Let me know where he's going as soon as you find out."

Gallo nodded.

Sloan dismissed Gallo and took a seat at his desk. His father's old contacts were paying off, it seemed. If he could get Victoria Marshall to make her movie with him, he might be able to get out of the drug business after all. Surefire box office hits don't come along all that often, but this was one of them. It would take his production company to the next level, and he could leave a legitimate powerhouse business to his son. And not put his son in a situation like he was in now—deciding who to kill, what new territories to take, and too many other choices that could put him behind bars for life.

Sloan knew he could handle Victoria. What he was most worried about was who hired the man in the bar who was protecting her. That could throw a wrench in all of Sloan's plans if he didn't handle it now. That's why he was willing to go to lengths he hadn't before. He had to make it in the movie business. No matter what he had to do to make it happen.

Sloan's phone rang. It was Clint Hues.

"Clint, give me the good news." Sloan was already way ahead of Clint, but he would hear him out all the same.

"I found him. The man at the bar. Lawson Raines."

"Nice work. But you're too slow. I already found him, and I'm taking care of it."

"What? I told you I had it under control." Clint was upset.

"But you didn't. So I controlled it."

"Okay, well, I can take care of him right now," Clint said.

"I already told you, you were too slow. And too sloppy at the meeting. I'm not used to such amateurism. You're fired, Mr. Hues."

When Sloan was pressing END on the call, he heard Clint begin to shout. It didn't matter to Sloan; everything was going according to plan, and that was all that mattered. What didn't matter at all to him was some Hollywood fixer's job status, and definitely not some stranger in a bar. He knew Gallo would find out who this Lawson Raines was working for; then everything would be handled, and Victoria's movie would be his.

11

——————

CLINT SLAMMED THE PALM OF HIS HAND AGAINST THE steering wheel. When Marty Sloan originally had come to him for help in the Hollywood circles, he almost turned him down. And this was the reason why. A man like Sloan was used to pulling the strings, and he's used to doing it with the men he already trusts. Clint's instincts told him that Sloan would use the men who already worked for him if things got serious, and he was right. Not only did Clint get embarrassed in the bar, now he was fired. Absolute worst-case scenario for a fixer. Now he was going to have to regroup. In a major way.

"That's not good," Jenny said from the passenger seat.

Clint shot her a look that could kill. His insides were sizzling.

Jenny pointed out the front window. "There goes Raines."

Clint watched as the man who'd started this downward spiral pulled into the parking lot at Victoria Marshall's office. Who the hell was this guy, and what was his business with Victoria? At the moment Clint was so enraged he almost didn't care about either answer. He just wanted Lawson to pay for getting involved at all.

"What are you going to do now?" Jenny said.

Clint took a deep breath. "I'm going to hit him where it hurts."

"Okay, but what good would that do?"

"It doesn't have to do any good. Sometimes it's just about revenge."

"Can I be honest?"

"When have you not been honest, Jenny?"

"Good point." She smiled. "Let's take a look at where we are. You get hired by a guy who's in the movie production business, but who is really a drug lord by inheritance. Shit goes wrong at the meeting he hired you for, which looks bad. Then he fires you after he figures out the information he asked you to find before you find it, which looks much worse."

"So far I love this story, Jenny. Please continue."

"Your sarcasm aside, that is where we are."

"Get to the point."

"The point is, what this does is next time someone considers using you for a job, this is going to come up. Everyone in our circle is going to know about this."

"It just gets better." Clint wasn't enjoying this.

"Truth hurts. And unless you give him something he doesn't already have and he rehires you, jobs will be tough to come by."

"Maybe I could find something out he wants, maybe I can't. That's a long shot."

Jenny kept going on her train of thought. "Long shot or not, it's the truth. So if he doesn't hire you back, just understand that everyone will know about this, making it hard for us to get jobs. You are sitting here worried about some random guy that has no effect on your future business anymore. Maybe you're focused on the wrong thing."

"Really? Do tell, oh great and knowledgeable one."

"So, if you kill Lawson Raines, or hurt his family, or kick his ass, you will feel better about yourself. But future employers won't give a damn. Right?"

"Okay." Clint thought he knew where Jenny was going. And he could already tell, as usual, she was going to be right.

"What they *will* care about is that you failed Marty Sloan and he fired you. So the only way forward is to do something about *him*. That's the only way you really get the respect back you'll need to continue doing what you do."

Clint turned toward her. "So you want to take out the leader of a long running drug operation? That your idea? You're right, that will get our reputation back. Which will be really helpful when they retaliate and we're both dead."

"You and I have both heard the grumblings. The guys who ran it for Sloan's father are the same ones running it today. Marty's just the default head because they had so much respect for Martin Senior."

"So what? That doesn't mean they want him dead."

"You sure about that?"

"Yes. I am."

"Okay, maybe not dead. But what about just out of the picture?"

Clint was quiet for a moment. He watched Raines on the phone in his car, but his mind was on Jenny's words. If he killed Marty Sloan, there was no question his thugs would retaliate. They would have to, to keep the respect of the business intact. But if somehow Clint could get him arrested, his men could have his operation, and Clint could circulate that he can fix anything if he could fix what happened with Marty Sloan. This would be a massive undertaking; he and Jenny would need a lot of help.

Jenny said, "You like what I'm saying, right?"

"We won't be able to do this on our own."

"We have a few people in the police department. You don't think they could help us?"

"Not with this. Sloan has more people in the police on payroll than we do. I can assure you of that. Besides, even if we could convince dirty cops to help us, if something goes wrong, the retaliation on their families would be too much for them to risk. We need someone who would want Marty Sloan to go down as bad as we do. Someone smart, but if need be, they can be as ruthless as we are too."

They watched as Lawson got out of the car and walked toward the entrance of the small office complex. Clint and Jenny looked at each other, then at Lawson, then back at each other.

Clint said, "I know what you're thinking, and it's out of the question."

"Is it?" Jenny smirked.

"Yes. It is."

"You know, Clint, your pride is going to be the death of you."

Clint didn't answer. His mind was working. Even if he could somehow get past what happened with Lawson, working with him was still a long shot. Clint had no idea who the man was. Moreover, he had no idea who he was working for. But he did know that Marty Sloan had it out for him, and if Clint and Jenny could find something strong enough to make sure Lawson had it out for Sloan too, it could work.

Jenny filled the silence. "You remember what I told you

he did in Vegas last year? You want smart and ruthless, I think he might have both in spades."

"Find out who he works for, and find something we can use to make sure he has a compelling reason to take down Marty Sloan."

Jenny opened her laptop and began plugging away. "On it."

12

"LAWSON RAINES. HERE TO SEE VICTORIA MARSHALL."

Lawson didn't know what he expected, but as he stood at the receptionist's desk, he supposed it was something nicer than this from a supposed "A"-list Hollywood writer, or producer, or whatever Victoria was. This looked more like your average CPA office. Complete with the plastic plant in the corner.

"I'm sorry, Ms. Marshall isn't in today, sir. Can I leave a message for her?"

"Just have her call me as soon as possible." He turned to leave, then thought maybe he should try to track her down. "You have any idea when she might be back?"

"She's out of the country. Last-minute location scout. That's all I can really say."

Lawson nodded, then walked back outside into the never-ending sunshine. He hadn't dealt with anyone in Hollywood before, so he had no idea how common something like this was. However, alarm bells in his lizard brain began to sound. He hadn't heard from her in two and a half days. And while she didn't owe him anything, he felt it odd that she wouldn't want to follow up with him after what happened. To try at least to understand what kind of danger she might be in.

Lawson's phone began to ring. Cassie.

"Hello?"

"I take it your meeting was a short one."

"You really are a great detective, Cass. I answer my phone shortly after I am supposed to be in my meeting, and you deduce that it was a short meeting. The PI firm is certain to be a success."

"What?" Cassie seemed surprised. "No, I meant because of the news."

"What news?"

"Victoria Marshall. She's been reported missing."

Lawson let that sink in for a minute as he got in his car and started it up.

"Lawson?"

"I heard you. What else did they say?"

"Nothing yet, but I'm digging on it. Seems her daughter reported her missing last night. Hadn't seen her since you dropped her off after the meeting at the bar with Mister Fixer."

This was exactly what Lawson had been worried about. He should have gone looking for her after the second time she didn't answer his call. But technically, there wasn't anything he could do about it. He wasn't her personal security, she had only hired him for the one meeting. Not to continue working for her. If that had been the case, he would have handled the last couple days entirely differently. He was only checking up on her now as a courtesy.

"So, just as a reminder," Cassie said, "the way a conversation works is I say something, then you say something."

"Have you found anything on Clint Hues?"

"Okay, we're switching gears . . . yes. Not sure who he is working for, but I have a phone number. I called it, it's just an answering service. Probably just a covert way of fielding calls. Most likely someone who needs his services says some sort of password or something."

"You leave a message?" Lawson said.

"Yeah, I just said Lawson Raines thinks you're a pansy and left your phone number."

"You're a real riot. Find out more about Victoria going missing and get back to me."

"Sir, yes sir!"

Lawson ended the call, and just as soon as he was about to pull out, he noticed a car across the street. The man behind the wheel was staring intently, but when Lawson looked his way, he quickly turned his head. Lawson didn't let on that he noticed. Instead, he pulled out of the parking lot onto Wilshire and watched in his rearview as the man pulled out behind him, just inconspicuously enough that Lawson knew for sure he was being watched. But it wasn't the work of a professional. He was making things far too obvious.

Lawson punched the gas and took a quick right turn, then immediately whipped into a parking lot and beside a large pickup truck. His car was hidden from the road. The man in the Mercedes sedan sped forward, obviously trying to see where Lawson had gone, and Lawson pulled back out onto the road after a few cars had passed and kept the Mercedes in sight. He knew that once the man realized he had lost Lawson, he would drive back to base, wherever base was, and Lawson could maybe get a look at who the man was working for.

After a couple aimless miles, the man in the Mercedes had circled back to a building not far from Victoria

Marshall's office. Lawson just kept driving by. He called Cassie.

"Miss me?" she answered.

"2425 Wilshire Boulevard."

"Hello to you too."

"See who it is. I was being followed."

"Followed? Let me plug it in."

"I have a feeling this will tell us who Clint Hues is working for," Lawson said.

"Why, you don't think it was Hues following you?"

"It was a Hispanic man. If Hues were following me, I think he'd do it himself."

"The office belongs to a Martin Sloan Jr."

"That was fast," Lawson said.

"Google is pretty nifty, Lawson. You should try it. Says it's the office for Sloan Productions LLC. Ring a bell?"

"Never heard of it."

"Me either, but Los Angeles isn't our beat. I'll look into it. Maybe give Frank Shaw a call. He might be able to—"

"No," Lawson said. "Don't even think about it."

"Okay," Cassie said, "let me just jot this down . . . Help Lawson with everything he asks"—she was drawing out her words like she was taking handwritten notes—"but don't use the only real local source of info we have. Got it. This will be easy."

Lawson didn't react to her sarcasm. "Let me know what you find."

"Copy. And listen, I was doing some digging on Taylor. Something's not adding up. You said she's in trouble because they threatened her sister if she didn't pay, right?"

"That's what Taylor said."

"Well, her sister seems fine to me."

Lawson was confused. "How could you know that? Google gives updates on how people are doing now?"

"Lawson, it's 2019. Everyone knows how everyone is doing. All the time. It's called Instagram."

"That doesn't help me."

"It's an app on your phone. People post pictures all the time. Taylor's sister just posted one this morning. She's in London, heading to the park to enjoy the sunshine, hashtag blessed."

"Hashtag?"

"Never mind. Point is, unless this cartel has people in London, Taylor isn't being honest with you about her sister being in danger."

Lawson still didn't understand. "Why would anyone post pictures of themselves where anyone can know where they are?"

"I don't get it either, but you may want to have a talk with Lexi about it."

"Lexi? She doesn't have Instacam."

"Insta*gram*. It's—yes she does. I follow her. Your house has made the photo roll several times. You really should pay more attention."

Lawson didn't hear the last line. All he could think about was the fact that if Cassie could look and see where Taylor's sister was, what would stop one of these assholes in LA from finding out where Lexi lived by her pictures on the app?

"I've got to get back to the house. Find out why Martin Sloan Jr. would be having someone follow me. Or at least why Clint Hues might be working for him."

"That's easy, but it's a big problem," Cassie said.

"Great."

"Sloan Jr.'s daddy was a made man."

"Was?"

"Yeah, that means Junior probably took over when he died," Cassie said. "And now that you ruined his meeting with Victoria Marshall, he and all his thugs are going to be after you. Nice work. You seem to be a magnet for pieces of shit."

"And you seem to have completely lost your filter. I'll meet you at your office after I go have a talk with the girls. I need some answers, and I need them fast."

13

LAWSON SWERVED INTO HIS DRIVEWAY, NOT EVEN BOTHERING with the garage. This was the first time he had been upset with Lexi since they'd reunited. He was glad it took him twenty minutes to get home. He needed that time to cool off. Even though it sounded like Lexi was just being a normal teenager, putting herself out there on the internet was a mistake. Especially with the seedy people in Lawson's past. Whether he liked it or not, what happened in Las Vegas was going to follow them forever.

When he walked through the front door, Lexi and Taylor were reading lines in front of the fireplace hearth.

"Dad! Taylor is SO good at this."

"Give me your phone."

Lawson got right to it. Lexi's face went from elation to shock.

"What? My phone?"

"Give it to me right now."

"Dad, what's wrong?"

She took her phone from her pocket and handed it to him.

"Show me this Insta-thing."

"Instagram? Why?"

"Just show me."

She took her phone back, tapped on the screen a couple times, then handed it back.

"What's wrong with you, Dad? What's the big deal?"

Lawson looked at her phone like it was in Chinese. "Show me the pictures you put on here."

Lexi moved over beside him, tapped again, then swiped her finger up and photos scrolled. Most of them were harmless, but then he saw the one of the front of the house. The house number showing plain as day.

"Lexi, you can't put pictures on here that show where your house is. Do you know how dangerous that is?"

"It doesn't say the street name."

Lexi was defensive.

"You don't think someone can figure that out by the look of the house and the surroundings? Delete your account, right now."

"Dad! I'm not deleting my account. You can't make me do that!"

"Delete it. I'm not playing. It's dangerous to—"

"I'm not deleting it! No!"

"Lexi—"

"Hang on," Taylor interrupted. "Maybe there's a way you can both be happy."

Lawson gave her a stern look. "You stay out of this. You and I are going to have a talk next."

Taylor put up her hands, politely suggesting he pump the brakes and calm down for a second. Lawson took a deep breath and let her speak.

"I'm not trying to get in the middle. Lexi, just delete all the pictures of anything that might remotely show your

63

location. Your dad is right. There are a lot of crazy people out there. Trust me, I know."

Lexi took back her phone and began deleting.

"Lawson, once she deletes those, I'll show her how to make her account private so only her friends can see her photos. It won't be open to the public. Okay? Then the two of you can sit down and go through the photos so both of you are satisfied that they are okay to be on there."

Lawson didn't really understand any of what Taylor was saying, but it sounded reasonable. Lexi looked up at him, and he nodded his head. She rolled her eyes, a reaction he supposed he'd better get used to. She was a teenager now after all.

"Taylor, you and I need to talk. Lexi, keep doing what you're doing. We'll be right back."

Lawson turned toward the stairs, and Taylor followed him upstairs to Lexi's room. After she walked in, he shut the door behind her.

"Have I outstayed my welcome?"

"Listen, Taylor, I agreed to help you because Lexi likes you. But I told you last night, if you weren't honest with me, I can't help you. You lied to me about your sister, and I'm having a hard time finding a reason not to throw your ass back out there where I found you."

Taylor's shoulders slumped and she looked down at the floor.

"And don't do the puppy dog routine, it won't work on me."

She looked back up at him and straightened her posture. "I'm not a child."

"You're not? Then stop acting like one."

"Who the hell—" Taylor stopped herself, realizing there

wasn't much she could say. She was the one who needed him.

"Why did you lie to me?" Lawson said.

Taylor turned away from him and walked over to the window. She slid something off her wrist, took her long hair in her hands and put it up into a ponytail. Lawson looked out the window; he didn't want the way she looked to sway him from being as harsh as he thought he needed to be.

"I'm sorry." She turned back toward him. "You're right. But I can't tell you why I lied to you."

Lawson opened the bedroom door. "Then you can get the hell out of my house."

The two stared at each other for a minute. Neither making a move. Then Taylor started to cry. She took a seat on the bed. Lawson stood like a statue. He was incredibly uncomfortable. He hadn't had a woman cry around him in far too long to remember. He honestly had no clue what to do. On one hand, he just wanted her to stop and tell him why she lied. On the other, he just wanted her not to be upset. Maybe there was a little of his old self in there somewhere after all. But no part of his old self was giving him any ideas about how to console her.

She continued to cry, and Lawson thumbed through his brain for what to do next. Of all people, Lauren's voice is the one he heard. Often when he needed answers, his late wife would whisper in his ear. In this case, she was telling him to comfort Taylor. Like he would if it was Lauren herself crying. She was still doing her best to make Lawson a better man, even though she'd been gone for over a decade.

Lawson moved slowly and sat next to Taylor on the bed. He awkwardly put his hand on her shoulder.

"You don't have to do that. I lied to you. Even though you helped me when I needed it most."

65

"Tell me what's going on. Maybe I can help."

Taylor looked up at him. Her emerald eyes were swimming in tears. Most people looked unattractive when they cried, but not her. Lawson couldn't imagine a situation where this woman could ever be unattractive. Seeing her hurt, he felt something inside him that he hadn't in a long time.

He wanted to kiss her.

"But . . ." Taylor stopped to stifle more tears. "I still can't tell you. Only two people in the world know this about me. Well, apparently more now, which is why I'm in trouble."

"I can't help when I don't know what's going on. You understand that."

Taylor nodded. "I know. Okay. Just bear with me—"

Lawson stood from the bed and looked toward the window.

"What's wrong?" Taylor said.

"Sirens. You don't hear that?"

Taylor cocked her head. Then a terrified look came over her. "Did you call the police?"

Lawson watched as two police cars hurried onto his driveway and came to a stop just outside his house.

"Stay here. Unless whoever shot you told the police you were here, there's no way they could know."

"Dad!" Lexi shouted from downstairs just as the sounds of banging on the front door made it to Lawson.

He rushed past Taylor. "Don't move." He jogged down the stairs and looked at Lexi. "It's fine. Just don't say anything."

Lexi nodded.

After more banging on the door, Lawson opened it. Two police officers were standing in front of him, one of them holding a pair of handcuffs in his hand.

"Lawson Raines?" the short and stocky one said.

Lawson nodded.

"You're under arrest. Keep your hands where I can see them."

It never even crossed his mind that they could be there for him.

14

THE EMPTY ROOM, COLD BY NATURE, WITH ITS CONCRETE
floor, single table, two chairs, one of them empty opposite
Lawson, and a camera perched in the corner, sent chills up
his spine. It was all too familiar being brought in like this,
and the nostalgia wasn't pleasant in the least. And just like
last time, Cassie had to be there for Lexi when he was
arrested, but at least now she wasn't a two-year-old child.

Though Lawson wasn't expecting it, he supposed he
should have. He knew the video of the bar fight was circu-
lating. The police had tracked his face and found him in the
system. It didn't take them long to trace him to the house in
the Hollywood Hills. A lot of things were swirling through
his mind. Victoria Marshall disappearing, Martin Sloan Jr.
having him followed, Clint Hues and his band of misfits
seeking revenge, and the thing that Taylor was about to tell
him in the bedroom were all eating away at his conscience.
But the thing gnawing at him most was disappointment in
himself.

Lawson's plan was to lie all the way low after getting
Lexi back and surviving the nightmare in Vegas. He had

done a good job of it for a year. But he really stepped in it when he took the phone call from Victoria Marshall. It had been like a domino effect of falling mishaps ever since.

The door to his holding room opened, and just when he thought things couldn't get any worse, they doubled down. Time hadn't been good to Frank Shaw. The brown hair he used to have now looked Just For Men black, the lines on his face read like a map, and his eyes, they just looked tired.

"Lawson Raines. Long time no see," Frank said as he took a seat across from Lawson.

"Not long enough."

"You just can't seem to stay away from trouble, can you? You must be one of those people who just don't feel alive unless they're miserable."

"What is this, Frank? Did you have me brought in because I hung up on you earlier?"

"First off, I'm here to do you a favor. I didn't have you brought in. That bar fight with known criminals did that for you, and it was the police who brought you in. But I already got you cleared. I was just trying to see if I could—"

"Does that mean I'm free to go?" Lawson interrupted.

Frank shook his head, pulled out a cigarette, and lit it. "You mind?" He took a long drag and puffed a cloud of smoke into the air. "What are you chasing here, Raines? 'Cause I'm here to tell you, you're messing around in the wrong circles."

Lawson's mind was telling him to get up and walk out. His skin was crawling just being in the same room with this guy. But while he had him there, he may as well use it to his advantage. Of course, if Frank Shaw could ever be an advantage to anyone.

"What do you know about the Victoria Marshall disappearance?"

"Why, she your girlfriend?"

Lawson just stared while Frank took another puff. He couldn't stand the fact that Frank was getting enjoyment out of this, but it was clear that he was.

Frank said, "I don't even know who she is. Just what I heard on the news, same as you. But I do know who Clint Hues is. Been building a file on him for a while now. Not the kind of guy a man would want his daughter bringing home, that's for sure."

"What about Martin Sloan?"

"Martin Sloan?" Frank repeated. "The movie producer?"

"Never mind." Lawson stood.

"All right. Settle down."

Lawson sat back down.

"Word is, he's a softy, but I know for a fact he's not. You asking for Victoria Marshall?"

"Why, are they connected?"

"You mean you really don't know?"

Lawson was tired of constantly playing catch-up. He'd already made up his mind that when he walked out of the police station he was going to go on the offensive.

"Clearly not."

"That meeting you broke up was for Sloan. Clint Hues has been seen leaving Sloan's office on a few occasions. A couple of my sources say Sloan wants a film that Victoria has the rights to. Must have sent Hues in to persuade her to sell it to him. Anyway, what's it to you? Why do you care?"

Lawson's wheels were turning. He didn't understand why, if Hues was working for Sloan, Sloan would have someone else follow him. Something was off about what Frank was saying.

Lawson sat back. "Then it sounds like Victoria Marshall's disappearance is pretty obvious, isn't it?"

"You think Sloan kidnapped her? You haven't been in this town long enough, Raines. Nothing is what it seems."

"So you know that Sloan tried to strong-arm Victoria, and when it didn't work she went missing a day later, and you don't think there is a connection?"

"I don't know anything for certain. All of what I'm telling you is third-party information. From informants, not known knowledge. You expect me to stir something up over a movie deal?"

"No, Frank, you are doing exactly what I expect. Nothing."

Frank put out his cigarette and stood. His brow furrowed and his voice growled. "Tread carefully, Raines. My favor only goes so far. You got a raw deal in Vegas and I'm trying to throw you a bone here. Don't bite the hand that feeds you."

"Two cliché dog lines in a row. You watch too many cop shows, Frank."

"Okay. I tried to help you. I know you have a daughter at home and I was trying to help you keep her safe—"

Lawson couldn't stop his reaction to hearing Frank mention Lexi. He reached as he stood and took the collar of Frank's shirt in his hand, nearly pulling him across the table. Two policemen rushed in along with a woman dressed in a business suit. Lawson held onto Frank's shirt until they ripped his hand free. His eyes remained locked in.

"You want me to lock him up?" the police officer asked Frank as he straightened his shirt.

Frank stared for a moment longer. "No. Let him go. The piece of shit will end up back in here on his own in no time, I'm sure." Then he said to Lawson, "Don't call asking me for help when shit hits the fan. You just burned this bridge."

"Just stay out of my way, Frank. Once again I'll do your job for you. For old time's sake."

Frank didn't respond so his partner did. "Frank bought you time, Lawson. You should be thanking him."

"Yeah? Who the hell are you?"

"I'm his partner, Claudia Henderson. You do realize you were the last person seen with Victoria Marshall? From your background, I don't have to tell you that you are prime suspect number one, do I? Frank vouched for you with the detective, but if Ms. Marshall doesn't turn up sometime today, you can bet they'll be beating down your door again. If you know anything about where she might be, I suggest you tell us now. Or there won't be someone to bail you out next time."

Lawson didn't know what to say. Everything she said was true. He picked up his plastic bag of belongings that Claudia had laid on the table and walked past the police officers.

"One final warning," Frank said.

Lawson stopped at the door but didn't turn around.

"Whatever your involvement is in this, get out of it. Take a little vacation while this gets sorted out. Maybe just move back to Kentucky."

Lawson twisted the handle and walked out. He didn't know what to say, and if he did, he wouldn't have said it anyway.

15

SEEING AS THOUGH THE POLICE HAD GIVEN LAWSON A RIDE TO the station, he had to call Cassie to come and pick him up. It was best anyway, because if he wanted her help before, now he flat out needed it.

"Okay," Cassie said as she turned onto the main road, headed back to Lawson's house. "So we need to find Victoria Marshall."

"Yeah, and we need to find her today. Otherwise, you'll be working on this while I'm sitting in jail."

"Bailed out by Frank Shaw. That's gotta sting."

"It's just plain weird is what it is." Lawson squinted into the sun. The sky beyond the buildings was as blue as a lonely heart. "That man would never do me any favors. There has to be something in it for him."

"Well, you said his partner, Claudia, seemed pretty sharp. Maybe she's been a good influence on him."

"Maybe hell hath frozen over."

"Yeah. Maybe. But it doesn't matter. What's important is finding Victoria, or at least finding out who took her."

"Martin Sloan Jr.," Lawson said.

"Certainly looks like it on the surface. Drug trafficker turned movie producer. Seems like the kind of thing a man like him would do with those resources and a penchant for getting his way. But don't you think he would know it would seem a little obvious?"

"Why would he think that?"

"He had to know that a fight like the one at the meeting with a high-profile criminal and movie producer would get some attention from the authorities. Don't you think he'd assume the police would be able to put Clint Hues and him together?"

"Probably," Lawson thought about it. "But you have to understand the kind of man Sloan is. He's used to being above the law, used to his father being above the law. Sometimes that leads you to bad decisions."

"I don't buy it." Cassie turned up into the Hollywood Hills, not far from Lawson's house. "It's too obvious. There's something else going on here."

"And sometimes the most obvious thing *is* the solution." Lawson spun his phone in his hand. "Sloan kidnaps Victoria, holds her hostage until she signs over the movie rights. How could Victoria prove she didn't just sign it over to him once he let her go?"

"Umm, because she was kidnapped. Signing a document under duress doesn't make it legal."

"It does when you tell the police you weren't kidnapped. Victoria has a daughter. You can be damn sure Sloan would threaten her with her daughter's life."

"Then she can't say anything," Cassie agreed with Lawson's line of reasoning. "Signing over the movie rights will be the only way to ensure her daughter stays safe."

"Right."

"So, now what? We just go beat down Martin Sloan's door? Demand he hand over Victoria Marshall?"

Lawson didn't respond.

"Lawson?"

He wasn't hearing Cassie speak to him. When they rounded the corner, all of his senses broke down when he noticed there was no off-duty cop car sitting in front of his house.

"Where the hell is Eric?" Lawson's pulse began to pound.

"I-I don't know. He was supposed to be here until this evening!"

Cassie sped up and jerked the car into the driveway.

"Whose car is that?"

Lawson didn't respond. Instead, he jumped out of the car and ran around the black Dodge Challenger sitting in front of his garage. Three strides later he exploded through the front door, and his mind froze when he saw a strange woman and Clint Hues sitting opposite Lexi on the living room couch.

"Hey, Dad! What's wrong? You look scary."

"Lexi, get upstairs, now."

Clint leaned back on the couch and spread his arms out on the pillows. "Geez, relax, Lawson. Just an old pal come to say hello."

Lexi said, "He said you told him to wait for you here. Said you were getting out of jail and everything was going to be okay."

"Upstairs, Lexi. Right now. And shut your door."

"God, Dad. I can't do anything right."

As Lexi stormed off, Cassie walked in the front door behind Lawson. Her weapon drawn. As soon as he heard

Lexi's door shut, Lawson bolted for Clint, rage pulsing through his veins. Clint's smug look disappeared, and he held a hand up as a stop sign just before Lawson could get to him.

"I just saved your daughter's life."

Clint was no small man, but Lawson picked him up by his shirt and tossed him over the couch. Clint scrambled to his feet, and Lawson stepped over the couch.

"You'd better talk fast or the beating I gave you the other night will seem like a vacation."

Clint bowed up; he wasn't a man used to being rag-dolled. The woman with him stepped in between them and tried to calm both parties. "Just hold on a second." She looked at Clint. "I tried to tell you this little stunt of waiting for him in the house with his daughter was a dumb idea."

Clint straightened his shirt. "No it wasn't. I needed to show him—" Clint looked at Lawson. "I needed to show you how vulnerable you are. You've got some powerful people coming down on you. Time to tighten things up. LA isn't where you come from. Cops are bought and sold here every day. You can't trust anyone."

Lawson's chest was heaving. Seeing his daughter sitting with this stranger had spiked his adrenaline, and frankly it scared him to death. He felt a hand on his arm, and he ripped it away.

Cassie took his arm again. "Okay, Lawson, let's calm down. Hear what he has to say." Then to Clint. "It better be good, though, cause I'll fucking shoot you for involving Lexi in this."

Cassie's normally playful rhetoric was gone. Lawson assumed she was just as rattled as he was.

"All right. I get that it was a lot," Clint said. "But I'm telling you, it was necessary."

Cassie spoke for Lawson who was still trying to talk

himself down from tearing Clint's head off. "You said you saved Lexi's life. What do you mean?"

The woman with Clint spoke. "Can we just sit down and talk about it?"

"No." Lawson was blunt, but his emotions were back under control. "Spit it out." His eyes hadn't moved from Clint's since he walked in the front door.

"We have a mutual enemy now is what I meant. Marty Sloan."

Lawson was taken aback. "You mean, your boss?"

"Sort of," Clint said. "Look, Sloan obviously wants you to pay for ruining the meeting with Victoria. I'm not sure why the movie she has means so much to him, but I don't get paid to know these things. Nor do I care. What I care about is life after working with Sloan."

"He fired you, didn't he?" Lawson said.

"Because of you. Which made me want to retaliate, but working together seemed the smarter option."

"You mean the only option."

"Look," Clint said, moving into car salesman mode. Lawson didn't like this guy, but he did want to hear what he had to say. "You and I aren't all that different, the way I see it."

Lawson let that one slide.

"We'll do whatever it takes to get things done. I did my homework on you. Sloan's operation is bigger than you, and me too, but together we could maybe make something happen."

"You still haven't told me how you saved my daughter. And like Cassie said, it better be good."

"Sloan wanted her kidnapped. He wanted to use her as leverage until you could persuade Victoria Marshall to sign over the movie."

"Bullshit." Lawson wasn't buying it. "He already kidnapped Victoria, he doesn't need me."

Clint's face scrunched in confusion. "Kidnapped Victoria?"

Lawson could tell Clint was caught off guard.

"He would never do that. He's smarter than that. Sloan would know the police could tie the meeting gone wrong with Victoria back to him through me. Kidnapping her would be too obvious."

Lawson looked over at Cassie. "Don't." He knew she wanted to throw in an "I told you so." To Clint he said, "So if you're fired, how do you know all of this about Sloan wanting to use me?"

"I know you noticed the man in the Mercedes following you today, didn't you?"

A chill curled up Lawson's spine. He waited for Clint.

"I know you did, because he's terrible at it."

"Who is terrible at it?" Cassie said.

"Hector. He works for Sloan, but he used to work for me. It's how I got hooked up working with Sloan in the first place. I called Hector after Sloan let me go, and he told me all about it."

Something still didn't seem right to Lawson. Probably the fact that Clint had rolled in here the way he did and used Lexi as a pawn. But everything he was saying was adding up.

"So why tell me this?"

"Like I said, Raines, we have a mutual enemy, and alone there is nothing we can do. But together, I can clear my reputation if we take him down. And once Sloan is gone, your daughter will be safe. He has a son, and they are close, so he knows you will do anything to ensure her safety. Believe me, working with you is the last thing I want to do.

But I'm a big-picture kind of guy, and this is the only way we both get what we want."

Lawson looked over at Cassie. She shrugged her shoulders. He knew she wouldn't like working with a Hollywood criminal any more than he did, but Clint might be right.

There might not be any other option.

16

THE MASSIVE WINDOWS IN LAWSON'S LIVING ROOM LET IN THE tangerine light of the fading sun. After Clint and Jenny left, Cassie and Lawson had been hashing out the best way to move forward. Cassie had also been working some angles at the police department. Not only trying to get some information about Victoria's disappearance, but doing what she could to see what the detective on the case was going to do about Lawson. He and Cassie both knew how it worked. If there was no other information coming in, the detective would have no choice but to question Lawson. He should have already done it, but apparently Frank Shaw really had put in the good word.

Lawson and Cassie hadn't really come to any conclusions, mostly because they didn't have any leads. They didn't know anyone in LA, and they certainly didn't know anyone who knew Victoria Marshall. Cassie was going to try to contact Victoria's daughter the next morning. See if she could shed some light on any ideas of where her mother could be. In the meantime, they needed to find an in, someone with more information on Sloan and his operation. Or at least where he could be holding Victoria if he had in fact taken her. Clint was adamant that Sloan wouldn't have done it, but Cassie had convinced him at least to ask the right people some questions to see if they knew anything about her being held somewhere.

The next trick was going to be finding something on Sloan if he had not kidnapped Victoria. If Clint and Lawson were going to satisfy both of their agendas—Clint having Sloan put away in order to clear his own reputation, and Lawson getting rid of Sloan to keep himself and Lexi safe—they would have to trip him up somewhere and bring the police down on him. Clint was clear about how difficult this would be, what with all of the police on Sloan's payroll. However, he did say that Hector didn't mind sniffing around his bosses operation and would relay any openings Clint and Lawson could possibly exploit.

For Lawson, the problems ran even deeper than that. At the same time he was worrying about Sloan, he also was invested in helping Taylor. He needed to talk to her, alone, and really find out what was going on. Whatever it was she was about to tell him before he was arrested, he knew it was going to shed more light on the reason she'd gotten herself into the mess that got her shot. And he knew it was going to be a different story than the one she told about her sister, he just didn't know how bad this entire mess was going to get. If the last couple days were any indication, everything was more than likely going to end up worse than he thought.

All of the details aside, his main concern was keeping his daughter safe. And though he knew she was always safe when she was with him, he didn't feel that she was safe at their house alone. As far as Lawson knew, Sloan and his men didn't know about Cassie. And they certainly wouldn't know where Cassie lived; he wasn't even sure he did. And he trusted Cassie not only with his own life but also with Lexi's. She would die to keep her safe. So he was sending Lexi along with Cassie so that he could get things cleared up with Taylor without interruption. He needed to make some progress on at least one of his problems. Since Taylor and he would be alone, it was the best place to start.

As Cassie and Lawson were finishing their conversation, Lexi and Taylor made their way downstairs. Lexi was already packed. She wanted to stay with Taylor, but she understood that things were complicated and agreed to go along with Cassie. Lawson stood as Lexi came over to give him a hug.

"I'm sorry if I made things worse by putting pictures of the house on Instagram, and by letting that man in today."

Lawson gave her a squeeze. "It's all right, Lexi. We're both learning together. We'll figure it out."

Lexi nodded.

Lawson tried to ease Lexi's worry. "And don't worry about any of it. I'll take care of Taylor, and I'll make sure nobody else like the man who came here today comes here ever again. Now go and make Cassie run lines with you. You've got another round of auditions coming up."

Cassie laughed. "Well, thanks. Now I have to follow Taylor Lockhart. No big deal."

"You'll be fine, Cassie," Lexi smiled. "I'll make you that drink Dad makes you."

Taylor said, "You know how to make cocktails?"

Lexi smiled and nodded.

Lawson shrugged his shoulders. "I never claimed to be Father of the Year."

"Have Dad make you one, Taylor. They're Cassie's favorite. I bet you'll like it too."

"I'll have to see if I can get him to." Taylor smiled at

Lawson.

Weakness wasn't a thing a man like Lawson Raines felt very often, but Taylor's smile could melt steel.

Lawson turned from Taylor to Lexi. "All right, you two get going. Call me when you get to Cassie's."

"I'll text you. No one calls anyone anymore, Dad."

"Yeah, Dad," Taylor said, and winked.

Lawson must have made some sort of face, because the look on Cassie's face was like she could see right through him and she knew what effect Taylor was having on him. Lawson didn't like it.

"Bye, you two." Cassie smiled.

Taylor said, "Lexi, don't forget, don't be afraid to look stupid. Bring yourself into your character and something real will come out."

"Thanks, Taylor. You're awesome."

Cassie and Lexi left on that note, and Lawson was left alone with Taylor. When the front door shut, the two of them stood in silence for what seemed like an awkwardly long amount of time. Lawson felt really uncomfortable. He always did around strangers, especially since being released from prison. But with Taylor there was this electricity, and it was enough to make him nauseous.

"How 'bout that drink?" Taylor finally ended the suffering.

Lawson didn't even acknowledge her words; he just headed to the kitchen and began mixing. He was going to make his a little stronger than usual. Though it was hard to make a drink stronger than bourbon neat.

"I know you want to finish the conversation we started earlier, but it's clearly been a long day for you. Can we just give ourselves a break for the night? We aren't going to solve anything right now anyway."

Though Lawson had no idea what they would talk about if they weren't talking about the issues at hand, it did sound good to give it a rest. Rather than answer her question, he simply finished making her drink and handed it to her. Her green eyes sparkled in the yellow light above the kitchen island. It gave her tanned skin a glow. She had taken the time to fix her hair, and the golden-brown waves fell down below her neckline. She was still wearing the tank top she had on earlier in the day. He thought about asking her if she wanted a T-shirt, but the words couldn't form as he sipped the Blanton's bourbon in his glass.

"You don't talk much, do you?"

Lawson ironically only shook his head.

"Lexi told me about what happened to your family. I'm sorry. I know all too well the pain of losing someone close to you. It changes you forever."

Lawson took another drink. He looked at Taylor, and even though she was talking about what happened to Lauren, he couldn't think past Taylor's lips.

"You hungry?"

It was all he could think to say. His brain was scrambled looking at Taylor. Listening to her. The way she moved, he could understand why millions of people would be captivated by her on film.

"Is that what you do when you're uncomfortable? Change the subject?"

Lawson's demeanor changed. Who was she to be so forward? "Look, as you have already come to know, I'm not much of a conversationalist. Especially when it comes to things that are so personal."

"Now you know how I felt in the bedroom earlier. I was about to tell you something that only a handful of my closest friends know about me."

Lawson did understand. He turned and opened the refrigerator. "I don't have much in here, but Lexi, having the palette of a forty-year-old, always keeps Havarti cheese and grapes on hand. Some fancy crackers too. That work?"

"Love cheese and grapes. Sounds great. How 'bout I find a movie since you aren't much of a talker. Any specific genre? Let me guess, you'd love something like *The Fugitive*."

Lawson brought a plate and his drink into the living room. He turned on the television and handed the remote to Taylor.

"That's a good one. My wife and I—"

Lawson stopped himself and looked up at Taylor. She didn't look away from the channel guide on the TV. "It's okay, Lawson. You can talk about her. My therapist said it helps keep their memory alive when you do."

Lawson swallowed hard. His entire body was itching like he was having an allergic reaction to intimacy. With Cassie it was easy. They were like best friends, always taking playful shots at each other. But being there with Taylor was altogether different. Something he hadn't experienced in over twenty years, not since he and Lauren first started getting close, all the way back in high school. But there was also something about Taylor that made him feel comfortable.

"Lauren and I used to love *Wedding Crashers*."

Taylor whirled around, a look of shock on her face. "Get the hell out of here. You? *Wedding Crashers*?"

Lawson smiled. He understood how that could be shocking if you only knew the 2019 version of him. "Oh yeah. I wasn't always this way."

"What way? Rigid? Emotionless? Addicted to working out?"

She was so much like Lauren it scared him. That is exactly the way she used to rag on him. Call him out and make him feel uncomfortable. Lawson couldn't respond. His tongue was tied.

"I understand." Taylor winked. "When things are out of control, you overcontrol everything you can."

She was really something.

"All right, okay." Lawson played it down. "How about that movie. Any movie. Anything would be better than being psychoanalyzed by the woman with the gunshot wound in her shoulder."

Taylor made a face as if his words stung a bit, then smiled, then looked away at the television. "Okay. Touché, I guess. But look what I found on Video On Demand."

Lawson looked over to the TV, and a picture of Owen Wilson and Vince Vaughn filled the screen.

"Feel like crashing a wedding or two?" Her smile radiated. "Or did I hurt the big strong man's feelings?"

Lawson huffed and walked around to sit on the couch. He took a sip of bourbon and a bite of cheese and cracker, then sat back while she continued to stare at him, waiting for a response.

"Are you going to start the movie or not?" he said.

Taylor smiled and plopped down beside him. The next couple hours were something that Lawson never thought he would experience again. But it was something he needed more than he knew. The movie flew by, and then she introduced him to *The Hangover*. Together they ate, drank, shared high fives, and laughed until they couldn't laugh any more. And it was a good thing they took that much-needed break, because the next day was going to test every last ounce of Lawson's resolve.

17

A golden ray of sunshine needled at Lawson's closed eyelids, seemingly wedging its way inside. After a couple helpless blinks, one eye finally opened. A few blinks later, so did the other, and the fog slowly lifted that had been draped in front of them. He almost jumped in reaction to seeing Taylor's head lying heavy on his lap. They must have fallen asleep—passed out really. Lawson couldn't remember the end of *The Hangover Part II*. His hand was resting on her shoulder. As he removed it, he slid it down her arm. Taylor's skin was soft and warm. His touch roused her.

She sat up slowly, giving her arms a stretch; then after a yawn, she gave him a smile. "Morning, handsome."

Lawson scooted one cushion over, putting a little distance between them.

"Sorry if I was snoring," she said, her smile as bright as the sun coming in the window behind her.

"If you did, I didn't hear it."

"You want some water?" They both said it in unison, and

they both stood up at the same time. Too close for comfort for Lawson, but he didn't move.

Neither did she.

"That was fun," she said. Then she tucked a loose strand of hair behind her ear. "I needed that."

Lawson, in typical Lawson fashion, didn't say a word. He just nodded.

Taylor took him by the arm and pulled him closer. There was a heat between them, so intense it erased his mind, and Lawson just stood there staring at her lips. As she raised herself onto her toes, she took her right arm and placed it around his shoulder. Just as she was beginning to lean in, Lawson heard his phone vibrating from afar and the moment between them was shattered.

Lexi.

"She never checked in!"

Lawson practically shoved Taylor out of the way to get to his phone. He ran to the kitchen. Why was his phone on vibrate? It was *never* on vibrate!

He picked up his phone and his stomach dropped. Twenty-one missed calls from Lexi. And seven more missed texts. His heart was on the floor. What had he done?

He tapped on the missed calls notification and dialed Lexi. She picked it up in the middle of the first ring.

Lexi was frantic. "Dad! I don't know where I am! I've been calling all night! They took Cassie!"

"Lexi, are you okay? Where are you? What happened?"

He had heard her say she didn't know where she was and the words *They took Cassie*, but apparently it hadn't registered yet.

"I don't know! Some kind of park, hiding in a green tube slide, but I don't know where. I ran when they took her.

They tried to get me but I ran! I think they're still looking for me!"

Lawson's blood pressure was through the roof. He let his little girl go all night in trouble. And for what? A pretty woman and some movies? He was furious with himself but he had to focus. "What's around you? Tell me what you see."

Taylor came running over, reaching for his phone. He shoved her away. "What are you doing? Can't you hear she's lost?"

"I can help! Give me your phone. I can tell you exactly where she is."

"What? How—hold on, Lexi, I'm coming, baby."

Taylor took the phone from Lawson and put the call on speaker. "It's okay, Lexi. Is your Find My iPhone connected to your dad's?"

Lexi was crying. "Yeah . . . yes. Cassie linked them for us."

Lawson had no idea what they were talking about.

Taylor looked up at Lawson. "Go get the car ready, I can take you right to her."

Lawson ran for the garage. As soon as the door was high enough, he pulled the car out, spun a one-eighty, and opened the passenger door. Taylor came running out and jumped in the passenger seat. "Turn right out of the driveway. Go straight until I tell you to turn!"

Lawson mashed the gas pedal and the car spun its wheels out of the driveway.

"We're on our way, Lexi. Just sit tight!" Taylor said.

"We're on our way. Don't move!" Lawson shouted at the phone.

Taylor hit mute on the call and turned toward Lawson.

"It's okay. She's okay. We know exactly where she is, all right?"

Lawson nodded, but her calming words had zero effect on the adrenaline rushing all through him.

"Dad," Lexi said through the phone, "I'm sorry if I'm the one who got us into this. Is Cassie going to be okay?"

Cassie.

In his frantic state to get to his daughter, the words *They took Cassie* never had a chance to hit him. Lawson swerved around the tight turn of the road he was descending, and out of the corner of his eye he saw Taylor unmute the call. But he didn't have words. Taylor gave him a tap on the arm and a nod, a suggestion to give his daughter some reassurance.

"She . . . Cassie is going to be fine, sweetheart. You know I'll find her. None of this is your fault."

"But I put those pictures of our house on Instagram. Is that why they came to take me? Is that why Cassie is in trouble?"

Lawson came to the stoplight at the bottom of the hill, and Taylor pointed for him to turn right.

"Lexi, none of this is your fault. Don't worry—"

"Dad, I hear someone."

Lawson's blood ran cold. She said it in a whisper as if they were close to her. "Lexi, don't say anything else, just keep your phone on. I'll be there to get you in no time!"

"Turn right!" Taylor shouted. "It looks like she's in Plummer Park. It's right up here on the left."

Lawson took the turn fast, and the car wobbled as he straightened it out. He reached across Taylor and pulled his spare Sig Sauer from the glove box. There wasn't a lot of green space in West Hollywood, so it wasn't hard to spot the entrance to the park. He cut across oncoming traffic and pulled into a loading zone just in front of the park and was halfway out of the car before it was fully stopped. There was a building with a sign that read Plummer Park Community Center.

"The park is behind the community center," Taylor said. She had sidled up to him. "I've been here before. That's where the slide will be."

"Get back in the car." Lawson kept it short. He followed her instructions and moved around the right side of the community center. He felt her leave his side, and he focused on the row of shrubs and trees at the edge of the building. He walked with his gun down by his side, but it was obvious to the few people out exercising that morning that he wasn't out for a leisurely stroll and they scattered at the sight of him. He came to the trees and with two steps through them, the green tube slide quickly came into view.

But so did the two men who were now only a few feet from it.

18

THE TWO MEN APPROACHING LAWSON'S HELPLESS DAUGHTER hiding in the slide had their backs to him. In a matter of seconds a few things occurred to him. He could shoot them both dead where they stood. A tempting act for a father protecting his daughter. The problem with that was twofold. If both men were dead, finding who was responsible for trying to kidnap Lexi, and finding Cassie, would be greatly hindered. Without being able to question at least one of them, Cassie would most certainly die. The other issue would be proving why they were righteous kills. Most likely the two of them had criminal records, but chancing it would mean risking the rest of his life behind bars—therefore rendering the saving of Lexi's life pointless, because he couldn't protect her from the inside.

He would certainly take that risk if there was no other way, but they were obviously intent on the slide, so they would never see him coming.

Lawson tucked the Sig at the small of his back and surged from the trees. His heart was racing out of control and his stomach was in knots. He hopped the small fence that sequestered the children's play area from the rest of the park, and just as Lexi let out a scream when one of the men reached inside the slide, Lawson grabbed the back of that man's head and pounded it against the hard plastic slide. The boom of the blow echoed in the slide, and Lexi screamed again. Lawson moved on to the second man who was reaching for his gun.

"Run, Lexi!" Lawson shouted as he wrapped his hand around the wrist of the second man's gun hand. He raised it toward the sky, and the man squeezed off a round that rocketed toward the clouds. Lexi screamed again, and through Lawson's ringing ears he could hear her scrambling inside the slide. Lawson kept his grip on the man's wrist as he slid his right hand to the back of his neck to hold him in place. He drove his right knee into his groin and the man released a grunt of breathless pain. Lawson moved his right hand to the barrel of the gun and ripped it from the weakened man's hand.

As the now-gunless man doubled over in pain, Lawson turned and put the gun in the face of the first man who had just begun to advance after regaining his wits. Lexi popped out of the tube slide just behind the man who now was holding up his hands.

Lawson shouted through labored breath, "The car is on the other side of the building. Go!"

Lexi didn't even glance over her shoulder; she just hopped the fence and ran for the street. Lawson was left alone with the two men who'd intended to take his daughter. Alone with the two men who must know where his only friend had been taken. The side of him that had been forced to emerge in prison, the monster he had to become to survive there for ten years, the one he'd managed to bury for the past year, had just made its way to the surface.

"Take out your gun and throw it on the ground," Lawson said. He was no longer breathless. Now that Lexi was safe, he had collected himself. His tone was calm but dead serious.

The man didn't hesitate. He tossed his gun across the playground, and Lawson shocked him when he followed that by tossing the gun he'd taken from the second man in the same direction.

"Where is Cassie?"

The man answered with a step toward Lawson, making the mistake of cocking his fist back before throwing the punch. Lawson snapped a jab to the man's nose, cracking it at the bridge. Instead of throwing his punch the man moaned in pain, grabbing his nose with both hands. Lawson took the moment to turn and uppercut the second man in the mouth, who was still bent over recovering from the previous groin strike. On impact, his legs gave out and he fell to the ground. As the sting of the blow radiated in Lawson's knuckles, the man spit out a tooth as he swam near unconsciousness.

The man with the broken nose had a smear of blood on the front of his white button-up shirt. He was clearly no stranger to a fight because instead of retreating he moved his hands from his nose and put them up in a defensive boxing stance. Tears welled in his eyes from Lawson's jab to his nose. But he was not afraid. In fact, he moved forward first.

One of the most important things Lawson learned in prison was to keep emotion out of a fight. No matter how bad they hurt you, no matter how dirty they fought, keeping your head meant having the best shot at protecting yourself. And while he never fought men in prison who'd tried to harm his daughter, during every fight he had in prison, he saw the blank face of the man who murdered his wife. If Lawson could keep emotion out of it in those situations, he could do that here as well.

The man opened with a jab–right cross combination. Both landed to Lawson's arms as he held up a protective guard. The other imperative thing Lawson learned surviving jail was that there are no rules in a street fight; rules are meant for a ring. What he was doing was not a valiant sport; it was kill or be killed. With that lesson at the front of mind, the second time the man moved forward, as soon as his front leg planted, Lawson delivered a low kick and pushed the man's kneecap out the back side of his leg. He folded like a tent to the ground. Lawson stepped forward and soccer-kicked the man in the forehead, causing the lights to go out.

The man behind him was still spitting blood, but he had managed to sit up and was now leaning back against the slide.

Lawson stepped toward him, towering over him. "Where's Cassie?"

The man spit some more blood, wiped his mouth on his sleeve, and let out a sigh. "You're going to kill me anyway, so what's the use?"

"You lead me to Cassie, I'll let you live to watch me kill whoever ordered you to take her and my daughter."

The man was quiet for a moment. His partner was still unconscious on the ground behind Lawson.

"Then *they* will kill me. Either way I'm dead. Might as well get it over with."

"It won't be hard to find out who you are, probably just need to check your wallet."

Though he was defeated, the man managed a bloody smirk. "So what? I just told you I'm dead either way."

"I see you're wearing a wedding band." Lawson nodded toward the man's hand.

The man looked down at his ring finger, then back to Lawson.

Lawson's face hardened. "Need I say more?"

By the sunken look the man gave, Lawson knew he didn't need to say another word.

"You move, I'll shoot you."

Lawson walked a few paces away from the two mangled men. He pulled his phone and called Lexi.

"You okay, Dad?" she answered.

"I'm fine."

"I'm in the car with Taylor. Hurry back so we can go home."

"We can't go home, Lexi. It's not safe. Let me talk to Taylor."

He heard Lexi hand the phone to Taylor.

"You all right?" she asked.

"I'm fine. You still want my help? Looks like you might be in more danger with me than without me."

"I'll take my chances. What should we do? I'm happy to stay with Lexi."

For the first time, especially now that Cassie was gone, he was happy to have Taylor around. He didn't know what he would do with Lexi without her. Because he was about to walk into the lion's den, and his daughter couldn't be anywhere near it. It wasn't that he trusted Taylor—he knew she was hiding something—it was more that he didn't have a choice. And despite her situation, he could tell that Taylor was, at the very least, a good person.

"Take Lexi to a hotel, somewhere away from here. Go to the beach or something. There is cash in the glove box."

"It's okay. I have a hotel I go to when I need to get away. They're always discreet."

"Text me which one. Right now I have to find Cassie."

"Don't worry about Lexi, she'll be fine with me."

"I'm afraid I really don't have a choice."

19

LAWSON ENDED THE CALL WITH LEXI AND IMMEDIATELY FELT the sharp sting of worry. What was he doing? He didn't even know Taylor Lockhart, and now the most important thing in his life was literally at her mercy—again. Even in the face of knowing she was hiding something, however, his instincts were still telling him he could trust her. And when he looked down the barrel of his Sig at the two men on the playground, he realized, like he just told Taylor, he really didn't have a choice.

Sending Lexi off with a stranger was certainly something he would never do under normal circumstances. But making these two take him to whoever their boss might be wasn't merely the only way to find Cassie; it was the only way he could ensure that these people wouldn't keep coming after him and Lexi. The thing that pissed him off the most was that all of this was over some random meeting with a filmmaker at a casting call for Lexi. Now all of their lives hung in the balance. He truly thought after all that happened in Vegas that he was finished with this life. Now here in LA, due to random events, he was just as bad off as he was a year ago, if not worse. Maybe Cassie was right: maybe he really was a magnet for terrible people. Either way, he had to see this thing through. It was the only way out the other side.

Lawson stalked toward the two damaged men. "Get up. Let's go to your car and let's go meet whoever's in charge."

The two men didn't put up a fight, and they didn't say a word as they shuffled like injured dogs off the community center's property toward their waiting SUV. Lawson got in the back of the Chevy Tahoe, instructing the two men to take the front so he could see them at all times. Lawson confiscated both of their phones so they couldn't sneak anyone a heads-up. He didn't really have a plan. There really wasn't time for one. The man with the busted nose drove the SUV out of the street parking space.

"Who hired you?" Lawson said. "And what am I walking into?"

The two men never had a chance to answer the question. A hailstorm of bullets were hitting the driver's side of the car before the sound of the automatic weapon had even registered in Lawson's mind. The SUV swerved right as the driver slumped dead onto the steering wheel. Lawson was too large to fit down in the floorboard, so the only thing he could do was pull the lock, open the door, and dive out. He was lucky that the SUV had swerved because it was rolling over a patch of grass in front of the street-side homes, and though it was a jolting drop to the ground, he rolled to his feet and began running between the houses without ever coming to a full stop.

In his periphery, he saw a car jerk onto the side street that ran parallel to the house he was running past. Someone had been watching him. He didn't know if the men who shot up the SUV were after *him* or the men in the front seats until he looked back over his shoulder. Because there was a privacy fence on his left, he was forced to make a quick right toward the car that had turned to follow him. As soon as he did, the car was waiting on the next street about thirty yards from him. As the car door opened, he aimed his pistol while still running. Just before he pulled the trigger, he recognized the blonde woman that emerged with a gun of her own in hand.

Cassie.

Lawson froze as she pointed the gun in his direction. Though he knew the gunmen were hot on his heels, what he saw was so shocking to his system that his mind completely shut down.

"What are you doing, Lawson? Run!"

Cassie fired several times. He could almost feel the bullets moving by him as he instinctively ducked.

"RUN!" Cassie shouted again.

This time he could tell she was looking beyond him. His body caught up with his brain, and he turned, fired a few defensive shots, then made a run for the car Cassie was driving. Cassie continued to fire behind Lawson to cover him. As soon as he jumped across the hood, she stopped and got back in the car. Lawson got in the passenger side just as the men came running around the house and began firing. Cassie hit the gas and the Honda Accord fishtailed as it sped away.

"What the hell is going on, Cassie?"

Cassie jerked the steering wheel left and turned back out onto another main road.

"I don't know."

Lawson looked over and noticed dried blood on the side of Cassie's head.

"Are you okay?"

Cassie continued swerving around cars, pulling away from the scene they'd escaped from.

"They knocked me out. Lexi and I were getting out of the car to go into my apartment, and someone came up from behind and popped me in the head. That's the last thing I remember. Where's Lexi? Please tell me they don't have Lexi!"

When she turned left onto Santa Monica Boulevard, the car almost ended up on two wheels she was driving so fast.

Lawson said, "Slow down, you're gonna get us killed. They aren't behind us."

"Is Lexi okay?" Cassie was frantic. Only one other time had Lawson seen her this way. The day Lauren was murdered out on the lake.

"She's fine." Lawson made an effort to sound calm, hoping it would rub off. "That Find iPhone thing or whatever you did saved her life. She got away and hid in the park. Taylor knew how to use it and it led us right to Lexi. Just as they were about to get to her. How did you know where I was?"

"I-I didn't. When I escaped the moron they had holding me, I took his car and followed those two that shot up the SUV you were in. I don't have a phone or anything, so it was the only thing I knew might lead me back to Lexi. Then I saw you jump out of the truck. I just reacted and turned off the road to try to get to you. Where is Lexi? Do I need to go back to the park?"

"No, Lexi's okay. She's with Taylor."

Cassie whipped her head toward Lawson, concern etched on her face. "But she lied about her sister. You think you can trust her?"

"Calm down. It's all right. I mean, look at the two of us . . . You really think there was another option? You were kidnapped and I have people shooting at me. The actress seemed the lesser of the evils."

"The actress who lied, got shot in your driveway, and oh by the way is a total stranger . . . And yet, I see your point."

Lawson took a deep breath and rubbed his hands over his face, trying to calm himself now, and trying to stop all the swirling thoughts. They needed to land on a direction to go in, right then, even if it was the wrong one.

"We have to find out what happened to Victoria Marshall," Cassie said.

"We're on the same page. Whoever took her is responsible for all of this."

Cassie turned into a gas station and put the car in park. She took in a deep breath and exhaled slowly to calm herself.

"But we've got nothing."

Lawson turned toward her. "Maybe not. We've got you."

Cassie didn't get it.

"Whoever took you more than likely took Victoria too, right?"

Cassie thought about it. "Maybe. But why would they try to take me and Lexi? That makes no sense."

"To get to me." Lawson rolled down the window to get some fresh air. "Whoever took Victoria obviously thinks I still work for her. So they think I am looking for her. It's the only thing that makes sense to me."

"It doesn't at all to me. The police know she's missing. So that means whoever took her knows the police are looking for her. What are they going to do, kidnap everyone's family in the police department too, so they don't come looking for Victoria? Something isn't adding up. It has to be Sloan."

"Clint said it wasn't." Lawson didn't sound convinced.

"And you believe him?"

"I don't know."

"Sloan is the only thing that makes sense," she continued. "He would be afraid that you, or whoever he thinks you work for, would go to the police and tell them about the meeting. How he tried to strong-arm Victoria. Linking him to the kidnapping, right?"

Lawson thought about it. There were so many variables. One thing that was sticking in his craw was the fact that the only person who really benefited from Cassie and Lexi being kidnapped would be Clint Hues.

"Clint wanted us to help take down Sloan, right?" Lawson asked.

"Right."

"Well, I agree with him, and you, that it would have been stupid for Sloan to kidnap Victoria. The police would easily connect the dots to him after the meeting at the bar. But I don't necessarily buy the fact that Sloan would think kidnapping Lexi would make me persuade Victoria to do anything. Why would he believe I could have any influence over her? I don't even know her."

"And besides," Cassie said, following her own line of thought, "the timing of whoever tried to take us last night doesn't match up at all."

"How do you mean?"

"It's common knowledge now that Victoria has gone missing. What good would it do Sloan to take Lexi to try to make you persuade Victoria to sign over the movie rights? If Sloan really didn't take Victoria himself, that means she is still missing, making it impossible for you to be able to talk to her. Therefore you wouldn't be able to persuade Victoria to do anything, giving Sloan no reason to kidnap Lexi."

Cassie was right.

Lawson said, "Either Clint was wrong about Sloan kidnapping Victoria, or he lied about Sloan wanting to kidnap Lexi so he could make me want to go after Sloan, to use me to help him get what he wants."

Cassie agreed with a nod. "But how do we find out which is true?"

"Like I said earlier, we have you. Take us back to where you escaped from, and we'll find who took you. That will be all the answer we need."

20

Cassie and Lawson doubled back to the office building Cassie escaped from earlier. It wasn't far, just a couple miles down Hollywood Boulevard. The sun was inching up the sky toward late morning. Lawson was a sweaty mess, in the same black button-up shirt and black chinos he'd been in for two days. When he went to wipe the sweat from his brow, the smell of Taylor's perfume on his arm still lingered.

"It's just up here on the right," Cassie said. "What's the play?"

"We'll take it slow. How did you leave the guy who was holding you here?"

"I handcuffed him to the handle on a safe in the office."

"Let's just pull into the parking lot if there is one, wait for a minute to see if we get lucky."

Cassie did as he suggested. The parking lot was off to the right of the small office building. She pulled into a space in the back. It wasn't Sloan's office, but that didn't mean it wasn't one of his employees' offices. Cassie backed in so they had a view of the entrance. No one would be able to go in or out without them seeing. Lawson laid his pistol on the dashboard. A quick grab if necessary.

"C-note says it's Sloan or one of his guys," Cassie said.

"I'm not in the mood for games," Lawson said. Never taking his eyes off the entrance.

"How'd we end up here?"

"We drove from Santa Monica Boulevard."

"Okay, smart-ass. You know what I mean."

Cassie was doing that thing where she nervously filled the void. One of her oldest habits. Lawson did know what she meant, but he really had no answer. It was astonishing they were in such a predicament.

"I guess I took the wrong job," Lawson finally answered.

"What the hell could be so important about a movie that all of this is necessary? I mean, the way things are going down, you would think it's a twenty-million-dollar cocaine deal you interrupted."

"I suppose if it's a movie that would be a box office hit, the stakes are much higher than twenty million, aren't they?"

"Yeah, I guess you're right." Cassie sighed as she opened her window further. The small breeze through the car felt fantastic. "Some of those big films do over half a billion when it's all said and done. Maybe we are looking at this from all the wrong angles."

That got Lawson's attention. For the first time since they parked, he looked over at Cassie. "How do you mean?"

"Well . . ." Cassie took a moment to organize her thoughts. Lawson thought she was her most likable when her wheels were spinning. A smart woman is always more attractive. Even if that woman is like your sister. "If we both believe all of this is because of a movie, shouldn't we be talking to someone who works for Victoria? I mean, we do have an ace in the hole here. Taylor freakin' Lockhart is with your daughter. Couldn't she get just about anyone to open up about a project?"

That hadn't occurred to Lawson. But he didn't see how it could help now. "Aren't we past that, though? We don't really have time to organize a setup where Taylor goes out to investigate. This thing is coming down on us right now."

"Yeah," Cassie said, "but it's Taylor Lockhart, Lawson. A phone call from her would get the right employee, or agent, frothing at the mouth . . . Call her."

"We're kind of in the middle of something here."

"Just call her. Check on Lexi, ask Taylor how we can get more info on this coveted movie. Tell her you think the same people might be involved in shooting her. Whatever it takes."

Lawson hadn't thought about Taylor's situation in a while. It really was another reason he trusted her. All that she had going on, and she was putting it on the back burner while Lawson cleared up his own mess. Did she have a choice? Maybe not. But Lawson would think that someone like Taylor, a full-blown movie star, would be a lot more selfish about a situation. Then the thought occurred to him that she never once offered to pay him for his help. He wouldn't have taken it if she had, but why hadn't she? People with money always try to solve problems by throwing money at things. For a fleeting moment, a very peculiar feeling moved through him. He couldn't put his finger on what it was, but it was there. Either way, he had to focus on the situation at hand, and if she could help, he needed to try. He pulled up Taylor's number, pressed the call button, and put it on speakerphone so Cassie could hear. He hated it, but when she answered, her voice made him long to see her.

"Lawson, is everything all right?" Taylor answered.

"I found Cassie. We're okay. You all safe? Lexi doing okay?"

"We're at the Malibu Beach Inn. Lexi is on the balcony watching the waves roll in, having a room service cheeseburger and fries. I'm having a bourbon from the minibar. Trying to calm my nerves."

"Good. I need your help."

"Anything."

"What do you know about Victoria Marshall?"

There was a longer pause than Lawson would have liked.

"Um, uh, why? Why do you ask?"

Taylor sounded like the question rattled her. Lawson felt a slow drip of worry leak into his mind. "What's wrong, Taylor?"

"No, nothing. Just wasn't expecting a question about her. I've worked with her a couple times. What do you want to know? Is she in trouble?"

"Not sure." Lawson played it close to the vest. "But there is a man involved in this that we think might be trying to hurt her."

"Victoria? Why?"

"We think it's over a movie."

Another lengthy pause. Lawson could hear waves crashing in the background, and a breeze blowing against the mike periodically interrupted the silence between them.

"Taylor?"

"Yeah, sorry. I think I know what movie you're talking about. And I think I know the man you're talking about too."

Cassie and Lawson looked from the phone at each other in shock. Lawson said, "What? How?"

"It's kind of big news here in Hollywood. Well, it was about six months ago anyway."

Cassie spoke up. "Can you elaborate?"

"Yeah, sure. All I know about it is that Carl Goldberg died in the middle of a deal. And the question of who held the movie rights became a big lawsuit here last year when one of Victoria's partners died too."

"Carl Goldberg?" Lawson said.

"Yeah, sorry. Forgot you're not much of a film buff. The last few movies he wrote were massive hits, so that's why it's such a big deal who gets the rights."

Cassie and Lawson nodded, as that answered why Sloan wanted it so bad.

"Okay, and who was the lawsuit with?"

Cassie jumped in. "Let me guess, Martin Sloan Junior."

"Yeah, that's right. They were both going to work on it together because for some reason Carl was adamant about working with Sloan. I don't know the reason, but speculation around town was that Sloan and his partner forced Carl to work with them. That's the only reason he would be adamant about working with Sloan. Some mafia-style stuff. Stuff that sounded more like a movie than the movies themselves. Anyway, Carl's only stipulation was that Victoria Marshall was involved too. That way he at least had someone he'd worked with before to share his vision on the movie."

Lawson followed. "So when Carl died, there was a fight for who got the movie."

"Right," Taylor said. "And when Sloan's guy died, he lost the majority and that's when the fight for the movie between Sloan and Victoria started. It's still being litigated as we speak. You think Victoria is okay?"

Lawson ignored her question. "Any idea who this third partner was? Sloan's guy who died?"

"Yeah, some real dirtbag from Las Vegas. Let me think, what was his name?"

Lawson could feel the blood drain from his face. His stomach knotted up and he began to sweat. When Taylor said "dirtbag from Las Vegas," the conversation with Victoria at Lexi's audition flashed in his mind and nearly made him sick. He knew the name Taylor was about to say before she said it.

"Umm, something De Luca maybe?"

Lawson could feel Cassie's eyes on him. Nero De Luca was the reason Lawson's wife was dead. And Lawson was the reason Nero De Luca was dead. But before Lawson could put words together, before he could start to entertain the ideas of how this could relate back to him, a car pulled into the parking lot and drew away Lawson and Cassie's attention. It was a black Dodge Challenger.

Lawson looked over at Cassie. "Clint Hues."

21

Before Cassie could stop Lawson, he was already out of the car and halfway to the Dodge Challenger, which Clint had barely had time to park.

"Lawson!" Cassie shouted.

But it was too late. When Taylor said the name De Luca, a host of horrible memories flooded his system. The death of his wife, the ten-year prison sentence, the ten years of Lexi's life that he missed, all of it put Lawson back in the headspace of a year ago when he was running down Nero De Luca. However, since Nero De Luca was dead, Lawson's only potential target for channeling that anger was just now stepping out of his car, and somewhere in the back of Lawson's mind, he knew he was going to kill him.

Clint emerged from his car, a worried look on his face. "You okay, big guy? You don't look so good."

"I'll show you what happens when you try to kidnap my daughter."

Clint's worried look turned to shock. So much so that his genuine surprise kept Lawson from punching him. Instead of doing massive damage, Lawson grabbed Clint by the lapels of his leather jacket. He lifted Clint up and slammed him down on the top of the hood.

"What are you talking about?" Clint shouted. He twisted his head trying to look at Cassie. "You'd better call off your dog or I'm going to kill him."

Lawson held him there.

Cassie spoke for Lawson. "This your office?"

"Yeah, why?" Clint's voice was strained. Lawson had continued to tighten his grip.

"Wrong answer." Lawson pulled Clint off the car and threw him a few feet away. Clint hit the blacktop hard but rolled up to his feet. He pulled a gun and pointed it at Lawson. Lawson reached for his, but in his rage he'd left it sitting on the dashboard.

"This how you want to play it?" Clint said.

Lawson could see in Clint's eyes that he was through getting manhandled by him. As easy as it was for Lawson to push Clint around, he knew that Clint was not an easy man. He knew that if push came to shove, Clint would pull that trigger and use his years of resources to cover it all up and walk away a free man. Lawson had to switch off his primal instincts and start tapping into some rational thinking.

Cassie started to back away from the scene. Lawson knew it was to get his gun from the dashboard, and so did the woman who was with Clint. She pulled a pistol of her own and trained it on Cassie.

"That's far enough," she said to her. Lawson didn't remember ever hearing the woman's name.

Cassie held out her hands. Then she switched on her rational brain and did the talking for Lawson. "Listen, I was just kidnapped. You're telling me you all had nothing to do with that?"

Lawson watched Clint's reaction closely. He genuinely looked surprised.

"Kidnapped? You?" Clint said to Cassie.

Cassie nodded.

"Why would you think I would've had something to do with that?"

"Because they took me here, and held me here. The moron I was able to escape from is still handcuffed to your safe in your office. That might be why we think you're involved."

"There's a man handcuffed to my safe? In my office? Right now?"

"Yeah." Cassie gestured toward the car she'd taken when she escaped. "And that's his car."

"I don't know that car." Clint started walking toward his building. "I've been set up. Someone is trying to make it look like I did this. I just proposed yesterday that we work together. Why would I kidnap you today?"

Lawson looked dead into Clint's eyes as Clint walked by. "Because you want it to look like Sloan is doing this so we will help you take him down."

Clint stopped and got in Lawson's face. He had to look up a bit to meet his eyes. "You know what, I've seriously had about enough of you. I don't know who you think you are, but you aren't going to stand there and accuse me and not pay for it."

"Yet here I stand," Lawson said with his jaws set and his fists clinched.

The woman with Clint stepped in between them. "Are you guys for real? Good God, you are the most cliché men I've ever seen. 'Hey, I can beat you up.' 'No, I can beat you up.' You might as well square up and have a pissing contest." She put her hands on both of their chests and pushed them apart. "We are wasting time fighting with each other. Let's get in here and see who this is. Then let's use all that macho bullshit to go get who is really responsible for all of this."

"I already know who is responsible," Clint said. "Sloan. Going after anyone else is a waste of time."

Cassie had gone back to the car to get Lawson's gun, and as she walked by the three of them toward the entrance to the office, she said, "Okay, well, let's just go find out then."

22

THE FOUR OF THEM STOOD STARING AT THE HANDCUFFS dangling from the handle of the safe in Clint's office.

"Well"—Clint stood from his bent position where he was checking out the handcuffs—"whoever it was, we'll never know now."

Silence fell over the room. Nobody knew what the next move was, because nobody fully trusted each other. While everyone was focused on the man no longer handcuffed to the safe, Lawson couldn't stop thinking about the connection between Nero De Luca and Martin Sloan Jr. It made complete sense that they would be connected. A lot of crime families from different territories scratched each other's back from time to time. Lawson figured De Luca's and Sloan's fathers probably worked together first, back in the heyday of organized crime. The other question burning all through Lawson was, is this connection why Cassie and Lexi were kidnapped? Could it be that it was no longer about the movie or the meeting Lawson interrupted at the bar? When Sloan looked into who Lawson Raines was, and found out, was all of this now about what happened to his old friend Nero De Luca?

"Clint," Cassie said, "is there somewhere Lawson and I can talk in private?"

"Jenny's office is right next door."

Cassie tugged on Lawson's arm, and it broke his trance. He followed her into Jenny's office and shut the door behind him.

"I see those wheels turning, Lawson. You're thinking about Sloan and De Luca, aren't you?"

"How could I not be?"

"I know . . . Bad shit follows you around like a hungry puppy. You noticed that? You ever thought about saging yourself? Clear the bad juju?"

"You don't think Sloan came after you and Lexi because of my connection to De Luca, do you?"

Cassie took a deep breath and walked over to the window that overlooked the street. She lifted one of the blinds and squinted into the sunshine. "Why would the guy trying to hold me here use handcuffs?"

The question caught Lawson off guard, but it sparked something in his subconsciousness. He couldn't put his finger on it, so he let Cassie talk.

"The guy holding me, when I woke up, he didn't seem like a criminal. He seemed like a guy almost uncomfortable to be holding me there. I got him talking, he didn't give anything away, but he was too quick to want to help me. When I asked to go to the bathroom, it was easy to turn the tables on him and cuff him to the safe. Too easy. And right when I locked him to it, I remember thinking even then that it was weird that he used handcuffs. Not a zip tie, not a rope, not duct tape—handcuffs."

The third time she said it brought up the image of the

man's gun on the playground that Lawson confiscated. He remembered having a similar split second like Cassie just described when he realized what kind of gun the man was carrying. A Glock 22. A popular gun, but also the standard issue of the LAPD. The only reason he knew that fact was from a discussion he had with a fellow agent in Vegas who used to be LAPD. They had an entire conversation about Beretta versus Glock, and the agent's argument was that if the Glock was good enough for the LAPD, it was good enough for him.

"You think they were cops, don't you?" Lawson blurted.

Cassie let go of the shade and turned toward him. "Why? You too?"

"The man in the park trying to get Lexi had a standard issue Glock 22. Didn't really register to me until what you said about the handcuffs."

"So, what does this mean?"

"Maybe nothing," Lawson said. "Maybe everything. Sloan has cops on the payroll, you heard Clint. Maybe we should ask him?"

Cassie obviously agreed because she walked right by him, out the door, and back to Clint's office. Lawson walked in just in time to hear her question.

"How often does Sloan use cops to do some of his dirty work?"

Clint smiled. "The handcuffs, right? Jenny and I were just talking about the same thing. He uses cops all the time. Has them all over the city. But listen . . ." Clint's tone changed and he eyed Lawson. "I ain't telling you shit else until you apologize for the parking lot."

Lawson actually laughed. It was an involuntary reflex.

Cassie put her hands on her hips. "I've been trying to get this guy to apologize to me for something, anything, for over thirteen years. Guess we'll just say our good-byes right now."

"I wasn't talking to you." Clint didn't find it funny at all.

Lawson stepped forward. He didn't like the tone Clint took with Cassie. Cassie stopped Lawson by putting the palm of her hand to his chest. She came right back at him. "I don't really give a slippery shit if you were talking to me or not. You came to Lawson for help, not the other way around. So unless you look out that window and see pigs flying through the Los Angeles smog, swallow your pride and tell us what you know. Otherwise, deal with Sloan yourself. We'll make do on our own."

"This how it works, Raines? She does all the talking for you? You just heel like a trained puppy?"

Lawson moved Cassie's hand from his chest. "It is how it works. She keeps me from breaking your neck."

"Seriously?" Jenny spoke up. "You guys don't see that you're basically the same person?"

"Sure," Cassie said. "Except for the whole Clint is a life-long criminal and Lawson is a lifelong law man. Honestly, are you serious?"

Clint scoffed, "I'm the criminal? Excuse me, but I'm not the one who murdered my wife."

There are a lot of things that set Lawson off. A lot of things a man could say to provoke him. He's a hothead, so it wasn't hard. But those words, saying that about the love of his life, that will get you killed. Lawson stepped around Cassie; she already knew that would trigger him. He flipped the desk over that separated him from Clint like it was made of paper. Two steps later he buried his fist in Clint's stomach so hard that the air from Clint's lungs would have blown that same desk over.

Lawson went to bring his knee up to meet Clint's forehead as he bent over, but Jenny managed to put a shoulder in him hard enough to knock him off balance. Clint used it as his chance to strike. He lowered his head, rushed forward, wrapped his arms around Lawson's waist, and tackled him to the ground. Clint was stronger than he looked. Even off balance, Lawson would be able to keep most men from taking him down. There must have been a wrestling background somewhere in his past.

Lawson got his hands up just in time to block the elbow that Clint threw from on top of him. Another came right after that. Lawson was no expert in jiujitsu, but he had picked up enough from some men in prison that he knew to buck his hips to get Clint off balance. This was enough, and he was able to push Clint off with a shove. They both came to their feet at the same time, Clint throwing a quick jab that caught Lawson on the left cheek. Clint went to follow it with a right cross, but Lawson parried it and delivered a left elbow that hit Clint in the left shoulder, knocking him clean off his feet.

Lawson advanced to finish the fight, but Cassie stepped in, wrapping him in a bear hug and pushing back with all she had. Jenny did the same when Clint got back up to his feet.

"I should let him kill you for that comment, asshole!" Cassie shouted.

"This isn't doing anyone any good!" Jenny shouted. "This is what they wanted, whoever tried to set Clint up by taking Cassie here. They want you to fight each other instead of fighting them. Now stop it! It has to be Sloan! He's the only one who knows you two even know about each other!"

Both men pushed toward each other one last time, but the women held their ground.

"She's right, Lawson," Cassie struggled to push him backward.

Lawson didn't say anything, but he stopped pushing forward. Everyone was quiet for a moment. Lawson tried to calm himself but he was seething. Rational thought dies when blind rage is induced. An ill word about Lauren would always have that effect.

Clint had finally cooled. "Look, for God's sake, all I want is for Sloan to go down. I don't know you or what happened to your wife, and you don't know me or why I do what I do. But saying things about a man's late wife is wrong and I'm sorry."

That was good enough for Lawson, but he wasn't sticking around to hug it out. He turned his body toward the door, and his mind toward Marty Sloan.

23

LAWSON WAS WALKING QUICKLY DOWN THE HALL TOWARD THE exit of Clint's office building. Cassie was taking two steps to his one to keep up.

Cassie said, "So is this the part where you do your Lawson thing and just bust in someone's house, or office, without any plan whatsoever? The thing that gets me shot at and almost killed just for being with you?"

Lawson just kept walking. Man on a mission.

"Lawson. I—"

Cassie ran into the back of Lawson. He had stopped abruptly at the exit without warning.

"No," he said. "It looks like this is the part where I become a fugitive."

Lawson felt Cassie step out beside him. She watched with him as two police cars—full lights, full sirens—came screaming into the parking lot.

"They here for you or for me?" Lawson heard Clint say from the other end of the hallway behind him.

"Me. And there's no way I'm talking myself out of this one. After being the last to see Victoria Marshall, and now

BRADLEY WRIGHT

I'm sure I fit the description of the big guy fleeing the vehicle that just got shot up. I have to get out of here."

Cassie's face was blank. "You can't run from the cops. It will only make things worse."

"Worse than being in jail while Sloan is trying to kidnap Lexi?"

Cassie made a "hmm" face. "Good point." Cassie turned to face Clint. "Got a car we can borrow?"

Clint waved them both toward him. "Only car we have here is mine, in the parking lot with the cops. But there is a door on the other side of the building. I'll try to distract them while you make a run for it."

Any worry that Clint was responsible for Lexi and Cassie's kidnapping was just erased. Lawson began walking toward Clint; then he stopped and turned to Cassie. "You can't come with me."

"Bullshit. Sloan kidnapped me and tried to get Lexi. We're doing this together, whatever that means."

"Cassie, this could ruin your career."

"Lawson, yours and Lexi's lives are on the line, and you think I give a damn about my career? Do we even know each other?"

Lawson turned back toward Clint. Clint started a fast walk to the opposite side of the building. "I'll call you after they leave and let you know how bad it is. Meanwhile, if you're feeling frisky, Sloan always has a lunch meeting on Saturdays at the Library Bar over at the Roosevelt Hotel."

Lawson didn't respond. His mind was busy being thankful that Cassie was coming along and calculating how to get out of there without getting caught. When they reached the exit, they heard police pounding on the door at the other end of the building.

"I locked it," Clint said, smiling. "You can never be too careful."

Lawson pushed open the door and stepped out into the sunshine. Instead of running, he opted for walking, as if he was supposed to be there.

"You know the detective is probably watching in an unmarked car, don't you?" Cassie caught up, hooked his arm with hers, and walked beside him onto the sidewalk.

"Probably."

"Plus, you're six foot three, two hundred and forty pounds. Pretty easy to spot."

"So you're saying we should run?"

"I'm saying we should run."

Just as the last word left her lips, across the street an unmarked car emerged from an alley, a blue light flashing on the dash. It was forced to settle in momentarily behind a string of traffic. The only time Lawson would ever think LA traffic was spectacular. Cassie got the jump on Lawson, tearing across the street, forcing cars to react to her instead of the opposite. She was fearless. A few steps and a couple dodged cars later, Lawson had caught up to her and they were running down an alley, dodging hipsters with e-cigs and dumpsters jutting from both sides. Lawson felt good about the move to run across the street, until another police cruiser screeched to a halt about fifty yards in front of them, blocking their western exit from the alley.

Even without knowing exactly what the surrounding streets looked like, he knew they were trapped. You don't send three cruisers and an unmarked car for questioning. They were there to arrest him again. Maybe for Victoria's disappearance, maybe for the shooting on the street earlier, but probably for both. An old Ford Crown Victoria came out of the side street and almost ran them over; the front end just missed clipping Cassie's right leg. Lawson grabbed Cassie's shirt and yanked her to the right, but another cruiser stopped sideways in front of them, blocking them in. Lawson prepared himself to be taken in. At least this way Cassie would probably go free.

The window of the Crown Victoria rolled down, and a familiar face came into view. Lawson was frozen, unsure if this was good or bad.

"Well, don't just stand there . . . I suggest you get in." It was Frank Shaw. His smirk was a mix of pride and braggadocio. The face of a man who knew he'd won.

Lawson had no choice but to get in. Even if Frank meant to turn right toward the police station and turn him in, it would be no different than if Lawson refused: he was dead to rights either way. Getting in the car at least gave him a chance. The *whoop whoop* of the police cruiser's siren at the edge of the alley drove that notion home. Cassie looked at him in a way you look at a man who was just told by his wife that she was leaving him: with absolute pity. She knew how much it would sting getting in the car with Frank.

Cassie opened the door and they both climbed in the back. As soon as the door shut, Lawson's world was flipped upside down. The fact that Frank Shaw had been the one to bail him out again completely faded from his mind when he saw who was sitting in the passenger seat on the other side of the safety cage.

Victoria Marshall.

24

LAWSON'S FIRST INSTINCT WAS TO TRY THE CAR DOOR HANDLE. He knew it wouldn't open but tried anyway. There was a reason Frank and Victoria were driving this car; it had been modified to keep criminals in.

Frank picked up the mike on the radio. "This is Special Agent Frank Shaw. Stand down, I've got him. Good work, ladies and gentlemen. I'll bring them in."

The car was silent for a moment as Frank drove away. The police cruiser let him pass, and Frank turned out of the alley. Lawson didn't know where they were going, but he knew it wasn't to any police station. Not with Victoria Marshall riding shotgun. He knew as soon as he saw her sitting there that whatever story had been pushed to the media about the big movie and all of its partners—the story Taylor had told him—was probably all wrong. It wasn't Sloan who wanted Nero De Luca in on the production of the high-profile film; it was Victoria.

Lawson couldn't hold his tongue. "So, how long had you been seeing Nero De Luca before I jammed a knife through his throat?"

Cassie's head swung in Lawson's direction, and Lawson could see Frank's eyes jump to his in the rearview mirror, but Victoria just sat in silence, staring at the busy street in front of them.

"I always knew you were dumb," Frank said. "But I didn't know you were clueless. You're here, nowhere to run, and you're smarting off? Provoking the woman who holds your fate in her hands? If nothing else, you've got balls."

"And what about you, Frank? How much did she have to pay you for your help?"

"Shit, I'd pay her to see you go down. If it wasn't for you, I'd still be back at home in Vegas where I should be."

Lawson was quiet. A thousand things were churning in his mind. The only question mark he had left about what went down in Vegas was who tipped De Luca off more than eleven years ago that Lawson was coming for his father. All this time he thought it must have been the head of the Vegas FBI division who'd been responsible. Now it seemed it could very well have been Frank. But how in the hell did Frank become connected to Victoria?

Lawson was still baffled by the fact that this tragedy in his life was still haunting him. After all he'd been through, after all the time that had passed, his ghosts were still trying to drag him to hell. He wasn't going anywhere without a fight. No matter how high the odds were stacked against him.

"All right," Lawson said. His thoughts had come together. He switched off the part of his brain that felt like the victim and tapped into the skills that made him one of the best detectives and FBI agents in the country. "You tried to kidnap my daughter. You kept me out of jail twice. And I'm still alive. Let's skip all the runaround and get right to the part where you tell me what I need to do to keep you from killing me, shall we?"

That got Victoria's attention. She shifted in her seat and faced sideways so she could get a look at Lawson in the back seat. The car stank of smoke; this was apparently Frank's car. The sun was coming in heavy through the windshield, spotlighting the frozen skin on Victoria's face. Lawson knew she was in her fifties, but her Botoxed skin, long and straight dyed dark-brown hair, and supple injected lips made her look no more than forty-nine. "So there are some brains inside that brawny exterior."

Lawson made no response. He had only known Victoria for a short time, had only had a couple conversations with her, but as she looked at him, something was different about the way she was acting. He couldn't put his finger on what it was, so he chalked it up to the fact that she just wasn't the woman he thought she was. Still, it was very odd.

"Too bad those brains didn't kick in before you got yourself stuck in this situation."

"What situation am I in exactly?" Lawson leaned forward.

"If you can keep your wits," she continued, "one that you can walk away from free and clear. Just make the decision now to save the hero shit for another day and you should be all right."

"You mean the kind of hero shit that led me to staring into your old boyfriend's eyes as he gagged on a steel blade? It was fun seeing him leave this world and head straight to hell. Wish I had it on video."

Lawson felt a pinch on the outside of his right thigh. He looked over at Cassie, and her face was begging him to stop provoking Victoria. But Lawson knew what Cassie didn't—

that Victoria wanted something from him or both of them would already be dead.

"I have a feeling you already know what situation you're in," Victoria said.

Lawson did know, but he wanted her to say it. "Pretend I don't."

"I've been trying to figure out a way to get the rights to *my* movie out of litigation, and keep it out of Marty Sloan's hands. I'm sure you already came to this conclusion."

Yes, Lawson had realized it, in fact right when he sat down in the backseat and saw her in front of him. He nodded.

"But I have no shot in the courts. Sloan has too many people on the payroll. Though I was intimate with De Luca, a very powerful man, a while back, the day he died so did my connection to people like Clint Hues or anyone in De Luca's organization. So I had no way to fight Sloan. If I didn't act fast, I was going to lose the movie. I've had my lawyers prolonging the court battle as long as possible until I could find another way. Then one day I called to check on Johnny, and he accidentally gave me a wonderful idea."

Johnny was Nero De Luca's son. Lawson had used Johnny's naiveté to get to his father. They left on good terms, in spite of the way things ended. Johnny was all but being held hostage by Nero, so Johnny was happy to be free of that existence.

Victoria continued her long-winded story. She sounded very proud of herself as she talked about her ties to the De Lucas. "He spoke very highly of you, Lawson, which still makes my skin crawl. You killed his father and the kid still loves you."

"What's that say about his father?"

It looked like he'd hit a nerve, but Victoria's face was so frozen he really couldn't tell.

"As I was saying . . ." She collected herself. "I asked whatever had happened to you, and Johnny said he really didn't know. Except he saw on your daughter's Instagram that you had moved to Los Angeles, and that Lexi seemed to be happy about it."

He really didn't like hearing Lexi's name in all of this.

"So I wished him good night and looked up little Lexi Raines myself. He was right, she did seem happy. Far too open with pictures of her house, but happy."

Lexi would be devastated if she knew they had tracked down Lawson because of her Instagram. Lawson was tired of the long story. "Can we please edit this script and get to the point?"

"Fine. When I saw that Lexi had been posting pictures working with acting coaches, I knew I had found the kind of man who could get me what I wanted. The kind of man who didn't wait around for the law to get things done."

Cassie spoke for the first time. "There are plenty of people like that here in LA. Why not just hire one of them?"

Lawson had already put that together. "Because they can all be traced to criminal activity in the city. If she has me do her dirty work, no one would know to look for me. As a bonus, whatever I end up doing for her, she can pin on me in the end. And a guy like Frank Shaw can help her do it."

"Well done, Mr. Raines." Victoria's tone was flat. "I'm impressed. So do you have any idea how you'll persuade Marty Sloan to drop the lawsuit and sign the movie over to me?"

Lawson shook his head. "Your plan to blackmail me into helping you backfired, remember? I got Lexi free. I'm not doing anything for you."

"Ah, Mr. Raines, I'm afraid you are underestimating me. I had Frank here really dig into what happened in Vegas. Nero made two fatal mistakes in trying to manipulate you. First, he underestimated you. I will not. Second, he didn't have any insurance. He tried, but Lexi got away from him. When he got her back, he made the mistake of holding her at his own home. Not keeping enough distance."

Lawson didn't like how Lexi was the common theme. A little prickle of worry began needling at the back of his brain. The good thing was, he knew where Lexi was and that she was safe. "I don't see your point. You're even further behind than where Nero was, so how can you say he got it wrong? He at least had Lexi, you don't even have that to hang over my head."

Victoria turned the rest of the way in her seat, making a point to look directly into Lawson's eyes.

A crooked smile grew over her face. "You sure about that?"

25

THE WARM OCEAN BREEZE FOUND ITS WAY THROUGH THE OPEN sliding glass door that led to the balcony and blew the hair back off Taylor's shoulder. The smell of salt was rich, but as she stared at the text from Victoria Marshall, the only thing her senses could register was fear. Her stomach was in knots. She jumped up from the bed, ran to the toilet, and vomited all the room service food she'd just eaten. She ran a washrag under cool water, wiped her mouth, then dabbed her forehead. She stepped out into the room and saw that Lexi was still nibbling on her fries, watching the seagulls floating by.

What the hell am I going to do?

This question had come to mind at least a thousand times over the last day and a half. Ever since she'd actually met the man whom Victoria had described as a monster. He couldn't be further from that. Lawson may have his demons, but he was a good man. You could tell that by how sweet his daughter was. There was no way she was going to let Victoria have Lexi. Blockbuster return to the movies and blackmail be damned. No set of incriminating photos, and no movie role, no matter how much it would springboard her back into the spotlight, would be worth it.

Her cell phone let out a chirp on the bed. Then three more chirps in succession. More text messages. She took a deep breath and walked over to her phone, and on the lock screen it showed that all the texts were from Victoria. If she was sick before, opening her phone took it to a whole other level. Victoria's first text was asking for her and Lexi's location. The second text was a warning: *Don't forget, there is more than just a movie role at stake here.*

That text was followed up with three pictures. The first two were of her naked, in a sexual position with her now dead fiancé. The third, a picture of her laughing while she did a line of cocaine off a woman's ass. She had no idea how Victoria got the photos, but they were all career damaging, if not destroying. As if her career could stand any more. She rushed back to the bathroom and vomited twice more. The first two pictures didn't scare her. It was the third that wrapped her in fear. That was the lowest point in her life. She was at the end of a long downward spiral after her fiancé killed himself, and that photo brought all of that past right back to the present. She had battled her way back from who she was in that photo. It was a long, hard fight. She hadn't touched a drug in a long time; that part of the story she told Lawson was true. The part she didn't get a chance to tell him yesterday was that the girl in that photo died that night, and though Taylor had nothing to do with it, if anyone found out she was there, she would be ruined. Maybe even sent to jail.

She didn't even know the girl. She was so out of her mind in those months that she could hardly even remember them. But seeing these pictures brought it all back. Her phone alerted her that another text had come in.

Another message from Victoria: *Tell me where you are, right now, or I send these to the tabloids, and the police.*

Taylor laid her phone on the bed and walked over to the balcony. She took a deep breath of the salty air as she watched Lexi kicking her legs back and forth as she enjoyed her Coke. Victoria's promise when she came to her with this sinister plan was that Taylor would never have to do anything. She was just there on the off chance that what Victoria had set up fell through. She assured Taylor numerous times that Lawson would be taken without her help, which was the only reason she agreed to the whole crazy ordeal. Victoria knew that Lawson wasn't a bad guy. Taylor should have seen it sooner. Victoria was actually banking on Lawson being the good guy that he was. She knew if Taylor was shot on his property that he would take care of her. That he would let her in. Why hadn't she seen this before she got involved?

"I never had a choice," Taylor accidentally said out loud. She was so inside her head that it just slipped.

"What was that, Taylor?" Lexi turned and smiled. Her blue eyes matched the blue water beyond the rail.

"Nothing, don't worry about it. How was the burger?"

"Really good. But the fries are even better. You were right, truffle fries are the bomb!"

"Good, I knew you would like them."

"Is everything okay, Taylor? You seem like something's bothering you."

Taylor forced a smile. "I'm fine. Just hope everything works out."

"It will. I told you, my dad will fix it." Lexi tucked her windblown hair behind her ear. "Thanks for watching me. I know I don't need it, but it makes my dad feel better. He worries about me a lot."

"Your dad is a sweet man."

Lexi smiled, looked out toward the water, then back to Taylor. Her smile had changed, turned into something bordering on ornery. "You think he's hot, don't you?"

The question caught Taylor by surprise, and instantly brought her back to the moment she and Lawson had in his living room where they'd almost shared a kiss. A grin grew across her face. "Why would you say that?"

"I can tell by the way you look at him. Besides, my acting coach goes on and on about him. It's gross, because I'm his daughter, I don't want to hear that. It's different for you, because I can tell he likes you too."

For the moment, the sick feeling left Taylor and Lexi's words gave her a glowing feeling. "Why's that?"

"Same reason. He looks at you different. But of course he does, you have movie star good looks. Dad is just in really good shape."

"All right. Well, anyway . . . You wanna go check out the beach?" She changed the subject as fast as she could.

Lexi jumped up from her chair. "I'll get my shoes!"

Taylor was right, she didn't have a choice before. But now she does. And she wasn't going to let someone bully her into putting this young girl in danger. She walked over to her phone and without another thought, she texted Victoria Marshall exactly what was running through her mind . . .

Send the pics to whoever you want. Then go straight to hell.

26

THE FIRST THING LAWSON THOUGHT OF WHEN VICTORIA SAID the words *You sure about that?* was the moment when Cassie told him that Taylor was lying about her sister being involved with her drug problem. He didn't want to believe that Taylor could be capable of such lies, but Victoria just finished explaining the entire scenario. From start to finish. How he'd been duped. How everything, from the shooting to Taylor having drug dealers extorting her, was all a lie. Lawson hadn't seen any of Taylor's movies, but he could certainly see why she was a popular actress. The performance she put on for him was Oscar worthy. And because she was with Lexi, it broke him in two.

"I'll do whatever you want me to do."

It was the only thing he could say to Victoria. Didn't matter how he really felt, he needed her to believe him. His little girl was vulnerable, and there was nothing he wouldn't do to keep her safe.

"I knew you'd see things my way."

Frank pulled the car into FBI headquarters. Lawson

knew it was because they needed to put on a show. If Frank wasn't going to take Lawson to the police station, the detective on the case would obviously start asking questions. FBI had rank over LAPD, so all he would have to say is that they needed to ask Lawson some questions before they handed him over to the police. Lawson knew they would parade him in the building, just in case there were any eyes watching; then they would let him out the back door. What they would want him to do exactly when they let him go was what he was waiting to hear.

"All right, Raines," Frank said. "You know the drill. We'll take you in here, take your phone, then let you out the back. On the other side of the building is a Ford F-150. Keep your pistol you've got with you, 'cause we know it's not registered anyway. Cassie, there is an unregistered Glock in there for you. Also in the glove box is a cell phone for each of you. It only has the number to my burner phone and the number of both phones programmed in it so you can communicate with each other. We have them mirrored, so if you make any other calls, we'll know, and, well, I don't have to tell you what will happen if you do, right?"

Lawson got the picture. "Just tell me what you want so we can end this thing."

Victoria turned toward him once again. "It's real simple. I want the movie signed over to me and the litigation dropped. Or Sloan dead. Doesn't matter to me. I'll leave that up to you."

Lawson didn't hesitate. "Done," he said.

They got out of the car, and Frank walked Lawson and Cassie into the FBI offices. Once inside, Lawson and Cassie handed over their cell phones. Frank walked them to the back door. "Just do what we're asking you to do and I promise nothing will happen to your daughter."

Every fiber of Lawson's being was screaming at him to strangle Frank to death right then and there. For what he might have done eleven years ago that led to the death of his wife and for what he was doing today, putting his daughter in danger.

Lawson took a long and hard look into Frank's eyes. "It will be done before the day is over."

"There's a GPS tracker on the phones and on the truck. So I'll know where you are at all times. Frank opened the door and handed over the keys to the truck. Lawson and Cassie found the truck, got in, shut the door, and started it up.

"Lawson?" Cassie said. Her voice was soft, not wanting to poke the bear.

The rumble of the truck's idling engine filled the cabin. The air blowing from the AC vents had begun to cool. Lawson's insides were a nuclear bomb with a short fuse; he could feel that he was about to explode. Cassie let him sit in silence. If he didn't calm down, he wasn't going to be able to unscramble his mind to start to piece together a plan. The hardest part of all of it was not knowing Lexi's exact situation. So until he did, he would have to assume the very worst and work off of that.

"Take a deep breath, and let's start to figure this out." Cassie kept her voice calm. She had to know Lawson's fuse was about a millimeter long at that point.

Instead of cracking, instead of beating the steering wheel or taking out his pistol and wiping Frank Shaw off the face of the earth like he really wanted to, he listened to his partner. He took a long, deep breath in through his nose and slowly let it out through his mouth. He put the truck in drive and pulled out of the parking lot.

"Roosevelt Hotel?" Cassie said.

She already knew the only play they had. He already knew he had the best partner in the world. And he knew he was going to need her more than ever if they hoped to get out of this situation.

"I'll take your phone with me when I go in to talk to Sloan, if he's even still there. Frank will think you stayed with me. He already knows Sloan's routine, so he won't think anything is off when *we* are at the hotel for a while. You're going to have to steal a car and run it blind. You won't have a phone. Do you know where you'll start?"

"You sure you don't want to be the one looking for Lexi?"

"It's all I want, but I have to deal with Sloan."

Cassie nodded. "You know how you're going to play it?"

"Not yet."

"I'm sorry this is happening to you, Lawson. This is the last thing you deserve. You've been through so much. I—"

"Let's stay focused, Cass. How are you going to find Lexi? You can't be gone from me very long."

"I'll go to the only place I think we can get help."

"Clint Hues?"

"Clint Hues," Cassie confirmed.

Lawson took another deep breath. It was bad enough he had put his daughter back in harm's way, but it was worse that he had to rely on someone as untrustworthy as a Hollywood fixer. But if he could get Clint's motivation steered in the right direction, there could be no better ally in this town than someone like him. Even though it was clear at that point Clint had been lying about Sloan trying to kidnap Lexi, Lawson needed him. Any retribution would have to wait.

"Remember when he said Marty Sloan had a son?" Lawson said. "Said they were close."

"Yeah . . . And?"

"You have to convince Clint to kidnap him while I'm here with Sloan."

"*What*?" There was real shock in Cassie's voice. "You can't be serious."

"Cassie, if you think it through, you'll see it's the only way."

"I'm not thinking that through. I'm not asking Clint to do that. It's a child. You should know better than anyone—"

"That Sloan will do anything to get him back." Lawson finished Cassie's sentence with his own words.

"That's a big hell no, Lawson. I can't believe you. This isn't who you are."

"No, it's who I have to be to keep my daughter safe. Open your mind, Cass. Look at the alternative."

Cassie scoffed as she shook her head. "There has to be another way."

"There is another way, and you know what that is, and you know it will be worse for Sloan's son if that is the route I have to take. But I'll take it if I have to."

"You mean kill Sloan."

"Yes. The only other option is to kill Sloan, but it is a much worse option. For the kid who loses his dad forever, for Lexi, me, and you."

"How would that be worse for me, Lexi, and you? And I'm not convinced it wouldn't be better for the kid to lose his scumbag drug dealer of a dad."

"Yes, you are. And you know exactly why it would be worse for all of us too. Don't play dumb. We'd be on the run forever from Sloan's entire army of thugs. You don't want to admit it, because it's a horrible thing to do to kidnap a child, but you know it's the best way forward. The *only* way forward."

When Lawson turned onto Hollywood Boulevard, the Roosevelt Hotel wasn't far. If he didn't get Cassie on board with this, there was no way he could pull it off.

"Look," he said, "if we are the ones who kidnap Sloan's son, we know he won't be hurt. I'm sure Clint has met him before, he can tell the boy that his father needed Clint to pick him up today and entertain him because his dad and his mom had something important come up. Right? We're in control, nothing will happen."

"No, Lawson, Clint will be in control. We don't know what he might do to Sloan's son."

Cassie was right, but hurting a child would get him put away for a long time, so Lawson knew it wasn't something Clint would do. Regardless, it was a risk Lawson had to be willing to take. His daughter's life was on the line. Morally right or not, Lawson would slaughter an entire city to keep her safe.

"Besides," Cassie continued, "we don't know that I could ever convince Clint to do it. Kidnapping is no small crime. He gets caught, he's doing hard time. It's too much of a risk."

"Clint is desperate. He would never have come to me for help if he wasn't. In order to work again, he has to take Sloan down. Ruthless is what this guy does for a living. If you sell it right, he'll do it. I know he will."

Cassie didn't say anything else. They valeted the truck at the hotel entrance, and the two of them walked in together.

"Okay. I don't like it, but okay. I agree it's the only way. I feel disgusting."

"Come right back here after you talk to Clint. We can't chance you being gone too long."

Cassie handed Lawson her phone so Frank would believe they stayed there together, and was on her way.

Lawson switched off that part of the plan in his mind; his focus now was what exactly he was going to say to Marty Sloan. He wasn't sure what it would be, but he was sure it was going to have to be good.

27

TAYLOR EXCUSED HERSELF FOR THE FOURTH TIME ON HER beach walk with Lexi. Lexi opened the bag of potato chips Taylor told her to bring and began feeding a small gathering of seagulls. The sun was high in the sky, and the sand between Taylor's toes was beginning to warm. She took out her phone, and for the twelfth time she dialed Lawson's number. She had also sent a few texts trying to warn him about what was going on. She'd received nothing in return. And she was starting to really worry.

The phone continued to ring like every other time she'd called. She moved in a circle on the beach as she waited, and when her turn brought her around to the hotel they were staying at, she could have sworn she saw a man's leg as he went back inside a hotel room from the balcony. Her hotel room.

She did her best to count the rooms, trying to figure out if it really was hers, but did it really matter? She wasn't going to take Lexi back to that room now. Though she didn't tell Victoria where she was, in the back of her mind she almost knew it wouldn't matter. She probably had police able to track her phone somehow. She heard Lawson's voice telling her to leave a message, but she didn't. A pit formed in her stomach as she looked back at Lexi enjoying the birds. It occurred to her that what Taylor had done might have ruined this poor girl's life, and her father's.

Taylor ended the call and walked back over to Lexi. Her mind was working on who she could call to help her get out of this mess. The problem wasn't that she didn't know anyone who could help; the problem was that she didn't know anyone she could trust. Everyone in Hollywood knew everyone else. And word always got around. What she needed was someone who made a living being discreet.

Taylor stopped just before she reached Lexi again and turned her back to her. She needed the guy who'd helped keep her clear of what happened the night the girl in that photo died. The night of the picture that Victoria had tried to blackmail her with. Her then-agent had called him a fixer. She pulled her phone from her pocket and searched her contact list for the number. She couldn't remember the guy's name, so since it was all she knew him by, she scrolled to the *F*s in her contacts. Sure enough, there it was: FIXER.

Taylor pressed the call button, but as soon as she looked up, she found that her suspicions about a man being on her balcony were correct. Two men had just walked off the hotel's pool deck and onto the beach. And they weren't wearing surfing gear either. Taylor tucked her phone in her pocket and sprinted back to Lexi.

Lexi saw her coming. "Oh no, what's wrong?"

Taylor grabbed her by the hand and yanked her in the direction opposite the hotel as well as the two men coming toward them.

"We have to run."

28

———————

"YOU WANT ME TO DO WHAT?" CLINT COULDN'T BELIEVE what he was hearing. He was already reeling from learning that Victoria and some FBI agent were working together to blackmail Lawson into taking down Sloan, so hearing Cassie tell him she needed him to kidnap Sloan's son was a lot to take in. Especially when it wasn't more than a half hour ago he finally got rid of the cops who'd come to his office looking for Lawson.

"I know it sounds crazy," Cassie explained, "but it will work out for all of us. Believe me, if there was any other way, I wouldn't be here telling you this."

Clint shook his head, taking a minute to consider what she was saying. At that point, what Lawson Raines needed didn't really concern him. His daughter being in trouble didn't help Clint get rid of Sloan. However, what he was trying to calculate was if he took Sloan's son, would it help get Sloan out of the picture? He knew Sloan and his son were close. He had only been to Sloan's house a handful of times, but it was easy to see how much he cared about him.

"I don't mean to rush you, but Lawson is with Sloan right now. We don't have a very big window to make this happen."

"No," Clint said.

"No?" Cassie seemed confused.

"Yeah, no way I'm doing that. Even if I pull it off, and Lawson gets what he wants out of it, he could easily turn around and spill it all to the cops, pinning everything on me. So, yeah, the answer is no."

As Cassie took that in, his wheels started spinning. Was there a way he could use any of this to blackmail Sloan himself? Either by taking him out or getting back in his good graces? He would need to talk to Jenny about it as soon as Cassie was gone. He needed to bounce some ideas off her, because he wasn't sure what was the best way forward.

Cassie didn't know what to say. She honestly hadn't expected Clint to say no. Lawson was going to kill her if she didn't make this happen, but in a way she was relieved. She understood why Lawson would be willing to go this far to save his daughter. But the thought of kidnapping a little boy, even knowing he wouldn't be harmed, made her skin crawl. So did a lot of things lately, like sitting here in this scumbag's office practically begging him to help her. She was finished with it, and she knew she could find another way.

She uncrossed her legs, and just as she was about to stand up and tell Clint to screw himself, Clint's cell phone rang and his reaction to the number calling him shocked Cassie.

"Taylor Lockhart?" Clint said, looking down at his phone. He looked over at his partner Jenny. "Taylor Lockhart is calling me, can you believe that? Haven't heard from her since her agent called me to bail her out of that party disaster a while back." Then to Cassie. "I've got work to do. Come up with something else, find something on Sloan, anything, and we'll be ready to help. Otherwise, it sounds like you all have your hands full."

Cassie did the only thing she could think to do. She pulled the pistol Frank left her in the pickup truck and pointed it across the room, directly at Clint's head.

"What the hell are you doing?" Clint dropped his phone on his desk and instinctively held up his hands. "Are you crazy?"

Cassie held the gun on him with her left hand, and pointed to Jenny with her right when she saw her move for her gun. "Don't."

Jenny froze. Cassie hardened her tone. "Give me the phone." When Clint didn't move, she shouted, "Now!"

Clint slid the phone over to Cassie, and she picked it and answered the call. "Taylor, it's Lawson's friend Cassie. If you hurt Lexi, I'm going to kill you!"

"Cassie? Cassie! Thank God! How did you get this phone?"

Taylor sounded like she was out of breath. Thank God? Why would she be relieved to hear Cassie on the phone if she was working with Victoria?

"Where's Lexi?"

Clint started to stand, until Cassie re-extended the pistol in his direction, letting him know to stay back.

"She's with me. But they are after us. Cassie, I did something really bad. I—"

"I know. We are trying to clean up your mess right now. And it doesn't look good. Where the hell are you? Who is after you?"

"Victoria. Her people, I mean. How do you know—"

"Taylor, I don't have time for this, and it sounds like you don't either. I just need to know, are you with Victoria? Are you working for her?"

"No—yes, I mean, I was, but no, not now. I couldn't do what she wanted me to do. I was stupid. She has something over me. Something I thought only two people in the world knew. Please help us—help Lexi—what do I do?"

Clint and Jenny still looked dumbfounded. At least that was the expression their faces were swapping. Cassie kept the gun on them while she tried to get things straight with Taylor.

"Are you really in Malibu where you told Lawson you were? At the Malibu Beach Inn?"

"Yes, but they found me. I swear I didn't tell them where we were. Victoria tried to make me but I wouldn't. They must have tapped my phone somehow."

"Yeah, she has the FBI helping her. Do you know anyone in Malibu? A place you can hide?"

"If I can get away from them, shouldn't I just go to the police?"

"No, Taylor, no police. We don't know who we can trust."

"I don't know what to do. They're catching up to us. We're on the beach, there's nowhere to go!"

Taylor was really out of breath at this point. Cassie felt a thousand miles away from Lexi. With them all the way in Malibu, she might as well be. Cassie was racking her brain to try to find a way to help her. To help Lexi.

"The SOBA Recovery Center," Clint said.

"Taylor, keep running, give me just a second," Cassie said.

"I'm at the pier! There's nowhere to go!"

Cassie heard Taylor's words, but she was keying in on Clint. "How does that help?"

"It's where I had her go to talk to someone about her drug use." Clint spoke fast. "Taylor knows where it is. If she's at the pier, she'll have to double back, but it's not far. A guy I've done a lot of favors for owns it. I'll call him and tell him to look out for her."

Cassie spoke to Taylor now. "The SOBA Recovery Center. Clint said he'll have a guy watching for you to come in."

"SOBA? But it's on the other side of the hotel. They'll catch us!"

"It's all I've got. Get there, I'm on my way. Just get to the main road and stay out in traffic. They can't do anything to you in the middle of the road." She covered the phone and looked up at Clint. "Can he really keep her safe?"

"He'll do what he can. He owes me."

"Taylor, you've got to get to SOBA . . . Taylor?"

The call ended. Taylor heard Cassie say SOBA. All she could do was hope she could get Lexi there safely.

"Can you take the gun off me now?" Clint asked.

Cassie lowered the pistol. "Why are you helping?"

"She called *me*, remember? I need all the clients I can get right now."

"Bullshit." Cassie saw through his statement like it was written on glass. "Why are you helping?"

Clint motioned with his hands, moving them from high to low, telling her to lower her gun. "That's not bullshit, it's true. But . . . I also need Lawson's head in the game here. If I help you secure Lexi, he can concentrate on helping me with Sloan. You know that's all I care about here."

"Well, he's with Sloan right now, already doing your dirty work. Helping Lexi is the least you can do."

"It's already done. Roger will keep them safe until you get there. No matter what."

Cassie put her gun down. She needed to get back to the Roosevelt Hotel before any of Frank's men could tell she was gone. But she needed to go to Malibu even more. It's what Lawson would want her to do. She just hoped it didn't really jam him up with what he was trying to do with Sloan.

29

Lawson checked his watch for what must have been the thirtieth time. Sloan's men had told him to wait in the lobby, that he was in a meeting, and they would see if he wanted to talk to Lawson when he was finished. Considering Sloan would have to walk by him to exit, he still felt like there was a chance to sit down with him. The time waiting wasn't all bad. Lawson had needed a few minutes to find his angle. He felt pretty good about the plan he'd formed, but he wouldn't know until he could actually feel Sloan out.

Two men, clearly not part of Sloan's movie operation but the more seedy ventures, walked toward Lawson. One of them looked familiar, but Lawson couldn't place him. He could tell by their determined stride and scowling faces that Sloan had declined to see him. Lawson had prepared for this scenario. Drug Thug number one opened his suit jacket just wide enough to let Lawson know he had a pistol tucked in his belt line. Lawson stood, looking down on both of them.

Lawson played offense. "Before you tell me Sloan

doesn't want to see me, and that he actually wants me dead, I need you to let him know that his family is in danger."

The Hispanic man, the one with the gun, reached for it, letting his hand rest on its handle. "Are you threatening Mr. Sloan? That's not a very smart way to get what you want."

"Not a threat," Lawson said. "Just trying to warn him that someone—not me—wishes to do his family harm. But if you don't want him to know that, I'll just be on my way." Lawson turned to his left but Drug Thug One stopped him by grabbing his arm.

"Why didn't you tell me this when you first got here?"

"Because I was trying not to alarm anyone, but now it seems necessary that Sloan is alarmed."

The two drug thugs stepped back. Drug Thug One said something to Two, and Two walked back toward the bar.

"Just wait here for a second."

A few seconds passed, and Two walked out of the bar, nodded toward One, and several people moved out of the bar where Sloan was having lunch. Drug Thug One nodded toward Lawson. "Follow me."

Lawson walked to the entrance. Both of Sloan's men patted Lawson down, confiscating the two phones. He was happy he'd decided to leave the pistol in the truck. Lawson could see that the bar was empty now. Not even a bartender. He was going to get his time with Sloan, and he needed to make it count.

A bearded man at a table in the back of the darkened bar waved Lawson in. Lawson understood what tone Sloan was going to take before ever sitting down. He'd been looking for Lawson ever since Lawson ruined the meeting with Victoria Marshall. He wasn't going to be happy. The hardest part of this entire confrontation was deciding whether or not Lawson believed that Clint Hues was no longer working for Sloan. It was the crux of the entire plan. If Lawson sat down and said what he was about to say, and Clint had been lying and was still working for Sloan, the plan was dead. Not only that, but more than likely Lawson was dead too. Sometimes you have to take chances, and even though that is hard to do when your own life is on the line, in this line of work, it's just how things roll.

Sloan presented Lawson a seat by waving his hand toward the opposite side of the table. Lawson sat without saying anything. He would let Sloan facilitate the meeting. Lawson was better at counter punching, so he would be patient and wait for all the right moments.

Sloan was smug. "Of all the people I didn't expect to see today, you're the biggest surprise. Don't you know it isn't safe to seek out a man like me when I'm not very happy with you?"

Classic organized crime bravado. Lead with telling someone how powerful you are. Lawson had seen this a dozen times. They think making you feel weak will make it more likely you'll give them what they want. The last thing they expect is for you to show your own strength.

"Haven't you done your homework on a man like *me*?" Lawson said. "If you have, you'll know men like you don't fare well when I'm not happy with you."

Sloan sat back in his chair and smiled. The reaction Lawson expected. Sloan wasn't used to someone not willing to cower to him. Lawson had found over the years that resistance was actually something men like Sloan appreciated. They weren't challenged very often. It intrigued them. If of course they felt you to be a worthy adversary.

"Okay, you have my attention. Don't waste it."

Lawson continued to show his strength. "I really wanted

to walk in here and do to you what I did to Clint Hues in that meeting with Victoria. Maybe worse."

Sloan didn't seem affected by the threat. "But you didn't." Then he turned sarcastic. "To what do I owe this great act of mercy?"

"I decided Clint was lying."

That garnered a raise of the eyebrow. "You've been meeting with my former associate?"

"He came to me."

"And just what interesting things did he have to say?"

Lawson got right to the heart of it. "That you were going to kidnap my daughter."

Lawson scanned Sloan's face like a computer. In the FBI you learn to profile people. To look for subtleties in facial expressions, a deepening of breath, a twitch of the mouth, even a pounding jugular, but Sloan gave no indication that this statement affected him in any way. Lawson's read on him was no read at all.

Sloan brought his hands from his lap and sipped on what looked like an espresso. "And you didn't believe him?"

"I didn't really know what to believe. Guys like Clint Hues have no loyalty, except to furthering their own cause. So belief doesn't lie in his words, it's in his motivation."

"Let me guess." Sloan placed his napkin on the table. "His motivation was me."

It was time for Lawson to take some leaps. He needed to get to Lexi. "You know how this works. You fired Clint, he needs his reputation intact. He has a reason you already don't like me. You told him to find me and make sure I don't interrupt any more of your meetings."

Lawson paused, giving Sloan a chance to correct him. Sloan didn't.

"Then to make sure I help him bring you down, he told

me you are the one who tried to kidnap my daughter and my partner."

"So the two of you could work together to take me down. But again, you don't believe him. Can we wrap this up and get to why you believe my family is in danger? I told you, don't waste my attention."

"At first I did believe him."

"What changed?"

Time to jump off the ledge. "After I found my daughter, the two men who tried to kidnap her were taking me to who I assumed was you. After someone killed them in the street, and tried to kill me, it wasn't long before I got picked up by the real problem, Victoria Marshall."

Lawson expected that to get a bigger reaction. Sloan was still unfazed. He sat back in his seat again and checked his watch. "Mr. Raines, when I had my men look into who you are, and I found out it was you who took down my old business partner, I did want to find you. Not because I wanted to harm you or your family, but to keep Victoria from galvanizing you to come after me. I could have told you she would do anything to get what she wanted. Kidnapping your daughter wouldn't have surprised me. She learned that sort of behavior from Nero De Luca. I never liked that son of a bitch. He and I may have had similar operations, but we operate very differently. We were only together in business because of promises made by our fathers. Are you about to tell me what I agreed to meet with you about? Why my family is in danger?"

Lawson heard what Sloan was saying, but his mind stuck on something else. When Lawson was explaining what happened with the two men who tried to take Lexi, when he told Sloan someone killed them and tried to kill Lawson himself, it was lost in all the chaos––who the man was that would be shooting at Frank and Victoria's men in the front of the truck. And who'd chased Lawson through the streets as he fled from the vehicle, shooting at him before Cassie showed up and saved his ass. He never even considered who *that* could have been. How could he have missed that? And how much would it cost him for overlooking it?

"Something wrong, Mr. Raines?"

Something was wrong. *Very* wrong.

30

THE MALIBU SUN WAS HOT, BUT IT WAS THE NERVES AND THE
fear that were making Taylor sweat. This felt much more
like one of her movies than reality. And she would give
anything if someone would shout, "Cut!" The men were
gaining on her and Lexi. Lexi was doing great, they were
weaving their way through the crowd of people on the pier
fairly well, but the men coming after them were running
right through them.

Traffic was heavy, but there was a stoplight at the pier
entrance. Through one more row of people, Taylor could
see that the light was red. They *had* to make the light to give
them a chance.

"Come on, Lexi! Run!" Taylor shouted, giving Lexi's arm
a violent tug.

They both surged forward, knocking into a group of
women leaving the pier. There was no time for apologies.
Just as they reached the road, the light changed. Without
thinking, Taylor yanked on Lexi one more time, and they
ran out into traffic just as the cars began to move. They
made it past the first lane, but horns were already blaring. It

must have scared Lexi because she pulled from Taylor's grip and fell to the ground. Taylor turned and reached out a hand for her as she held up the other for the Cadillac in front of her to stop. Lexi grabbed her hand, and as Taylor pulled her up, she looked back at the pier; the two men had reached the edge of the road. The first man stepped forward and almost got smacked by the car in the first lane that was already on the move. He was forced to step back. Just before Taylor turned to maneuver across traffic, their eyes met, his telling her she wouldn't get away. She was sure her eyes told him—begged him—to leave them alone.

Taylor moved into the next lane, cars already moving around them. She let go of Lexi's hand and waved her arms frantically above her head. One car swerved, just missing her, and the next one slammed on the brakes and laid on the horn. Taylor held out both hands, asking without words for them to wait. She waved Lexi over, and luckily the cars in the last lane had already stopped due to all the commotion. Lexi surged past Taylor, and finally they were on the other side of the street, running toward the SOBA center a few blocks down.

Taylor glanced over her shoulder, and much to her horror the two men were already running parallel down the opposite side of the street, matching Taylor and Lexi's pace with ease. They weren't going to make it to the SOBA center before the men. And even if by some miracle they did, no one there would be equipped to stop the two men chasing them. Her head was pounding and she was scared to death. But she had no other alternative. She had gotten herself and Lawson's daughter into this situation, and she was going to get them out of it.

She had to.

As they ran, she scanned her mind for a different place

to go. She knew a few people in Malibu, but only as well as you can know someone in this town, which is not that well. Not enough to bail her out of a situation like this one. She didn't have a weapon to use to steal someone's car. But she did have one thing that *did* go a very long way in Hollywood and its surrounding areas.

Celebrity.

If she used her celebrity, though, the story would absolutely get out. At the point when men were chasing you to take you to even more dangerous people, the consequences of a story didn't really matter. Because the consequences of real life were potentially much, much worse.

The Malibu Health Club was just ahead on her left. She did a number of personal training sessions there while getting in shape for her last movie. The place was always busy, and if her trainer or someone she knew at the front desk wasn't there, she knew that several, if not all, of the people in the club would recognize her. She wouldn't be surprised if video of her running across the street in traffic just a minute ago was already being watched all over social media.

Social media.

Taylor couldn't believe she hadn't thought of it before. But it would have to wait until she and Lexi were safe. Just because people knew her didn't mean they could help, even if they were willing.

"We're going to the health club just up ahead, Lexi!" Taylor shouted.

Lexi had been looking across the street at the men chasing them. When she looked over at Taylor, there was nothing but fear on the poor girl's face. Taylor was so disappointed in herself in that moment for getting Lexi into this that she felt sick. She never thought it would involve kidnapping a sweet, innocent girl. Victoria had lied to Taylor, telling her no one else would get hurt, and now her feeling of sickness turned to anger.

Taylor turned left, pulling Lexi along, and ran up to the entrance of the health club. She glanced back as she opened the door, and the men had stopped, watching intently. There was no light or intersection. No crosswalk for them to get a break in traffic. This would buy Taylor at least a couple minutes. Maybe that would be enough.

Taylor opened the door and walked in. She could only imagine what kind of hot mess she looked like. For the first time in her life, she hoped it was as bad as she felt. It would only further compel someone to help. She turned the lock on the door, hopefully buying her more precious seconds.

"Hey, you can't lock that—Taylor Lockhart?"

This was a first: she was ecstatic to be so instantly recognizable. She hurried to the counter. The man who recognized her was young and fit. Typical for Malibu.

"Are you all right?"

"No, I need your help. We're in trouble."

31

CASSIE LEFT CLINT'S OFFICE IN A RUSH, BUT SHE DIDN'T leave the premises right away. There was something odd about the way Clint looked at Jenny when Taylor called. Cassie didn't know what it was, but it was enough to make her take pause. So instead of running directly to her car and booking it to Malibu, she ducked behind a nearby trash bin to see if Clint or Jenny would make some sort of move.

Not five seconds passed before Clint and Jenny came sprinting out of the office building. They ran directly for his car, jumped in, then sped out of the parking lot. Cassie ran for the BMW she'd taken from the Roosevelt Hotel valet parking lot and tore out onto the road to follow them. She had the advantage of Clint not knowing what car she was driving, so she let him lead her right to where he was going. But she already knew his destination.

Malibu.

What she didn't know was why. When she left, she told him she would handle it. There was no reason for him to get involved. He had bigger fish to fry. Sloan. And he wasn't going to have the help of Lawson after refusing to help with Sloan's son.

Cassie had no way to let Lawson know that Clint wouldn't be kidnapping Sloan's son. So if that was still what Lawson planned to threaten Sloan with, things were going to get worse—fast. As Cassie followed Clint from a distance, the question now was, who the hell was Clint working for? If for himself, why did he care about helping Taylor when so much was on the line for him with Sloan? Unless . . .

Cassie nearly hit a car coming out of a side street. She swerved around it, and her heart pounded as she kept Clint's Dodge in view. Her mind kept jumping back to Frank and Victoria, but mostly to Victoria's speech about insurance. She made it clear that it was what separated her from Nero De Luca, and it would be the reason she would succeed where De Luca didn't in getting Lawson to do what she wanted him to do.

The insurance Victoria had spoken of was Taylor Lockhart. Cassie had no idea why Taylor had been helping Victoria, especially with something involving an innocent young girl like Lexi. Cassie had to assume that Victoria wasn't up-front about everything with Taylor, which is how Taylor made it seem on their frantic call. But that didn't really help the situation now. What could help is knowing if the needling sensation at the back of Cassie's brain was based on fact or not. Had Victoria gotten to Clint? Is that why Clint was racing to Taylor—not to help her but to make sure Lexi became their hostage?

As she followed Clint onto the Santa Monica Freeway, in her mind she scanned every situation and conversation she'd had over the last two days. She and Lawson had missed something. Nothing jumped out at her, so she contemplated what they'd learned. They originally thought all of this was because of Sloan. It made sense, and it was what Clint wanted them to believe. Then they learned that Frank and Victoria were behind it all. However, they didn't learn that until the shoot-out on the street, which Lawson narrowly escaped. The two men who tried to take Lexi weren't so lucky. If it was Victoria who wanted Lexi, then those two dead men had to be working for her and Frank. So who in the hell killed them right in the middle of the street?

Cassie didn't know the answer, but she knew that was the missing link. Regardless, all she could do right now was try to protect Lexi. From Clint Hues, from Victoria Marshall, and from Marty Sloan. They were in a bad situation. Cassie felt almost helpless. All she could do was hope that Lawson could tap into that old detective magic he used to possess in spades. She could try to help Lexi, but Lawson was the one who needed to figure out how to end it. And he had to find out who was really pulling all the strings.

32

The Library Bar was quiet. All Lawson could hear were people outside the doorway to the hotel lobby hustling to wherever they needed to go. Sloan had asked him if something was wrong, but Lawson was too deep in his own thoughts to answer. So much so that he stood from the table. There was something on the tip of his tongue that his mind was reaching for.

"Mr. Raines, do I need to have you removed? Are we finished here?"

Lawson looked at him but didn't see him. "Can I get a drink?"

While Lawson could certainly use a drink, it was time that he really needed.

"Hector," Sloan shouted. "We are finished here. Please remove Mr. Raines from the hotel."

A lightning bolt shot through Lawson's body. When he turned around and saw Hector coming toward him, a flash memory of the man following him yesterday hit his mind's eye. The next frame of the memory was of himself running from the car that had just been shot up, then seeing Cassie and looking back over his shoulder. The same face approaching him now was the same one he saw firing at him from around the side of the house during the shoot-out. Hector. And Hector was the name of the man Clint mentioned who used to work for him.

Lawson held up both hands in a surrender position. As Hector and Sloan's other man reached for Lawson's arms, Lawson turned his open right hand into a fist and slammed it into Hector's forehead. When Hector reeled from the blow, Lawson moved his left hand to the second man's waist and grabbed him by the wrist before he could pull his gun. Lawson threw him a head butt to the nose—the benefit of being hardheaded, as Cassie calls him—and as the man reached for his nose, Lawson took his pistol and wheeled around just in time to match Sloan's own extended gun. Though Lawson had been the one fighting, Sloan was the one heaving for air.

"This isn't your thing, Sloan, put the gun down."

"You think I won't shoot you?"

"I think you can't afford to."

Sloan stood trying to calm his breath. The end of his gun was shaking.

"Me?" Sloan said. "*I* can't afford to shoot *you*?"

Lawson heard shuffling behind him. "Move again and I shoot him. Then I shoot both of you."

The shuffling stopped.

Sloan regained some of his wits. "What's the end game here, Raines? Kill us all?"

Lawson was confident, looking Sloan dead in the eyes. "Get you your movie, keep your family safe, keep my family safe, and erase the bastards who put this entire thing together."

"That's a whole lot of promises from one man," Sloan

said. "If you can do all of that, where do you suggest we start?"

"With Hector."

Lawson turned the gun toward Hector, who at the sound of his name reached for his pistol. Lawson shot him in the thigh just below the gun and Hector crumpled to the floor.

"Don't shoot me, Sloan. You're going to want to hear this."

Lawson moved over to Hector as he writhed on the floor in pain. He moved Hector's hand away from the wound, took the pistol from his waistline, then pressed his foot where the hole was already leaking blood. Hector shouted in pain.

"Who are you working for, Hector?"

Sloan's face was pale. It was very clear to Lawson why he wanted to be in the movie business. The blood was fake, unlike this scene.

"Mr. Sloan!" Hector shouted.

Lawson leaned, putting more of his weight on Hector's gunshot wound.

"I promise, this pain is nothing compared to what's next if you don't tell me right now. Who do you work for?"

Another shriek of pain.

The next thing Lawson expected to hear was the name Clint Hues.

"Okay, okay! Frank Shaw! I work for Frank Shaw!"

Lawson was shocked. How deep did this thing run? Granted, Frank had always been an asshole when Lawson was around him, but how did he devolve into this?

Sloan walked over and, before Lawson could stop him, shot Hector right between the eyes. Upon reflex, even though the deed had already been done, Lawson turned and knocked Sloan off his feet with a violent shove. Sloan sprawled on the floor, and his gun skidded off across the bar floor. This thing was going sideways on Lawson. If he lost Sloan to police custody now, he may not get the leverage he needed to gain the upper hand and stop Frank, or Victoria, or Clint. Everything had become so convoluted. If Lawson didn't pull it together, right then, he may lose his daughter again.

That wasn't going to happen.

Screams of fear from the crowd outside made their way into the bar. No question the cops had already been called. It may already be too late. Lawson moved over to Sloan and picked him up by his suit jacket.

"There's only one way out of this. My way. And it isn't going to be easy."

Sloan patted out his disheveled suit. "I'll do whatever it takes. I can't lose my family."

And that gave Lawson an idea. One that would certainly be met with resistance, but one that could potentially solve their problems. He'd had no respect for Sloan when he walked into the bar a moment ago. But a willingness to do anything for family, that was something he could work with. He didn't know if he himself could do what he was about to ask Sloan to do. But if it would ultimately save Lexi, there was no way he wouldn't.

"Give me your gun," Lawson told Sloan. "Are there any cameras in here?" He knew Sloan would know this. A man like him always knows who's watching. Except of course when one of his men, like Hector, betrays him.

"No cameras," Sloan handed him the pistol. "You used to be FBI, right? You know how these guys think? How this Frank thinks?"

"How did you let an FBI agent like Hector infiltrate your inner circle?" Lawson focused on Hector.

"FBI? Hector?"

"He said he worked for Frank."

"Hector has been around for a long time. He's never been FBI. I can promise you that. I shouldn't have trusted him, but I never thought he would rat. Frank must have something on him."

It surprised Lawson that Frank would do this on his own. Outside the FBI. He should probably stop being surprised by anything at this point.

"Okay, so why does Frank want you so bad that he'll break the law to trip you up?"

Sloan shook his head. "Now that, is a long story."

"You can tell me about it on the way to your son's school."

Sloan took a step back. "My son's school?"

Lawson wiped down Sloan's pistol. "What part of 'isn't going to be easy' didn't you understand?"

33

Unfortunately for Taylor, the man at the front desk didn't have a car. However, her celebrity had everyone in the facility's attention, and several of the men and women working out in the adjacent room came running to help when they heard she was in trouble. A couple of the bigger guys went to help hold the door closed while one of the women volunteered to sneak Taylor and Lexi out the back door and drive them to safety. Taylor didn't hesitate taking the woman up on it, and that's why she and Lexi were lying down in the back of a stranger's Mercedes Benz sedan, praying that the man who'd just rounded the corner of the building didn't see them duck down.

"Stay down," the woman said in a whisper. "He's at the far end of the building, but he's coming this way."

"I'm sorry I got you into this situation, ma'am," Taylor whispered. "I just didn't know what else to do."

"Call me Pam, and don't worry about it, honey. Believe me, I know there are a lot of crazy assholes in this town."

Pam was quintessential Malibu. Perfectly tanned, long

blonde hair, a forty-five-year-old face with a sixty-five-year-old neck.

"Is he gone?"

"No, he's coming right for us. How bad are these guys?" Pam said.

"The worst."

"Then hang on, honey, we're getting out of here."

Pam dropped the shift knob to drive and laid on the gas. Taylor peeked up over the console and watched as one of the men chasing them dove to get out of the way of Pam's car. Taylor looked back through the rear window, and the man was already on his phone. Pam took a hard left out of the back parking lot but had to hit the brakes before turning onto the Pacific Coast Highway.

"Damn traffic. I petitioned for a light to go in here months ago, and nothing. All the money my husband pays this city in taxes, and I can't even get a stoplight put in."

Taylor checked the rear window again. A man was running toward them away from the health club's front entrance, and the man Pam had nearly flattened came sprinting around the back of the building. Both men had guns in their hands.

"Pam, they're coming. We have to go."

Taylor looked down, and Lexi's face was buried in the seat, both hands covering her head. Terrified.

"Honey, I can only do what these damn cars allow me to do."

"Pam, they have guns!"

Pam laid on the horn and inched her way out into the road. Cars swerved around the nose of the Mercedes, narrowly avoiding a crash. Taylor looked back again, and the men were just a few feet away now and closing fast.

"Pam."

"I'm trying, honey."

"Pam!"

The men reached the car, and Taylor looked up through the back door window, staring directly at the business end of a pistol. At that exact moment, Taylor felt the car jerk forward; she heard two more horns around them and a lot of screeching tires, but the man with the gun moved out of sight.

"Hold on, girls!"

Pam turned the wheel and the car slid sideways. A couple more cars slammed on the brakes to avoid the heavy sedan. As they pulled away, Taylor took one last look back, happy to see the men stalking them moving farther away. But just before they were out of sight, an SUV pulled up and they started to get in. That must have been the call the man was making in the parking lot.

"Okay, I think we've lost them." Pam was beaming with pride.

"I saw them getting into an SUV. They'll be coming up on us fast."

Taylor and Pam met eyes in the car's rearview mirror. "Oh no they won't. This car may not be big, but it has one hell of an engine."

The Mercedes Benz's engine groaned as the car sped forward. Pam had been a godsend. The problem now was that Taylor had no idea where to tell her to go.

"Don't worry, we'll be at the police station before they can catch us."

"I can't go to the police, Pam."

Their eyes met again.

"What kind of trouble are you in, Taylor Lockhart?"

"I've been blackmailed. I made a mistake and got this innocent girl in trouble. I can't let them get her."

"If you can't go to the police, who's going to help you?"

"My dad." Lexi sat up.

"What's your name, darling?"

"Lexi."

"Lexi, I'm not sure your dad can find us," Taylor said. "He's not answering his phone." Then to Pam. "Is there somewhere you can take us? I know someone who can help. But I need to give them a place to meet us."

"I have a boat at the docks in Marina del Rey."

"I can't keep putting you in danger, Pam. You've already done enough."

"Sounds to me like you don't have a choice."

Taylor knew she was right.

"Can you get us there before they catch up to us?"

The car started going even faster. "I can sure as hell try!"

Lexi asked, "Who are you going to call?"

"I'd call Cassie, but she said she doesn't have her phone. But she was with the guy I called earlier. Even answered his phone."

"Who?" Lexi was concerned.

"I think his name is Clint, but don't worry about it."

"Clint? Clint Hues?"

"That *is* his last name, I think. How'd you know that?"

"'Cause he was at our house earlier. Dad doesn't like him. I don't think we should call him."

Taylor was confused. "At your house—wait, the man and woman who came to your house? When you told me to hide upstairs? That was Clint Hues?"

"Yeah, why?"

"We can trust him. If he didn't know I was there at the house, he can't be working for Victoria. She would have told him, so he would have known I was there with you."

Taylor pulled her phone and once again hit the contact named FIXER.

"Taylor," Clint answered on the first ring. "Were you able to get to the SOBA Center?"

"Is Cassie with you?"

"Cassie? No, but she's on her way to SOBA, I think. Are you there now?"

"No, we couldn't get there. They're chasing us! What do I do?" Taylor was still high on adrenaline, but she felt a rush of relief along with it. At least someone was coming to help.

"I don't know where you are, so I can't—"

Pam interrupted. "Tell him the Esprit Boat Club in Marina del Rey, and tell him to hurry."

"Esprit Boat Club in Marina del Rey. Are you sending someone?"

"No, I'll meet you there," Clint said. "We're on the 10 Freeway now."

"Hurry, they have guns!"

34

AFTER A MOMENT OF THOUGHT, LAWSON REALIZED HE wouldn't be able to go with Sloan. There was no time. He had to set the scene there at the Library Bar, then he had to get to Lexi. Fortunately, he had been able to convince Sloan to follow his plan—even though it involved a not-so-pleasant day for his son. While Sloan and his man with the broken nose reluctantly went to put that plan in motion, Lawson put Hector's gun in Hector's hand and fired off a couple rounds, at least making it look like he'd fired his own shots and maybe got what was coming to him. It was all going to be a tough sell, what with all the cameras watching in the lobby, but it would help when questions were asked.

Lawson took out the phone given to him and called Frank.

"Causing quite the commotion at the Roosevelt, I hear. Cops are on their way."

"I almost had him, Frank. But Sloan and one of his men got away. I did manage to take down a man Sloan called Hector. Ring any bells?"

Lawson wasn't going to let on what he knew.

"Hector Ramirez, sure. Longtime criminal. No surprise he works for Sloan."

Frank played dumb as well. Or maybe he was just dumb.

"Where's Lexi, Frank?"

"She's fine. Just get Sloan to sign over the movie and I'll tell you where she is."

"Tell me where she is and I might let you live."

"Threatening an FBI agent? That might not be—"

"I don't know where Sloan went," Lawson interrupted. The best way forward was to play along. Bide his time.

"That's my boy. Don't worry about that. I've got eyes on him."

"Let me know where he goes and I'll take care of everything. I have to get out of here."

"I'll text you the location," Frank said.

Lawson ended the call and immediately ran through the bar out into the hotel lobby. He had to hurry to see if he could find the person tailing Sloan, because he needed to make sure no one saw what Sloan was about to do. Especially not someone who could tell Frank. If they were going to have a shot at pinning the kidnapping of Sloan's son on Frank and Victoria, Sloan would need to have the chance to set it all up perfectly.

"Freeze!"

Lawson heard a woman shout behind him. It echoed in the lobby because the space had already emptied out after the gunshots in the bar. Upon reflex, he stopped. Because when you've done something wrong and that's what someone shouts, that's just what you do. Every fiber of his being sizzled, screaming at him to run. He didn't. But before he could turn around, he felt an arm hook around his.

"Walk with me."

Lawson looked over, and while he didn't know the woman ushering him out of the lobby, she was familiar. She wasn't forcing him along; in fact, her gun was nowhere to be found.

"I thought you said freeze," he told her.

"Just walk. Ask for your truck at the valet and let's get the hell out of here."

They exited the hotel, but of course there was no valet at the stand. They, too, had run for cover. Sirens rode the warm California breeze; they couldn't have been more than a block away. Lawson rushed to the key stand, found the F-150's keys, and the two of them ran for the truck. Lawson jumped in the driver's seat, and as soon as the woman shut the door, he held his gun on her.

"Where do I know you from, and what are you doing here? As you can see I'm a little busy."

The familiar woman with the short brown hair seemed entirely unfazed by the gun. " Start driving or the cops are gonna stop you."

Lawson looked in his rearview mirror. Nothing yet. But she was right, he needed to move. He put the truck in reverse and started out of the hotel parking lot.

"We met in the holding room yesterday when you were arrested and let go. I'm Frank Shaw's partner, Claudia Miles."

Damn. "So you're Frank's watchdog." It wasn't a question. More of a realization.

Claudia smiled. "Not exactly. I'm also a Department of Justice special agent. I was assigned to Frank a year and a half ago because rumor had it he wasn't playing by the rules. That surprise you?"

Lawson engaged the safety and set his gun in his lap. "What, that you are DOJ or that Frank is crooked? The answers are different. Yes and no. But why should I believe you?"

Claudia reached into her pocket and produced something from a hidden flap in her wallet. It was her DOJ credentials. "That help?"

Lawson was relieved. With Cassie not making it back to the hotel yet and no way to get ahold of her, he was happy to have someone with some knowledge of what was going on. She might even know more than he did.

"Were you the one tailing Sloan for Frank?"

"Yep. But I figured after your meeting with Sloan, which seemed to go in your favor, I should probably stick with you seeing as how you know where Sloan is going anyway, right?"

Lawson turned onto Hollywood Boulevard just as the police cruisers were rushing into the hotel. "Let's cut the shit, okay? My daughter is in danger and I need to find her."

Claudia cut right through it. "Frank got you released from police custody so you could help him take down Sloan. He's had a hard-on for him for as long as I've been his partner and, I can tell you, for much longer than that. A couple of Sloan's guys roughed him up real bad a few years ago. So much so that he lost his hearing in his right ear. And almost lost his job because Sloan had set him up and made Frank look like a fool to the Bureau."

"Frank's been looking like a fool to the Bureau since I worked with him in Vegas."

"I can imagine. Anyway, one of Sloan's men was Frank's informant, but he was playing Frank the entire time. The man you shot, Hector, that was Frank's retaliation. But when you popped up on the radar, Frank saw an opportunity to make sure Sloan went away for good. He knew what you were capable of when your family was threatened. He's trying to take advantage."

Lawson was furious. "You knew this, and you didn't tell me? My daughter could have been killed!"

"Now hold on. If I would have known your daughter was in danger, I would have stepped in. It was only a hunch for me that he wanted to use you. Frank has only been giving me the scoop on Sloan, said he was up to something and that I needed to follow him. Never said anything about you. I've been working on that independently. Since a couple nights ago when we first got the video of you at the bar. Then Frank started acting funny. So when he asked me to find you and Cassie, I did, but I looked with an eye as to why he might want you so bad."

"So you don't know about Victoria Marshall?" Lawson moved on.

"That she was kidnapped or missing? Yeah, I knew that. Did you do it?"

Lawson shook his head; then he snatched Claudia's phone from her hand and dialed Lexi's cell phone number.

"What the hell are you doing?"

"Trying to save my daughter. That okay with you?" Lexi's phone just kept ringing. "And you need to know, this goes much deeper than you think." The call went to voice mail. When he heard Lexi's recorded voice, his breath caught. He wasn't going to do anything else from that moment on but find his daughter and keep her safe. Frank and Victoria be damned. He would just have to bet on the hunch that Taylor wasn't capable of hurting Lexi. He ended the call and handed the phone back to Claudia. "Find out where my daughter is and I'll fill you in on just how far Frank has been willing to go."

"I'll make a call and see what I can do. Where are you going?"

Lawson's brain hit a land mine. "You said Hector was Frank's way of retaliating against Sloan. So Hector really did work for Frank?"

"Well, as much as a career criminal can work for an FBI agent. Why? He was an informant, so what?"

"No he wasn't." Lawson slammed his hand against the steering wheel. He had made another terrible mistake.

"Yes he was, I was there a few times when Hector met with Frank. What's wrong?"

"Hector is the one who shot up the car earlier. He killed two of Frank's guys and tried to kill me. If he was working for Frank—*really* working for Frank—and Frank wanted me to go after Sloan, he would never have tried to kill me."

"You're sure it was Hector?" Claudia asked.

"Positive. And I sent my partner into the lion's den without knowing it. To the man Hector really works for, Clint Hues."

"I'm officially lost," Claudia said.

"Apparently so was I." Lawson jerked the steering wheel and swerved onto the Santa Monica Freeway toward Malibu.

"What are you doing? We have to find Sloan!"

"Martin Sloan is the least of my worries."

Lawson floored the gas pedal. It just hit him: now that he had Claudia with him, he didn't need to wait for Frank to tell him where Lexi and Taylor were.

"I'll fill you in on everything I know. Just trace my daughter's cell phone. I get her out of this, I'll help you bring this entire thing down."

"What's her number?"

"It's the number I just called."

As Lawson swerved around traffic, using the shoulder when he had to, he filled Claudia in on Clint, Frank, Victoria, and Sloan. She needed to know everything so she could help him keep Lexi safe. Everyone who had something coming to them was going to get it, but only after Lexi was out of harm's way. His only hope was that Cassie was ahead of him in that matter and that's why she hadn't come back to the hotel. And his even greater hope was that Taylor Lockhart wasn't the woman Victoria was saying she was. That instead Taylor was the woman he thought he'd gotten a read on at his home. His daughter's life might literally depend on it.

35

THE DRIVE FROM MALIBU HEALTH CLUB TO THE ESPRIT BOAT slips in Marina del Rey would normally be about thirty minutes. However, the way Pam was driving—Taylor checked the speedometer and it said 110—they were going to be there in half that. If they made it without crashing. It wasn't like there weren't cars on the road, but Pam was weaving in and out of them like a show dog on a skills course.

Taylor still hadn't seen the black SUV come up behind them. Their speed in the Mercedes was keeping them at bay. But they wouldn't be far behind, and Taylor knew she needed to start thinking ahead. She had a thought earlier about social media. She hadn't been posting to it much lately, but whenever she did, inevitably the paparazzi magically showed up within minutes of where she was going to be. She pondered how she could use this to her advantage. Judging by what Clint had said on the phone, Pam's Malibu express was going to beat him to the boat docks by about five minutes. That would leave a five-minute window for the men chasing them to find her and kidnap her and Lexi. Or kill them. Whatever they were planning to do. She shuddered at the thought.

Lexi was being such a trooper. She said she was able be stay calm because what was going on right now was nothing compared to what happened last year in Vegas. Taylor had no idea what Lexi was talking about, but to be worse than their current situation, it must have been really bad.

Taylor opened her Instagram account, which was linked to her Twitter and Facebook accounts. She found a picture of the Esprit boat docks on Google, uploaded it to Instagram with the caption, "Never a bad day to be on the water," and added her location so anyone wanting a scoop would come running. This at least would create a good amount of people around her so the men wouldn't be able to touch her and Lexi until Clint could get there. She uploaded the post, and just like that, using those three popular social media platforms, over 100 million people knew where she was going to be. A curse any other time, but she was praying it would be a blessing today.

The next few minutes were filled with angst. Pam had tried to strike up a conversation a few times, but Taylor's mind couldn't stay with her. She was sweating she was so nervous. Her arm was sore from her gunshot wound, which now she figured she completely deserved. She was so disappointed in herself for being so desperate to suppress those photos and get the chance at a movie role. Though there was nothing she could do about that decision now, she was at least doing her best to get Lawson's daughter out of trouble. She'd felt a spark with him on that couch. But she supposed any shot at future sparks would fizzle once he learned what she'd done. She had to get her shit together if she made it out of this alive. No more feeling sorry for herself. Those days were over. A few more minutes of hellacious driving and nauseating nervous thoughts passed, and she knew they should be getting close.

"Well, here we are—what the hell?"

Taylor leaned forward when Pam's tone changed. Her social media trick had worked better than expected. There had to be at least a couple dozen people hanging out in the marina's parking lot. When Pam turned the Mercedes into the marina parking lot, the people parted like a bad comb-over, then quickly closed in behind the car to be the first to get that car-exiting shot. It was then that she remembered the patched wound on her shoulder. The white bandage stood out like milk on a dark hardwood floor in the tank top she was wearing. This would be fodder for salacious stories for days if she couldn't cover it up.

"This your doing?" Pam said. "Smart thinking. How'd you get them here?'

"Instagram."

"Ah, I have an account just to follow my granddaughter. I'll have to look you up!"

"I hate to ask, because you've been so kind, but do you have any sort of T-shirt or anything I could put on?"

"The bandage. Yeah, better not let these sharks see that. TMZ will be all over that." Pam reached toward the passenger seat. "Here ya go, hon. Might be a little big on you, but it'll cover you up."

Pam handed back a purple athletic zip-up. It was perfect. "When you find me on Instagram, message me. Let me take you to lunch or something for your trouble."

"I'd love that."

Taylor turned her attention to Lexi as she pulled on Pam's zip-up. "Don't answer any of their questions if they start asking. Let me handle them. I get along with them well. Probably know most of them. I'll just say you're a friend of the family. Okay?"

"Okay. You think this will keep those men from getting us?"

"I think so." Then to Pam, she said, "Thank you again, Pam. I owe you."

Taylor slid out of the car to a wave of camera clicks. The reporters were shouting her name, asking her questions, everything from "how have you been?" to "when's the next movie?" Lexi slid out behind her, but before Taylor could address the paparazzi, there was a commotion at the entrance to the parking lot. She shaded her eyes from the sun to see what she already knew it was: the black SUV. What surprised her was the blue light flashing in the front window. The police?

As the SUV pushed its way forward, the paparazzi moved out of its way. All of them shouting at the truck. Taylor's first instinct was relief. Naturally you always think the police are there to help. But if that were the case, then why had they been chasing her on the beach and all the way to the health club?

The SUV's front doors opened. Taylor grabbed Lexi's hand and began to back away from the distracted media. There were about twenty people in between them and the SUV. Two men exited the back, and Taylor's first instinct was quickly wearing off. She didn't know if they were really police or not. They certainly weren't in uniform. They were in casual clothes. Then she remembered something Cassie said. When Taylor was confessing about her connection to Victoria, Cassie had said something about Victoria having the FBI working for her. These had to be those guys. Every inch of Taylor's gut was screaming at her to run.

"Police!" the driver said, now fully out of the vehicle.

Taylor tugged Lexi's hand and began to backpedal. They were surrounded by boats, Taylor's heels now close to the first slip. There really was nowhere to go but toward the water. The men had the exit through the parking lot blocked. She saw the first gun raise as the paparazzi cleared a path for the determined men.

"Taylor Lockhart, don't move. You are under arrest!" the man shouted. "Get these people out of here!"

Taylor's foot found the boat slip. The three other men began to herd the paparazzi back. She knew the men couldn't hurt them as long as there were all these eyes. The problem was she couldn't let them take her and Lexi either, because the minute they left here, away from the cameras, there was no telling what they might do to her. Taylor deserved whatever was coming her way, but not Lexi. She shouldn't be here. This was Taylor's mess. Taylor just needed to buy a couple minutes. Then Clint would be here. He would know what to do.

She hoped.

"Come on, Lexi!"

Taylor pulled Lexi onto the slip that ran the length of the marina. It was a couple hundred yards long; all the other slips jutted out into the water away from it.

"Stop right there!"

Taylor heard the man, but she and Lexi were already running away. If she could get down the slip far enough, she might be able to jump onto a boat and hide long enough until help arrived. It was all she had. And with a glance over her shoulder, seeing the two men running around the entrance to the slip, she knew it wasn't much.

They were in serious trouble.

36

CASSIE FELT LIKE SHE HAD BEEN IN THE CAR FOREVER following Clint. Not knowing if Taylor had managed to get Lexi safely to the SOBA Center was like waiting for the doctor to tell you if your cancer had come back. She wasn't all that familiar with Malibu, but she knew they had a ways to go before they got there. That's why she was surprised when a couple cars ahead of her she saw Clint turn his car into a marina. She slowed down, and when she made it to the parking lot, she crept in, shocked by what she saw. A lot more people were there than should have been, most of them with cameras around their necks.

Cassie parked and jumped out of the car. She grabbed the nearest man with a camera and turned him toward her.

"What's going on? What's the frenzy about?"

"Your lucky day if you're with the press, lady. Taylor Lockhart is down there, running from the cops."

"What?" Cassie couldn't believe it.

"Yeah, like right now. A movie star running from the cops!"

So Victoria had Frank using officers from the police

department to run down Taylor. What the hell was Cassie going to do now? She felt confident with all the paparazzi there that the officers couldn't really hurt anyone. Then again, she couldn't actually see Taylor and Lexi, and there was a man with a gun keeping anyone from getting on the boat slips. Cassie felt helpless.

Where the hell was Clint?

Cassie searched the crowd of people. She had lost Clint's car once he turned into the marina; then with all the hysteria, she had forgotten about him entirely.

Gunshots rang out in the distance and froze Cassie. She was shocked to hear them, especially coming from the direction Taylor had gone running. The onlookers came running past Cassie toward the exit, knocking into her, terrified, but she did her best to move against the stream. Lexi was down there. If something happened to her, Cassie would be devastated. And Lawson, she would lose him forever too.

She passed a black SUV with a flashing blue light, and when she finally made it through everyone, she could see that the man who'd been keeping the paparazzi from entering the boat slips was lying facedown in a pool of blood. Up ahead on the ramp that ran the length of all the slips jutting out from it, she saw a man with a pistol extended in front of him moving past the rows of boats. Cassie stepped over the dead police officer, or FBI agent, whatever he was—he was in plain clothes so it was impossible to tell—and ran toward the shooter, pulling out the pistol Frank had left her.

She wished she knew more about what she was running toward. How many were after Taylor and Lexi, who they were, whom they worked for, what their intentions were. What the intentions of the man coming up behind Taylor and Lexi were. But she didn't. She was just going to have to be ready to do whatever she could to get to Lexi and protect her. That was her only motive. She wished Lawson had been the one to go to Clint's instead of her. Then he would be there running toward this chaos. She wasn't bad in these situations, but no one she'd ever worked with or around was better in them than Lawson. He would have known exactly what to do.

The man with the pistol moved to his right onto a slip that reached out into the water. Dozens of boats, big and small, were lined all the way down the same slip. Cassie rushed forward, and just as she placed her feet onto the slip, she heard more gunshots. A man—*Maybe it's Clint*, she thought—was mowing down the plain-clothed officers. The last two officers standing began to return fire, and she was forced to jump to her right to take cover behind the bow of a boat. Her skin was on fire. All the action was about a hundred feet away at the end of the slip, and she swore she saw a woman, maybe two, ducking for cover on the slip next to the water.

Any one of the errant bullets could hit Lexi. But adding to the already out-of-control chaos by putting her own bullets in the mix couldn't possibly do any good. Besides, who would she shoot at? Clint acted like he was going to help Taylor, but why would he go to this extreme? Killing cops, or worse, federal agents? What was happening? How had things become this bad?

Cassie poked her head out from behind the boat. Shots were still being fired, but she couldn't see Clint. She could only see two men firing off to their right and, much to her horror, two people covering their heads on the ground beside them. And now she could hear them screaming. Cassie didn't have another option: she moved forward, using the fact that the men beside Taylor and Lexi were distracted. She moved up, one boat at a time, running up then hiding behind each one. She came close enough to be able to take a shot. But she still didn't know whom to shoot at. It was possible that both parties in the shoot-out were worthy of being lethally stopped.

Cassie stepped out from behind one boat and took a knee. She aimed her pistol down the ramp at the man closest to Lexi. She might not know who the real criminal was, but she figured she should shoot the man next to Lexi. If she took him out, at least the bullets would be directed farther from Lexi, and that was a good place to start. Her sights danced across the midsection of the silhouette, and just as she was about to squeeze the trigger, she felt a bolt of pain at the back of her head.

Everything went black.

When her eyes opened a moment later, she was lying facedown on the ground. She tried desperately to stand, but it was as if she weighed a thousand pounds. She could have been dreaming it, but she swore the two men beside Lexi had just fallen back into the water. She blinked her eyes and again tried to stand.

Nothing.

A mere two or three feet from her nose lay her gun. She tried to move her arm, but it was glued to the ground. Things began to fog. The outsides of her eyes began filling with darkness. She watched Taylor and Lexi get to their feet, and she thought she saw their hands above their heads. Cassie tried to scream, but like her failed attempts at movement, she failed to make a sound. Had she been shot in the head?

Then she heard muffled shots from what seemed to be

behind her. But she couldn't be sure. She couldn't be sure of anything in that moment. She was on her way out.

That was when she saw a set of legs step out in front of her. She tried to look up, but she couldn't make it higher than the butt of whoever owned those legs. She heard voices shouting, but they were muffled to her ears. She was blacking out. The last thing she saw was the man at the end of the boat slip turn toward the pair of legs standing in front of her, and then muffled bangs came from his gun. The person in front of her dropped to the ground, and Cassie was then staring at the bottoms of a pair of shoes.

It was the last thing she saw.

37

LAWSON DROVE TOWARD THE MALIBU BEACH INN WHERE Taylor was supposed to be with Lexi. All the while he was running scenarios, worrying about Lexi and Cassie, and trying to reconcile why Clint would've had Hector try to kill him. Something about the Clint and Hector connection was off. Clint may very well have tried to kidnap Lexi to try to make it look like Sloan did it so Lawson would go after Sloan, thus forcing him to help Clint take him down, but why would Clint have had Hector try to kill him? That would be counterproductive for Clint. If Clint wanted Lawson's help, Lawson being dead certainly wouldn't do him any good. And why had Sloan been so quick to shoot Hector? He had been so out of his element just before that, that he could barely even hold the gun on Lawson. So much so that he was shaking. Then a minute later he could just walk up to Hector and shoot him in the head?

"Okay, we got the trace," Claudia said, still looking at her phone.

Lawson nearly jumped out of his skin. He was so deep

in thought, so entranced by the circle of lies surrounding him, that he had almost forgotten Claudia was in the car.

Claudia continued, "We're going the right way, but she's not in Malibu. She's in Marina del Rey."

"Marina del Rey?" Lawson said. Nothing was making sense.

"Yeah, just right up here on the right actually."

Lawson's heart was thumping. He thought he had another twenty minutes at least before he got to Lexi's location. The thought that she was right here excited him and terrified him at the same time. It meant that Taylor and Lexi had been forced from the hotel room. The hotel room where no one was supposed to know where they were. Victoria had been telling the truth. Taylor was working for her. Lawson was sick.

Claudia gasped. "What the hell is going on here?"

Lawson noticed the people running down the sidewalk, just a couple blocks from where Claudia was showing Lawson Lexi's location on her phone. His adrenaline spiked so hard he was nauseous. The people running were panicked.

"I don't know," Lawson finally said. "But be ready to shoot."

"Turn here," Claudia instructed.

A black SUV came careening out of the entrance to the marina they were turning into. The windows were dark, so Lawson couldn't see inside. His instincts told him to turn and follow that SUV. But they had Lexi's cell phone location, and it was close.

"Is it moving? Lexi's phone? Is Lexi in that Tahoe?"

Claudia used her fingers to zoom in on her phone. "No, the phone isn't moving."

Lawson continued into the parking lot. He was scared

to death of what he might find. He had no idea if it was good or bad that she wasn't in the SUV or that at least her phone wasn't in there. He was out of the truck before he even had it in park. One glance down at the entrance to the boat slips told him his worst fears might be coming true. There was a man lying facedown in a pool of blood. He tightened his grip around his pistol and ran for the entrance.

"You can't just run in there! There might still be a standoff!"

Lawson heard Claudia, but he didn't slow down. He hurdled the dead man and raced down the ramp. He glanced down each slip as he passed, and if he saw no sign of movement, he just kept running. He couldn't believe how far the ramp stretched. It was longer than any he'd ever seen. He passed his fourth slip with no sign of anyone, growing more aware that they might have just let the killer go by not following that Tahoe. He hoped with all he had that Lexi wasn't in that SUV. He hoped she was here with Taylor hiding somewhere. But nothing inside him helped him believe that was the case. Something horrible had happened there.

His mind jumped back ten years when he swam up on the boat he was renting. The blood running down the back of it. How he walked inside the boat and found his wife dead on the floor. His baby, Lexi, crying in her playpen. His life forever changed. Surely this couldn't happen to him again. He couldn't lose his daughter too. Not today.

Please!

As he pleaded internally to find Lexi, he finally noticed something on a glance down a boat slip. He skidded to a halt on the ramp and backed up. When he got back out from behind the nose of a boat, he saw three bodies lying on the ground fairly close to him, plus more bodies out at the water's edge of the slip. This was a massacre.

The sound of sirens jerked his head back toward the parking lot. Claudia was running toward him, and over her shoulder police cars were filing in. One of the bodies in front of him moved. Blonde hair.

Cassie.

Lawson sprinted toward her, maneuvering around a man lying face up on the slip. He hovered over her, slowly rolling her from her side onto her back.

"Cassie?"

He reached down and moved some hair out of her face. There was blood at the back of her head, but not a lot. Maybe she would be okay.

"Cass, can you hear me?"

She squinted, then began to blink, trying to bring herself back from unconsciousness. A moan of pain escaped her lips, and she took a deep breath.

"You're okay now," Lawson said.

Claudia arrived behind him; she gasped at the scene. He looked up and she was checking the body in front of him for a pulse. It was a man. Lawson couldn't tell much else.

"Lawson?" A painful groan carried his name from Cassie's lips.

"It's me. You're okay."

Then Cassie's eyes shot open. "Lexi? Where is she?!"

"I was hoping you could tell me."

She tried to sit up but couldn't. She pointed in the direction of the water. "She was there. With Taylor. Some men were trying to get her, but Clint was shooting them. Trying to stop them."

"Clint Hues?"

"Yeah, I think. But there was another guy. He came up

behind me." She rolled back to her side, squinting through the pain. "Him."

She pointed to the man who was shot right before she went unconscious. "Last thing I saw was Clint turning this way to shoot whoever that is. Clint must be with Lexi."

Lawson stood and walked over to the man that lay dead on his stomach. He bent down and turned him over. Clint Hues's blue eyes stared lifelessly up at him.

"I think you're mixed up, Cass. This is Clint. He's dead."

Lawson's wheels were turning. If it wasn't Clint who wanted Lexi, it must really be Frank. But he still didn't understand why Hector would try to kill him if he was really working for Frank.

Lawson said, "You don't remember who the guy was who shot Clint? What he looked like?"

Cassie was finally able to sit up. "I never saw his face. I just assumed it was Clint. I followed him here. He was going to help Taylor and Lexi. At least that's what I thought. Someone else must have been here already."

"It was the black SUV," Claudia said. "Whoever killed Clint must have been the guy leaving when we came in."

"He's got Lexi and Taylor." Lawson looked back toward the end of the slip. "You sure Lexi's phone didn't move?"

Claudia checked her phone where she had been tracking Lexi's phone. "It's still here."

"Who the hell is *she*?" Cassie groaned. "I leave you for five minutes and you replace me?"

"It's Frank's partner. Long story. Don't get up." As he was walking toward the water, he said to Claudia, "Go get ahead of this with the police. Make sure we can get out of here."

"On it."

Lawson stopped. "Did you happen to get the license plate on that SUV?"

"I did. And I've already got some people running it and trying to track it down."

Lawson nodded, then jogged down to the end of the boat slip. He sent up some silent prayers to Lauren, asking her to watch over their daughter since he clearly couldn't do it himself. Amidst the blood, shell casings, and a couple dead men floating in the water, he noticed Lexi's pink cell phone case at the edge of the slip. He walked over and picked it up. He hit the button that brought up her lock screen, and hovering above a picture of Lexi and her mother were the two missed calls he'd placed to her on the drive there.

The good news was that he didn't find her dead there on that dock.

The bad news was she had fallen once again into the hands of some men who meant to do her harm. And it was all because of him. Of all the places he could have moved his daughter to keep her safe, he had to choose Los Angeles. And the past he'd been doing everything possible to forget just kept returning to drag him back to hell.

Lawson didn't know who was driving that black Tahoe that had his daughter inside it. And he didn't know who that man worked for. But if he could just get his daughter back one more time, he and Lexi were going to disappear from these situations forever. No matter how far he had to run.

And the minute she was safe, every person who had said even so much as a "hello" to the people responsible for this were going to disappear too. Forever.

38

CLAUDIA WAS ABLE TO WALK LAWSON AND CASSIE RIGHT BY the police. FBI credentials tend to have those types of benefits. Her people had also found out whom the black SUV was registered to: the Los Angeles Police Department. It was easy to track because it was fitted with the LoJack recovery system, and they could watch every turn the Tahoe took. Lawson could see that it was driving on the 10 Freeway, heading back to Los Angeles. He could also see, in his mind's eye, his baby girl in the back, scared to death.

"Can't you go any faster?" Lawson said to Claudia from the backseat.

"I'm going a hundred miles per hour, Lawson. There isn't much more I can do. We're going to find them. Just hang on."

Lawson said to Cassie, "You should have gone with the police. Let them take you to a hospital."

"I'm fine. Just a headache. Let's just get to Lexi."

"I can't believe Taylor was working for Victoria." Lawson stared out the window. "I can't believe she could do this to Lexi. She just didn't seem the type."

"I don't think she is the type," Cassie said.

"Are you kidding me?"

"I talked to her on the phone when those men were after them. She was doing everything she could to get Lexi out of there."

"But she is the reason Lexi was in trouble to begin with."

"I know, and I'm telling you she made a mistake. She was being blackmailed and she let them convince her that no one would get hurt. She didn't even know Lexi would be involved."

"And you believe her? Why? Because you like her movies?"

"No, Lawson, because I heard her on that phone call. She was desperate. She would have done anything to make it right. I'm not saying she was innocent in this. I'm just saying she tried to save Lexi before they got to her."

Lawson shook his head and looked back out the window. The chain of events that had led to where they were was staggering. He was going absolutely crazy waiting in that car. Nowhere to go, nothing he could do. All the adrenaline from earlier was still lingering and it was driving him nuts. He felt a hand on his knee.

"Would you please stop?" Cassie said. "You're shaking the entire truck."

Claudia said, "The SUV isn't moving."

"Already?" Lawson perked up. "They haven't had enough time to get to LA."

"Well, it's stopped, and we're not far from it. I know how this sounds, but it looks like it's stopped right in the middle of the freeway."

Lawson's stomach dropped. That couldn't be good news.

He pulled out the phone that Frank had given him. He had felt it vibrating almost continuously out on the docks.

When he looked at it, he saw fourteen missed calls from Frank. Without thinking, he tapped on the missed call and dialed Frank back.

"Lawson, you'd better—"

"Stop talking." Lawson cut him off. "Right now my daughter is in the back of an LAPD SUV, with one of your men. You'd better tell him to let her out right now, or I will come for you until you're dead. I won't stop until then."

"It's not my man. All of the men I sent for Taylor and Lexi are dead. You're telling me it isn't you in that SUV?"

Lawson was once again blindsided. If Frank was right, and it wasn't his man with Lexi, there was only one other possibility.

"How do you know all of your men are dead?"

"The police on the scene reported back about the massacre you just left. I don't have to tell you that if it isn't you in that SUV, and it isn't one of my men, that it is absolutely one of Martin Sloan's."

No, he didn't have to tell Lawson that. The realization should have hit him the moment Sloan shot Hector with such ease. Lawson clearly had been out of the detective game for far too long. His instincts were completely shot. There wasn't just one person responsible for this mess; it was everyone he had ever suspected. All of them working a different agenda, but all of them working against him. Lawson understood in that moment that they hadn't just wanted him to help them get what they wanted. All of them —Sloan, Frank, and apparently Victoria Marshall too— they all wanted to use Lawson as a scapegoat. They had been planning all along that once Lawson got someone what they wanted, he would take the fall. Just like ten years ago. But it wasn't ten years ago. And he wasn't going to be anyone's patsy, and he wasn't going to lose his daughter either.

"Am I coming in clear, Frank?"

"What?"

"I just want to make sure you can hear what I'm about to say, loud and clear."

"I hear you."

"I'm not sure what resources you have left at your disposal, Frank. But you'd better call them in. All of them. Because you're going to need every last one of them to keep me from getting to you. And it still won't be enough. I'll see you soon, you son of a bitch. And I'll be the last thing you ever see."

Lawson ended the call. Before anyone in the car had a chance to react to Lawson's threat, Claudia swerved out to the shoulder to avoid the traffic standstill.

"What the hell is going on?" Cassie said. She was craning her neck to see the wall of cars through the windshield.

"Lawson, we are right on top of the SUV now," Claudia said. "I'm afraid it may have something to do with this traffic jam."

A second later the wall of cars to his left gave way to a wide open space in the freeway. In that space was a black SUV turned upside down right in the middle lane. Claudia drove up close to the overturned Tahoe. Lawson could see Taylor on all fours, halfway out of the back door, her upper body reaching back inside, feverishly pulling on something. Panic rushed through Lawson's body.

He jumped out of the truck and ran over to Taylor. He smelled gasoline and he could hear his baby girl screaming. He grabbed Taylor by her hips and pulled her out of the way so hard that she went flailing onto the concrete several feet behind him. He dove to the ground and crawled inside. Lexi was hanging upside down, trying to get her seatbelt undone.

"Daddy!" she screamed. Tears were running down her frightened face. They were mixed with blood coming from somewhere on her head.

Lawson reached in and pressed the release button on the seatbelt. But it was jammed. Maybe he was just that strong or maybe it was the adrenaline, but when he pulled on the seatbelt insert, it snapped right out of the buckle and Lexi fell into his arms. He pulled her from the Tahoe and walked over to the truck. Lexi threw her arms around his neck. The greatest feeling in the world.

"I'm sorry!" Taylor shouted. But Lawson just walked right by her. He didn't even look her way.

Cassie opened the back door of the pickup truck, and Lawson sat Lexi inside.

"Are you okay?"

"I'm okay, Dad."

"You're sure?" He wiped some blood from her forehead and the tears from her cheeks. "You're bleeding."

"I'm sure. I'm okay. Is Taylor okay?"

His daughter clearly didn't know that Taylor was responsible for this. But he knew it wouldn't have mattered if she did. She would still want to know if Taylor was fine. Lawson looked back over his shoulder at Taylor. She was bloody and crying, and somehow Lawson wanted to know, too, if she was okay. He looked back at Lexi and wiped away the next round of tears.

"She saved us, Dad. The guy driving us said we were both dead, and Taylor saved us. She jumped on him and got the gun away from him. The gun went off and she screamed, but she got it from him and she shot him when he tried to get it back. That's why we wrecked. Make sure she's okay, please."

Lawson looked back over his shoulder just in time to watch Taylor collapse to the pavement. Cassie and Claudia rushed over to her.

"Dad!" Lexi shouted.

Sirens were on their way in the distance. The trail of cars stretched back a mile at that point, and a lot of them were laying on their horns, not concerned at all with who was hurt but only with why they couldn't pass. Some were even driving around the Tahoe on the far end. But Lawson didn't see or hear any of it. His daughter was safe. And he had to make sure she stayed that way.

"Dad, let me go see if she's okay."

More tears. Lawson nodded and let her walk over to them. Lawson pulled his Sig Sauer and stalked back toward the upside-down Tahoe. There was nothing he could do for Taylor that the three of them couldn't. His mind had already shifted to what was next. Whom would he go after first? And finding out who this driver was and who'd hired him was a great place to start.

39

THE MAN HANGING FROM HIS SEATBELT IN THE DRIVER'S SEAT of the overturned Tahoe was dead. He was Hispanic, judging by the color of his skin and the name on his driver's license —Diego Acevedo. His name meant nothing to Lawson. Before turning back to help with Taylor, Lawson tossed both of the phones Frank had given him inside the SUV. He didn't need them, and he didn't want Frank tracking him with them either. Or with the truck, which also meant they needed a new car. He grabbed the phone lying on the interior roof just above the dead man's head. The last calls or texts this guy made would most certainly have been to whoever wanted to kidnap Lexi. Taylor may have not only saved Lexi but also inadvertently provided the key for Lawson's next move.

Before he could check the numbers on the phone, Cassie came running up to him. Police cars and ambulances were also pulling up.

"Lawson, Taylor's been shot."

Lawson couldn't put his finger on the feeling he had. Or why he had it. Taylor had put his daughter in grave danger, yet he still wanted to get her help. Maybe it was the fact that she took a bullet trying to save Lexi. Or was she just trying to save herself? He was confused on every level, but one thing was clear: even though he didn't want to, he cared about Taylor.

"Dad! Come here! Taylor's awake and she wants to tell you something!"

Lawson looked at Cassie. Cassie knew what he wanted without having to say anything. She went to find them a new ride while he went to see Taylor. When he got over to her, they had removed the zip-up she had on, and her tank top was red with blood from the gunshot wound in her stomach.

He took a knee beside her. "Save your energy. You're going to be okay."

"I'm sorry," she managed. "I'm sorry I—"

"Like I said, save your energy. If all you want to do is apologize, just keep it to yourself for now. Lexi's okay, that's all that matters to me. I'm going to get the paramedics over here."

Lawson started to stand, but she caught his arm. Her voice was hoarse. "I am sorry, but that's not the only thing I need to say."

Lawson leaned down to hear her. The bustle of the traffic was growing more impatient, and the police had yet to kill their sirens. Not to mention the news helicopter that was now hovering above the freeway.

"The man in the truck—"

"Don't worry, he's dead."

Taylor shook her head. "No, not that . . . I know him."

That piqued Lawson's interest. When he glanced up, the paramedics were opening the back of the ambulance. He figured he'd save some time, so he scooped Taylor up into his arms.

She took a deep breath and continued. "He's the guy. The guy who shot me in your driveway."

Lawson was walking her over to the ambulance. "But you said you had a bag over your face. That you never saw him."

She shook her head again and winced in pain. "It's his voice. I'm telling you, it was him."

Lawson nodded. "I'll get to the bottom of it."

"You have to believe me." Taylor paused to wince again and grabbed at her side. "I had no idea Victoria meant to do so much harm. I was stupid and desperate . . ."

Again she stopped, the pain overtaking her.

"Just get better. I'll handle the rest."

Lawson laid her on the gurney, and Lexi came running up, grabbing Taylor's hand. "You'll be okay, Taylor. You saved my life."

The paramedics wheeled Taylor up into the back of the ambulance. Lexi ran over to Lawson and threw her arms around him. He watched as Cassie and Claudia spoke to the police, trying to relay what happened.

"Do you think she's going to be okay?" Lexi asked. Her bright blue eyes sparkled in the late afternoon sun. Tears welled around them.

"I'm not sure, sweetheart."

Lexi buried her head in Lawson's chest. Once again his social cues were off. His daughter only needed a comforting statement from her father, but instead he increased her worry. He squeezed her and ushered her over to the oncoming Cassie and Claudia.

Cassie pointed to Claudia. "It's a good thing we've got her here. Otherwise, we'd be on our way to jail."

Claudia nodded. "I have a car. We need to get out of here. There's no telling what Frank might do next. We have to find him."

Lawson shook his head. "We have to find out who Diego Acevedo worked for."

"Who?" Cassie said.

"Diego Acevedo?" Claudia was surprised. "Martin Sloan's number one enforcer? Why?"

Lawson thumbed over his shoulder. "He's the dead guy hanging from the seatbelt. What the hell is going on, Claudia?"

"We have a file on him a mile long. Frank had an entire schedule surrounding what Diego was up to and who he was dealing with."

Lawson said to Cassie, "Taylor said he was the one who shot her in my driveway."

"What?" Claudia shaded her eyes from the sun. "Taylor Lockhart was shot in your driveway? What the—"

"I'll fill you in on the drive to Sloan's office." Then to Cassie: "If Diego works for Sloan, then Sloan had to be the one to set me up by having Taylor shot near my house. But Victoria claimed she was the one responsible for Taylor being involved—"

Cassie said, "And Taylor confirmed that when I first spoke to her, when she was trying to lose Frank's men in Malibu. Somebody is lying."

"No shit, Sherlock." Lawson quipped. "They all can't be working together. We have to find out who is either being blackmailed, lying, or both."

"Well, that ought to be easy," Cassie said, her sarcasm in full force. "Most people are really up-front about that kind of information."

Lawson looked at Claudia. "Any chance Frank has a special stash of files?"

"I'd say there's a good chance."

"Any idea where?"

Claudia took a moment to think about it. "Now that you mention it, maybe. But it won't be easy to get to because he always has it with him."

"You mean his phone?" Cassie said.

"No," Lawson said. "He's old-school, remember?"

"He's right," Claudia said. "He keeps a notebook. One of those with folders as section dividers. Never lets it out of his sight."

"Then that's where we start."

"Lawson, he just tried to kidnap your daughter," Cassie said. "You think he's going to hand you a notebook?"

"No." Lawson smirked. "But I can be very persuasive."

40

ON THE WAY TO FBI HEADQUARTERS IN LOS ANGELES, WHERE Claudia found out Frank and his notebook were currently positioned, Lawson filled in Claudia on any missing details about the past few days. Cassie chimed in as well. Lawson couldn't tell you what Cassie said after a certain point. He began spinning all the details in his own mind.

He started really piecing it together considering what happened at the marina. If it were really Frank's guys who had shown up in the Tahoe, which Claudia had confirmed was registered to LAPD, but then it was Sloan's enforcer driving it when it crashed, that meant that Sloan's enforcer took out all of Frank's dirty cops at the marina. In Lawson's mind that proved Frank and Sloan weren't working together.

And so did Claudia's earlier comment that Frank would do anything to take Sloan down. Not to mention the fact that Sloan had Frank nearly beaten to death, embarrassing him with the FBI. That made it even more unlikely the two would ever be on the same side. It seemed there's nothing

Frank wouldn't do, including breaking the law, to give Sloan some payback.

However, could the "nothing he wouldn't do" to get Sloan back also mean Frank would work with Sloan? Or at least pretend to be working with him?

Lawson shut out his surroundings and went deep into his head. Out the car window on his left, the city was a blur, but he paid attention only to his own thoughts. He recalled being in the car with Frank and Victoria and the moment when he sensed Victoria was acting odd. He closed his eyes and watched her talking to him. He replayed her speech when she explained how Johnny De Luca told her about Lexi's Instagram and how silly the entire story seemed. How forced her words sounded coming out of her mouth.

Forced.

That's how it felt to him. Forced, not odd. It had come across like it was scripted.

Lawson dove even deeper. To figure everything out he would have to decipher motivation. So he started with Sloan. What was it that Sloan wanted out of the situation? The rights to the supposed holy grail of a movie. So when he found out that Lawson, the man who took down Clint Hues at the meeting at the bar, was working for Victoria, that was where Sloan's involvement in Lawson's life began. That's when Sloan must have figured, if he could get to Lexi, he could use her to motivate Lawson to make Victoria sign over the rights to the movie. Then it hit Lawson as to why Hector tried to kill him and actually did kill Frank's men in the car after Lawson kept them from kidnapping Lexi. Because Hector *had* really been working for Sloan. And when Sloan found out it was Lawson who took out his buddy Nero De Luca in Vegas, all bets were off. That's why it was easy for Sloan to kill Hector at the Library Bar in the

Roosevelt Hotel: he didn't want Hector to say anything else because Sloan realized he was in real danger. That's why he shot Hector. Because if Lawson thought Sloan wanted him dead—that he wasn't just trying to get his movie rights for Victoria—Sloan would know Lawson would kill him right there in that bar.

So why did Sloan's enforcer, Diego, go to the marina and kill all of Frank's men to get to Lexi? Lawson figured it was like Victoria had said earlier. Insurance. If Lawson found out Sloan wanted payback for De Luca's death, he would be able to trade Lexi for his life if it came to that.

Then what about Frank? According to Claudia, his life's motivation was to take down Marty Sloan. She said he'd been going on about it for over a year and a half. That's a long time to hatch up a plan to take him out. Is that what happened? Is that how Victoria was involved? Insurance? It sounded like a word that Frank would use. A word that he would script Victoria to use.

"He took Victoria. She really was kidnapped."

Claudia and Cassie said in unison, "What?!"

Lawson leaned up between the two front seats. Cassie turned around with a bewildered look on her face, and Claudia had a hard time keeping her eyes forward on the road.

"Frank kidnapped Victoria, but he didn't tell Sloan. He's going to use Victoria to take down Sloan. But where Frank messed up was trying to use Victoria to get me to go after Sloan for him too. He got greedy."

"Lawson," Cassie said, "and I say this with all due respect, but have you lost your ever-lovin' mind? What are you going on about?"

Lawson decided he should back up, still trying to organize his thoughts himself. "The reason we couldn't—I couldn't—figure out who was the head of all of this was because there were two heads, and they were both fighting each other, but one of them didn't know it."

Cassie held up both arms, then let them drop. "Gee, that really cleared things up for us, thanks, *Detective* Raines."

He tried again. "Sloan and Frank have been working together."

"Bullshit," Claudia blurted.

Lawson continued. "*But* . . . Sloan didn't know Frank's *real* motivation. That's why we couldn't tell who wanted to kidnap Lexi, because they both wanted to. Just for two completely different reasons."

Cassie started to come around. "Okay . . . Do tell . . ."

"Sloan wanted to kidnap Lexi to use me to help him get Victoria to sign over the movie rights. Frank wanted to kidnap Lexi to get me to help him take down Sloan. Frank just made it seem like it was to *help* Sloan until he could compile all the things Sloan was doing and put him away for it. That's why Frank didn't tell Sloan he had kidnapped Victoria."

"What?" Cassie couldn't keep up.

"I know," Lawson sat back in the seat and took a long look at Lexi as she slept in the seat beside him. "It's complicated."

Claudia said. "So tell me again why Frank would kidnap Victoria?"

"Insurance."

Cassie looked back as if waiting for a big reveal. Claudia eyed him in the rearview mirror with the same look.

"Insurance against Sloan, and insurance against me if anything went haywire."

Cassie said, "Lawson, either land this plane or parachute out. We clearly don't follow so put it together for us."

Lawson nodded. "When Sloan and Frank involved me, Frank had already kidnapped Victoria. Think about it. Frank tried to kidnap Lexi but it fell through. That's why he showed up with Victoria. She was his insurance to keep me motivated to go after Sloan, and insurance to distance himself from any involvement. So he could tie Taylor Lockhart to someone else other than him. He didn't panic when Lexi got away from his men because he knew he had Taylor with her. That's why he had Victoria tell us that convoluted story about finding where I lived through Johnny De Luca. Victoria was never De Luca's woman, and she never called and spoke to Johnny about me. The meeting in the car was all bullshit. Frank got me released from jail so I could keep going after Sloan. That's why Frank showed up to keep the police from taking me into custody again when you and I ran from the police at Clint's office. And he made Victoria tell her lie about wanting to take me down for the De Luca thing. He wanted to make it seem like it was Victoria and De Luca that were close. But it was Sloan and De Luca that were the twosome in that movie deal all along. It's the only thing that makes sense."

"I still don't get it," Cassie said. "I mean, I understand why Frank would make Victoria lie to you. It would completely throw you off his scent and make her look like the puppet master. And it would make it plausible that she was the one who involved Taylor, because they had a connection. But why go through all the trouble?"

"Because Frank needed me," Lawson said. "He realized he wasn't going to be able to take Sloan down by the book, he wanted me to do to Sloan what I did to De Luca in Vegas. Just in case he couldn't make it look like Sloan kidnapped Lexi, he wanted to be able to put it on Victoria. He must have made Victoria come up with the Taylor plan somehow."

"I know how," Cassie said. "On the phone at Clint's office, Taylor said Victoria had something on her. Something that she thought only two people knew about. And Clint said she hired him over something about a party disaster. So Victoria must have tried to save herself by giving Frank something he could use to get Taylor close to you."

Lawson couldn't respond. He was stuck on what Cassie said about Taylor. That must have been what Taylor was trying to tell him in the bedroom before he was arrested. She was trying to back out of the situation then, but she never had the chance.

"Lawson?" Cassie prompted.

"Taylor was as much a victim in all of this as anyone else," he said.

"Okay, Lawson," Claudia said. "But focus, please. How does all of this explain how Frank was ever working with Sloan?"

Lawson put his train of thought back on the right tracks. "Diego Acevedo."

They were back in West Hollywood now. The car was quiet while Claudia turned onto Hollywood Boulevard. Lawson was letting them reel it all in themselves. It was so complicated that it was making his head spin too. The only reason he'd been able to pull it all together was because of Taylor telling him Diego was the man who shot her.

Cassie figured it out before Claudia. "Holy shit, you're right. If Diego Acevedo is the man who purposefully shot Taylor in your driveway to get this 'Taylor insurance plan' close to you and Lexi, Frank and Sloan *had* to be working together at some point. And Frank would have already had to have kidnapped Victoria, like you said. It's the only way Frank would have known anything about Taylor Lockhart—"

Claudia caught up. "And it's the only way Sloan's enforcer would have been involved with putting Taylor in play. Frank would have had to have told Sloan about Taylor. He probably told Sloan the FBI was investigating Taylor about what happened at this 'party disaster' Clint was talking about, and that's how Frank had something so bad on Taylor that she would go through with it. I know Frank, he probably sold it to Sloan that Taylor is an actress; if anyone could pull it off, she could. Frank knows how much Sloan loves movies, a fact he used to sell this whole ridiculous idea to him. And Sloan played along, probably thinking that once you, Lawson, got Victoria to sign over the movie rights, he could blackmail Taylor again and make her say that he had nothing to do with her little stunt. That it was Victoria who made Taylor go through with getting shot to fool Lawson into taking her in."

Cassie chimed in. "And all along, Frank knew he was never going to have Victoria sign the movie over. He was going to be able to pin the Taylor charade on Sloan because it was Sloan's man who shot her. Frank really thought this through. What a crazy deal. Only in Hollywood, I guess."

Lawson was once again locked onto a thought.

"Right, Lawson? Ha-ha. Only in Hollywood?" Cassie tried to get his attention.

Lawson was in another world. And again Victoria saying the word *insurance* came to mind. And then it hit him. "Victoria wasn't just a way for Frank to have a backup plan for keeping me involved in taking down Sloan. Victoria was the backup plan for taking down Sloan if I wasn't able to do it myself."

Lawson looked up at Cassie, who waited for him to elaborate. So he did. "Frank knew the situation between Sloan and Victoria. That they were in an ugly public battle over the movie. He knew that the police would see the clear motivation for Sloan, a guy with an already bad reputation, to kidnap Victoria to try to strong-arm her into signing over the movie rights. Frank getting Sloan to have Sloan's own guy Diego do the dirty work with Taylor just slam-dunked the possibility that the police would believe Sloan kidnapped Victoria. But there's just one problem . . ."

Cassie bit. "What? What is it?"

"Frank hasn't sealed the deal. Now that I'm not going after Sloan, and Frank knows it, he has to put the final touches on his Victoria insurance plan."

Claudia came on board. "And plant Victoria somewhere to make it look like Sloan kidnapped her."

"That's right," Lawson said. "The motive for Sloan to kidnap Victoria is so clear––for the movie rights––that the police would bite on it hook, line, and sinker."

Cassie said, "And Victoria will go along with it, she won't have a choice. She won't be able to tell the police Frank actually did it, because when Sloan goes to jail, Victoria will get her movie. Everyone wins but Sloan. The entire thing can be pinned on him. It is the perfect plan."

Lawson sat forward in his seat again. "Perfect except for one little thing."

"What?" Cassie and Claudia said together.

"Frank involved me."

41

CLAUDIA TURNED OFF HOLLYWOOD BOULEVARD INTO A parking lot that didn't mean anything to anyone in the car.

Cassie turned and faced Lawson.

As soon as Claudia put the car in park, she turned in her seat as well. "So what now?"

"I need a minute." Lawson opened the car door and stepped out.

He glanced up at the sign on the building: Pavilions, a grocery store. He remembered where they were now because he recognized the classic car shop across the street. Lawson had always had a thing for cars. The sun was still bright, but it was making its trek down behind the ocean, so the street was bathed in sepia tones. He walked away from the car, the sun hot on his shoulders. For the first time all day he rolled up his sleeves and took a minute.

A lot of things were running through his mind. The fact that Clint had been telling him the truth all along made him hate that he had to die. But Clint was no saint. He knew the line of work he was involved in and what the consequences were. He thought about how naive Taylor had been but how hard she fought to make it right. That led to the thought of wishing he'd gotten that kiss. And that led him to considering why he didn't just walk away from this thing right then and there. Cassie and Taylor were safe, he himself was still alive, and most importantly, Lexi was safe and with him again.

What drove him to keep pushing for a resolution was the fact that he believed one of these assholes, most likely Frank, would maybe get away with all of it. Not only kidnapping Victoria, not only shooting Taylor, but also putting his daughter in harm's way. And of course there was the fact that they had involved Lawson at all. Trying to use him for their gain—or Frank's revenge, as it turned out.

Lawson kicked the rock in front of him, and it skipped across the parking lot, toward Hollywood Boulevard. It's the only reason he saw Clint's Dodge Challenger swerve into the parking lot. Instinctively, Lawson reached for his Sig Sauer as the car pulled into the parking space right beside where he was standing. When the window began to roll down, he half expected to see a ghost. Instead, it was Jenny, Clint's partner. And it was clear that she wasn't happy.

"Should I leave my hand on my pistol?" Lawson said, standing at the ready.

"I followed you here from the marina. I saw everything. Including that son of a bitch murdering my best friend. Who is he?"

Jenny opened the door and got out of the car. Cassie came running across the parking lot. Keeping one hand on his gun, he held the other out for Cassie to wait.

Lawson knew she was talking about Diego Acevedo. "Who *was* he," Lawson corrected her. "He's dead now."

"Okay, so who did he work for?"

"Just let me worry about it. I'll take care of who he works for. They kidnapped my daughter. Someone has to pay."

Jenny moved forward and got in his face. "Tell me right now. I'm going to kill them. Clint may not have been a saint, but he saved me more than once in my life."

Lawson took a step back and took his hand away from his gun. Jenny was clearly hurting, and her adrenaline was at full throttle. Maybe he could use her to help him if she was hell-bent on doing something.

"Say something!"

"Okay, if you have to do something, I might have an idea. But it could very well get you killed. Especially if you don't listen to me."

Cassie walked over, and she was met with a strong shove. "You're the reason he's dead!" Jenny shouted.

She pushed Cassie again. Cassie had a big heart, but one thing Lawson knew about his partner was that she didn't like people touching her, and she had a hair trigger when it came to someone pushing her around.

"He died trying to save you! It's the only reason he went out on that boat slip!"

At the same time Jenny went to push Cassie again, Lawson noticed Cassie cocking back a right hand. Lawson stepped in and wrapped his arms around Jenny and lifted her off the ground. She began to kick and punch, but Lawson held her in place.

"Let go of me!"

Lawson said with a calm tone, "You want to help or not? This is exactly why I don't want you involved. You're too emotional right now. If you want to help, you have to calm down."

Jenny started to relax, and Lawson nodded at Cassie's right hand, telling her to lower it.

"Just let go of me."

Lawson let go, and Jenny walked a few steps away, trying to collect herself. "You think we can get who did this?"

"I know we can," Lawson said.

"Okay. I'm in. I'll do whatever it takes."

"Lawson, we don't even know her," Cassie said. "And we don't even know what we are going to do. Which brings up my vote that we do nothing. Let these two assholes destroy themselves."

Cassie had a way with words, not a good way most of the time, but a way with them all the same. This time, however, to Lawson they were pure gold. When Cassie said let them destroy themselves, a lightbulb went off in his head.

"Even though you didn't mean to be, Cass, you're a genius."

"I know. But . . . why this time?"

"We're going to do exactly what you suggested."

"What, walk away and do nothing?"

"No." Lawson smiled. "Let them destroy themselves. With a little bit of help of course."

Jenny said, "What do you mean?"

"Now don't fall for that," Cassie told Jenny. "There is no such thing as a little bit with Lawson Raines. Either he doesn't do a thing, or he's like a bull in an ultra high-end china shop. So just know that when you step in, it's going to get crazy."

Jenny looked from Cassie to Lawson, then back to Cassie. "Then what the hell are we waiting for? Let's get crazy."

42

"SO WAIT, WE AREN'T GOING TO THE POLICE FOR WHAT REASON again?" Claudia said.

The four of them were holding court inside the unmarked Ford Explorer, which Claudia's FBI credentials enabled her to borrow from LAPD back at the crash. Five if you count Lexi. Lawson wasn't happy that she had to hear these types of conversations, but there was just no way around it.

"Simple answer?" Lawson said. "Four 'cops' just tried to kidnap Lexi. The other reason is what I said earlier. The cops bring Frank or Sloan in, they will find a way out of this. One of them will anyway. So no cops."

"Okay, so what are we going to do?"

"Well, they both tried to use me to get what they wanted. So let's use me to get what we want. I go to Frank and tell him that I know that Sloan's enforcer, Diego, kidnapped Lexi and that I want Sloan for it."

Cassie said, "Okay, but why would he believe you now? What's in it for you?"

"A big part for Lexi in the movie when it gets turned

over to Victoria. I'll tell him it's the least he can do for me getting rid of Sloan and for him trying to use Lexi in the process."

Claudia said, "It's a reach, but he wants Sloan so bad he might go for it."

Jenny asked, "But how does that help us get what we want? You can go get Sloan without going to tell Frank first."

"Let me put it all together for you. Besides, going to Frank will keep him off my back while we pull this together."

"Okay, so what next?" Claudia prompted.

"Then I'll go to Sloan. Tell him I know that Frank has Victoria, and convince him that I believe Frank was behind all of it. And because he involved Lexi, I want him to pay for it. He already thinks I am working to get Frank anyway. Back at the Library Bar when Hector said he worked for Frank, I told Sloan to stage the kidnapping of his son and plant him somewhere remote. I was going to let that be what brought Frank down, but now that I know about Sloan and his involvement in all of this, I know he was never going to stage the kidnapping. He just wanted out of there alive, and he was happy to see me leave and go after Frank."

"All right," Cassie said. She was still unsure. "So you have them both thinking you're taking out the other guy. How does this come together?"

"I tell Frank about how I convinced Sloan to stage the kidnapping. Tell him I know where Sloan is keeping his son and that Frank can go get him and use Sloan's son to get whatever he wants out of him. Whether it's to get Sloan to turn himself in for all the things he had Diego do, or whether it's just to get whatever revenge he wants, I'll let Frank use his imagination."

"And Sloan?" Jenny asked.

"I tell Sloan where Frank is going to be once Frank's headed where I tell him Sloan's son is being held. Then Sloan can do what he wants with Frank. Either way, one of them is going to kill the other one, and because we know where it's all going down, we can be ready to move in and take down the man left standing."

The car was quiet for a bit. Everyone was taking in Lawson's plan.

"You really think you can pull all that off? Tonight?" Jenny said.

Lawson nodded to Claudia. "With the FBI's help, definitely. You just have to keep it from Frank."

Claudia nodded in return. "We can do this. I already know a good location for where we say Sloan's son is being held. I'll have a task force set everything up."

"So what do you need me to do?" Jenny still wasn't 100 percent on board.

"You were Clint's tech genius, right?"

"Right."

"We don't have time for Claudia to outfit us with tracking devices and cameras. But I'm assuming you have those things?"

Jenny perked up. "Oh yeah. I have stuff that is undetectable for you to wear. We'll catch the entire thing. And I have some GPS bugs so small it's hard to hold them."

"Perfect," Lawson said. "We don't have much time. Claudia, set a meeting with Frank for Cassie and me. Somewhere public. He's going to want to know why you haven't checked in. Tell him I recognized you outside the Roosevelt Hotel and that I have been forcing you to help me ever since. You'll have to really sell it. Then get a team to whatever location you choose. Let me know where before I see Frank so I can tell him that's where Sloan's son will be.

"Jenny, you can take us now and get me ready to capture everything Frank and Sloan say. We are going to need this evidence later, so I'm trusting you with maybe the most important piece of this. You said you wanted to help. Your camera and tracking work might just be the very thing that takes down these bastards responsible for Clint's death."

Jenny gave a devilish grin. "I am *so* in."

"What about Lexi?" Cassie said.

"I'll take her to headquarters," Claudia said. "She'll be safe in my office. And I have snacks and satellite."

Lawson looked her in the eye. "This is my entire world. You're sure she'll be safe?"

"She won't leave my side. And Alyson owes me a favor at the office. Plus I'll put a DOJ agent on the building to make sure she doesn't leave."

Lawson didn't like leaving Lexi, but if he could pull this thing off, he knew she would be much safer in the long run. "Okay. I trust you. Listen, I need a phone."

Claudia reached inside her purse. "Take this one. It's my phone I use to stay in contact with the DOJ. No one knows about it. I'll text you from my FBI phone so you'll have my number if you need anything, and I'll text the fake location as soon as it's set for sure."

Lawson nodded, then gave Lexi a hug and kiss good-bye. He hated leaving her, and she was scared to leave him, but it was the only way. Lawson watched as she and Claudia pulled out of the Pavilions parking lot; then he and Cassie got into Jenny's car and headed toward Clint's office to get fitted with all the technical gadgets. He could tell by the look on Cassie's face that she wasn't sold on Lawson's big idea.

That didn't surprise him, though, because neither was he.

43

THE NEXT HOUR WENT ABOUT AS WELL AS IT COULD GO.
Lawson thought multiple times, as Claudia was reporting
back about securing the site and the meeting with Frank,
that it would be about damn time for him to get a couple
breaks. He managed to get a status update on Taylor; she
wasn't out of the woods yet but her condition was stable. At
Clint's office, Jenny fitted Lawson with a button camera that
she attached to the lapel of his suit jacket. He'd retrieved the
suit jacket out of his car that he and Cassie had abandoned
earlier when they ran from the police. Frank was busy,
probably stashing Victoria somewhere, so in the gap before
the meeting with him, Lawson decided to go ahead and
see Sloan.

Sloan of course was wary at first. But Lawson knew to
play to his ego, which all crime bosses have; it's their
universal trait. Though his ego wasn't nearly as bad as De
Luca's was, Sloan still wanted you to know he was the man.
Lawson let him have that, and the explanation of everything
went well. He wasn't surprised to hear that Frank had Victoria. Yet Sloan didn't know Lawson knew he had worked

with Frank, so Sloan continued to play it off that indeed Frank was evil for doing such terrible things to Lawson and his daughter.

There were more than a few moments during the meeting where Lawson nearly lost his cool. To sit across from the man who tried to have you killed, and wouldn't have hesitated to have your daughter killed either, was another level of self-discipline. Something Lawson hadn't always been good at. He would have never been in that situation if he wasn't planning to take both of these bastards down. He could do just that if everything went according to plan. And if he could just keep his cool.

Thankfully, he did with Sloan.

Now Lawson and Cassie were sitting outside Lost & Found, a dive bar close to the Santa Monica Airport on National Boulevard. He wanted to be more open with Cassie about his meeting with Sloan, but with the camera attached to him and Jenny listening in, he just kept it surface and told her what the doctor had said about Taylor.

"You like her, don't you?" Cassie smiled.

Lawson didn't bite.

"It's okay. I know you do. If you didn't, you wouldn't be calling to check on her. Hell, you haven't called to check on me in months. I always have to reach out to you."

"You don't have a potentially fatal gunshot wound."

"Yeah, yeah," she teased. "I don't have those green eyes and that smile either."

Lawson looked over at Cassie with a smirk. "No. No you don't."

Cassie punched him in the arm and gave him a dirty look. Lawson just pointed out the front windshield.

"Showtime."

Frank waved the two of them over to follow him as he and two men with him walked into the bar.

"You sure we're doing the right thing here? Seems a little thrown together," Cassie said.

"Trust me," was all he said.

Lawson stepped out of Clint's car, a loaner from Jenny in case they needed a fast getaway, and stepped into the Hollywood night. The air had cooled and a breeze blew through, carrying the smell of broken dreams along with it. Or it could have just been the dumpster around the corner. Cassie caught up to Lawson and they both walked inside together. It was a dive bar, for sure. Complete with the ugly Christmas lights draped over the bar (even though it was months until the holiday), tile ceiling, and the quintessential pool table with the massive Bud Light signs behind it in the back. Lawson had expected the typical stale beer smell, but instead, all he smelled was popcorn. A pleasant surprise.

Lawson wasn't happy to be sitting down with Frank when what he wanted to do was murder him, but the same thing needed at his meeting with Sloan was needed here: patience and a cool head. Frank and his men were in the back, a paper boat of popcorn already under assault, and Frank waved Lawson and Cassie over to their table.

"Free popcorn, how could you not come here and drink?" Frank said. Butter glistened on the tips of his fat fingers.

Lawson was disgusted.

"Have a seat, you two. Let's talk about old times."

Once seated Lawson said, "Let's not and say we did."

"Fair enough. Where's the kid?"

Frank pushed the boat of popcorn across the table for

Cassie and Lawson. As if they were old pals sharing a beer. The man had always been clueless.

"I need some assurances first," Lawson said.

"You're making demands?"

"I am."

"On what grounds? You've got nothing on me."

"On the grounds that you tried to kidnap my daughter."

"Means to an end." Frank crunched some more popcorn, mouth open. "To hell with your daughter and to hell with you. I can make your life miserable."

Lawson's entire body warmed as a tide of anger rolled over him. He took a deep breath and calmed the brewing storm. He reminded himself what he was there for.

Lawson nodded. "Okay, but I need a second. I have to go to the restroom."

"Right now?"

"Yeah, Frank. Right now."

Lawson got out of the booth.

"Now hold on. Not without Sean going with you."

Frank nodded to one of his men who was at the high-top table beside them. Sean got up and ushered Lawson along. Just before Lawson reached the men's room, Sean gave him a shove in the back. "Don't get any ideas, asshole."

Lawson clenched his fists, then released. Another deep breath. He pushed open the door and Sean followed him in.

"A little privacy?" Lawson said.

"You ain't got nothing I haven't seen before."

Lawson turned his back on Sean for the toilet. "I'm not so sure about that."

"Funny man. Okay. Just piss and let's get back to the table."

Lawson did as he was told, and when he finished he

took a small piece of toilet paper, wiped his nose, then dropped it on the floor.

"So how much does Frank have on you to make you do his bidding? Or maybe cop salary isn't enough so you went dirty? Frank promising to keep you out of jail?"

"What did you just say to me?"

Sean was just as big as Lawson. But Lawson knew he wasn't nearly as tough. Lawson reached down to pick up the toilet paper and popped the button camera off his lapel that Jenny had installed earlier. It fell into the toilet, and he dropped the two tracking bugs in there as well, then put the toilet paper in right after that and flushed it all down. He turned to face Sean.

"Big guy like you isn't sensitive, is he?" Lawson smiled.

"You got something to say?"

"Frank tried to kidnap my daughter and my partner. My daughter is only thirteen."

"Fuck you and your daughter."

Lawson front kicked Sean's left knee cap, and it popped out the back side of his leg. Before Sean crumpled to the ground, Lawson caught him and held him up by his T-shirt. Through Sean's groans of pain Lawson managed to get a word in.

"Every single one of you is going down."

Then he pulled Sean's big head straight down onto his rising knee. The impact on Sean's forehead knocked him out immediately, and he lay on the floor like a crumpled beer can. Lawson washed his hands, adjusted his suit jacket, and walked back out into the bar. Frank stood up immediately when he noticed Sean didn't follow him out. The playful, cocky look was gone from his face as well.

"Where the hell is Sean?"

The other man with Frank stood as well, and puffed out his chest.

"He's not feeling so well. Says he needs a minute."

"Go check on him," Frank said to his man.

As soon as he walked by Lawson toward the bathroom, Lawson took a chair in his hands, turned with it, and smashed it over the man's head. The impact knocked him out. Before Frank could react, Lawson turned and put his gun under Frank's chin and, with his other hand, had an iron grip around Frank's hand that was reaching for his gun.

"You arrogant prick," Lawson said, glaring down at him. "You didn't even have sense enough to frisk me. And you thought you were going to be able to pull off a plan to use me to do your dirty work?"

Out of the corner of his eye, he could see the look of shock on Cassie's face. He wanted to clue her in earlier, but he couldn't with Jenny watching on the hidden camera.

"Raines, this is a huge mistake. Victoria will have someone after you in no time."

"Where, in make-believe land? You think I bought that dumb story you had her tell me about De Luca?"

Frank didn't say anything.

"Lawson, what are you doing?" Cassie asked.

Lawson turned Frank around, took his gun from his hip holster, and handed it to Cassie, then put his Sig Sauer to Frank's back. "I'm having Frank take us to where he's holding Victoria hostage. Once we have her, I have a feeling Sloan just might come to us."

Lawson poked at Frank's back and Frank walked forward. "I'm FBI, Lawson. You aren't going to get away with this."

The crowd that was left in the bar parted to make way so they could walk out. Cassie filed in behind them.

"You got it all figured out, don't you, Frank?"

"Enough to where people are going to know you took an FBI agent at gunpoint."

"Fair enough," Lawson said. They pushed open the door and walked out onto the sidewalk. "But Claudia will take care of me."

"My partner Claudia? You dumb shit. You think she'll vouch for you over me?"

"No, I think when we get to where you're holding Victoria, she'll just arrest you. I mean, she's been watching you for more than a year and a half. She knows you're crooked."

Frank turned around, and Lawson extended his gun. "What the hell are you talking about?"

"Who's the dumb shit now? She's DOJ, Frank. Tasked to put a file together on you because everyone was talking about how you'd gone rogue you were so thirsty to take down Sloan."

"Bullshit."

"Me giving her the details to your little kidnapping is just the frosting on top of the crooked cupcake."

"Go to hell, Raines."

"After you, Frank."

44

It was only after an elbow to the nose that Frank became willing to navigate Lawson and Cassie to Victoria's location. Cassie had found a T-shirt next to her in the backseat, and it was currently sopping up the blood running from Frank's nose.

From the backseat, Cassie said, "This was your plan all along, wasn't it?"

"It was," Lawson said.

Cassie scooted up. "Why didn't you tell me? I mean, I knew the plan you told us in the Explorer was mediocre at best, but I didn't know it was a decoy. Why do that? It was just us?"

"Us and Jenny," Lawson said.

"Yeah, so?"

"Her partner, Clint, worked for Sloan. That meant she did too."

"Worked, as in past tense."

"No—"

"Make a right here," Frank chimed in. The promise of another elbow kept his navigation skills on point.

"No what?" Cassie was impatient.

"He was working for Sloan when he got shot."

"How the hell would you know that? And don't say *insurance* again. If I hear that word one more time, I'm gonna lose it."

"Okay, since I can't say insurance, I'll say that he's the one who hit you on the back of the head on the boat slip."

"No," Cassie said.

Lawson said. "No? But how else did Diego Acevedo know Lexi and Taylor were going to be at that marina? You didn't even know they were there, right? You thought they were at the Malibu Beach Inn."

Lawson checked the rearview mirror and found Cassie shaking her head.

He continued. "The only person who knew was Clint, he had to have told Diego. That's why when you got there, Clint wasn't in front of you, right? He was waiting to let Diego take care of it. Like Sloan must have told him. He came in behind you to keep you from stopping Diego."

"Okay, I can see all of that. But tell me this, smarty-pants, why did Diego shoot Clint if they were working together?"

Lawson shrugged. "My guess? Clint only called Diego in on it at all to get back into Sloan's good graces. He was hedging his bets. If he couldn't get me to help him take Sloan down, he needed to get back to work for him so he didn't lose the reputation he so desperately coveted. Instead, Sloan wanted him gone for good. Probably knew from Hector that Clint wasn't the type to just roll over. So he told Diego to kill him too. You were just lucky Clint only knocked you out. He must have liked you."

"Was that you trying to be funny?" Cassie snarked. "You don't ever try to be funny, then you wait till my near-death experience to tell a joke? You're a piece of work, Lawson."

Frank spoke up. "One more turn and she's in the house three doors down. Two lights on above the garage."

Cassie went back to her figuring. "So anyway, that's Clint's story, but we're talking about Jenny. What made you think she was still working for Sloan? Enough to throw her this far off the scent?"

"Simple really. I just listened."

This time Lawson's glance in the rearview found Cassie rolling her eyes.

It didn't stop him from going on. "Jenny said she was going to kill the person responsible for Clint's death. Two seconds later she pushed you and told you he died because of you. It could have just been metaphorical, but I think she truly thought it was your fault. From the moment he died she blamed you for putting him in that situation. I think she probably called Sloan and told him in that parking lot that she was going to stay with us and help take us down."

Cassie rubbed her hand across her forehead. "That's an awful lot of leaps you're taking there."

"Yeah, I can see that. Would you feel better if I just said it wasn't worth taking the chance of letting Jenny hear the real plan just in case she was going to relay it to Sloan?"

"Yeah, it kinda does."

"Well, there you go." Lawson pulled into an open spot on the side of the road, a couple doors down from the house with the two lights over the garage. "Feel better about it now?"

"Whatever," Cassie said and got out of the car. Lawson and Frank followed. Cassie gestured toward Frank. "Let's just get Victoria so we can get this asshole started on his prison sentence."

Lawson walked over to Frank. "What are we walking into?"

"I led you here. She's in there. The rest is up to you."

Lawson hit Frank so hard in the stomach that he immediately vomited all the free popcorn he'd had back at the bar. "That's not how this works, Frank. I'll ask one more time, what are we walking into?"

Frank tried to speak, but he couldn't manage any words.

Cassie walked over and found Lawson's face in the streetlight. "For a smart guy, you're awfully stupid. You hit the guy with your lunch box of a fist right in the gut, knowing it will take his breath, then you want him to talk to you."

"Are you on my case because I didn't tell you the plan? Is that what this attitude is about?"

Lawson was having a lot more fun with his partner than he'd had in a long time. It reminded him of the days they were a team in the FBI. It was always easier to joke when it wasn't your daughter's life hanging in the balance. Somewhere in his head he had the thought that he might be able to work with her again. Maybe he should get the private investigation business going with her.

"Yeah, it's me with the attitude," Cassie quipped back. "Frank, I know he hits hard, but don't be a pussy. Take a deep breath and tell us who is in the house and where they are. Otherwise, we'll just shoot you right here and go in blind. No one, and I do mean no one, will give a parrot's pecker if you're dead."

Lawson smiled and let Cassie's line slide. It was good to be back. Even if there was a house full of dirty cops waiting for them and a crime boss on the way.

45

LAWSON AND CASSIE WALKED FRANK UP THE PORCH STEPS toward the front door. That's right, porch steps. The house was a Cape Cod, complete with the gabled dormers and shingle siding. Right there in LA. It occurred to Lawson for about the thousandth time since they'd moved there that a lot of people in Hollywood seemed awfully confused.

Lawson had a grip on Frank's left arm. "Okay, Frank. Call your man in charge and tell him to gather everyone in the kitchen. All of them. And put their guns on the countertop."

Frank was still recovering from the gut punch, but with labored movement he did as he was told.

"They're moving to the kitchen," Frank said. "Key's in my back pocket."

"You think I'm going to reach in your back pocket?"

Frank gave him a look, then dug in his pocket with his right hand and took out the keys. He extended them in his hand, and as Lawson went to take them, in an attempt to escape Frank balled the keys up into his fist with a key sticking out of his fingers. He jabbed up at Lawson's face, and the key sliced a gash in Lawson's left cheek. It took Lawson by surprise, and he faltered back a step. Frank had dropped the keys upon impact with Lawson's face, but he still was able to deliver a solid right hand to Cassie's forehead as she scrambled for her gun. It didn't knock her out, but it did knock her on her ass.

Lawson stepped forward, rage sparking from seeing Cassie get punched. This time it was Frank who took a step back. Then he turned to run.

He almost got away, but Lawson reached out, his fingertips just able to snatch the back of Frank's collar. He couldn't hold on, but it was enough to turn him. Lawson was on him in a blur, and he was able to step toward Frank with his left leg, then engage his hips to throw a punch with his right. The impact of Lawson's knuckles against Frank's chin sounded like a dry tree branch being broken in half. Frank was out instantly, and his body folded as it sailed backward toward the ground, then stiffened as he lay there unconscious. His neck strained and his arms were involuntarily held out in front of him as his brain tried to reboot.

"You okay?" Lawson rushed over to Cassie and helped her to her feet.

"He hits like a girl. Only reason it knocked me down was because I was already hit in the head once today."

"It might actually make you smarter."

Cassie looked up at him. Half of her disgusted, and the other half of her, Lawson could tell, was glad to have a piece of her old friend back. But she played it like that wasn't amusing at all. "Who are you?"

Lawson got serious. "Listen, we don't have long. We need to get in there and get Victoria. Then get the hell out."

"Why don't we have long? No one else knows Victoria's here."

"We drove Clint's car here."

Cassie might have just been hit again in the head, but she was quick on the uptake. "You son of a bitch. You knew tracker-happy Jenny would have a device on Clint's car . . . You thought this all the way through. You never intended on a meeting of Sloan and Frank at the fake kidnapping location, you always knew it would be where Victoria was being held."

Lawson smiled. "Insurance."

He pointed to the phone Claudia gave him that was sticking up out of the lapel pocket on the outside of his suit jacket. Just high enough so the camera lens could capture everything.

"You've been recording everything?"

"Even better, we're live streaming video. Say hi to Claudia. She's recording this from FBI headquarters."

Cassie laughed. "It's 2019, live video streaming on an iPhone is called FaceTime . . . Anyway, when did you manage that?"

"I texted Claudia earlier and told her to be waiting with a way to record a *FaceTime* call. After I disabled the douchebag in the bathroom at the bar and before I walked out, I connected with her on FaceTime, then put it right here." Lawson patted the pocket on his suit jacket. Proud that technology hadn't got the best of him that time.

Cassie looked impressed; then her expression changed to a squint. "Now I remember why I hated being your partner."

"You hated solving cases?" Lawson was really feeling his oats.

"No, I hated how you never told me everything. Déjà vu tonight, I guess. Can we go get this over with? Looks like Frank is waking up."

Right on cue, in the light shining from the porch, Lawson could see Frank stirring—a weary moan the accompanying tune. Lawson didn't so much as help him up, but pulled him up, and after Frank's legs buckled, Cassie and Lawson helped him up the stairs. Lawson picked up the keys with his free hand, and Cassie pulled her pistol with hers.

They walked into the home and could hear commotion at the back. Lawson assumed it was the kitchen and steered their walk that way, exchanging the keys for his Sig.

"You're not going to get away with this, Lawson," Frank said, slurring the words from his broken jaw.

Cassie spoke for Lawson. "What is this, an episode of Scooby-Doo? Who talks like that, Frank?"

Frank didn't have the energy to respond. He was all but broken at this point. Lawson and Cassie tried to pick up the pace, both understanding that time was running out. But they had also underestimated how quickly Sloan would have his men ready to respond, because just as they stepped into the kitchen, the sound of tires screeching to a halt just out front warned of ensuing chaos.

Lawson turned Frank and pinned him against the wall in the kitchen. The four men Frank had standing guard instinctively reached for their weapons on the kitchen counter. Lawson didn't have time to acknowledge them.

He grabbed Frank by the throat and punched the end of his Sig Sauer into his gut.

"Tell me where Victoria is, right now, or I will shoot you."

46

Frank Shaw must have seen in Lawson's eyes that he would in fact shoot him, so he told them Victoria was in the basement. As Lawson and Cassie raced downstairs to get her and avoid the oncoming shootout, they heard the men they'd left in the kitchen readying their weapons, and they heard at least two more cars pull up outside. Lawson hadn't meant to still be there when Sloan and Frank had it out, but it didn't look like there was going to be any way around it.

When Lawson and Cassie turned the corner in the basement, the bullet from the gun of one of Frank's men, who'd stayed behind with Victoria, came less than an inch from Lawson's nose before boring into the drywall beside him. He dove backward, taking Cassie down with him, and the stairwell kept them from eating any of the next three bullets the man fired at them.

"Any closer and I'll shoot her. Don't try me."

Lawson only got a glimpse of the skinny bald man standing behind Victoria, who was seated in a folding chair. He quickly scanned his view for a way to distract him. It was an unfinished basement. Smooth poured concrete floor, only studs and beams, no drywall. It was a fairly big open room, and Victoria and the guard were right in the middle. Lawson heard commotion and several footfalls above them. Lawson assumed the men were getting into a defensive position. He knew Claudia was watching, so he knew the police would be there any minute. But he had to make sure Victoria, Cassie, and he managed to survive until then.

Lawson and Cassie were huddled behind the steps, Cassie keeping watch up the stairwell to make sure they weren't surprised from behind. The outside wall, the only finished wall down there, stretched to his left. It wasn't a walk out basement like you see a lot of times in the rolling hills of Kentucky where he grew up. He was surprised there was a basement at all. He'd heard they weren't that common in Los Angeles. This was disheartening because even if Lawson was able to get Victoria away from this guy, they were going to have to go through whatever madness was going on above them to get out of there.

First things first, he had to get Victoria free. The only other thing Lawson noticed before he nearly lost his nose to the bullet in the drywall was a full-length mirror propped against a beam.

"I'm telling you, man, throw your gun out here and walk out with your hands up, or she's dead!"

That gave Lawson an idea.

"Okay," he said. "All right. Just don't hurt her."

As he spoke, he was working fast to remove his black oxford dress shoe.

"I'm just going to throw my gun out. Don't shoot."

He looked at Cassie, put two fingers to his eyes and pointed up the stairs. She nodded, letting him know she would focus on getting their backs.

"Here I go, don't shoot."

Lawson stood up, still hidden behind the stairs, and he could see the mirror directly across from him, maybe ten feet away.

"No sudden moves or she dies."

Lawson took his pistol in his left hand, getting it ready, and held the shoe in his right. He cocked his arm back, prayed that he could channel his inner Nolan Ryan, and heaved it sidearm as hard as he could toward the mirror. As soon as the shoe left his hand, he held the pistol with both hands and raised it to his eye level. He got lucky with the shoe. The wooden heel hit near the middle on the left side of the mirror and broke it just enough to where a few pieces shattered loudly on the floor.

It was the distraction he had hoped for. As the man instinctively turned his head to the crashing mirror, Lawson walked out from behind the stairs and aimed for the man's turned head, squeezing the trigger repeatedly until he saw one hit, making sure to aim plenty high enough so there was no chance Victoria could be shot. He was either going to miss the man's head, and deal with the consequences, or hit his mark and end the threat.

He squeezed them off so fast it was hard to tell which had done the trick, but he thought it was the third bullet of the six he shot that clipped the man's forehead, causing his collapse to the floor. Victoria's scream was almost as loud as the gunshots, and only a second later shots back and forth upstairs between Sloan and Frank's men made it to his ringing ears. It sounded like a small war above him.

"Suspect down," he shouted back to Cassie. It was an old reflex from their days working cases. It sounded weird coming out of his mouth.

"Stairs still clear," she reported. "But I don't think we have much time."

Lawson rushed over to Victoria and started to work on getting her free. Her face was wet with tears, and her normally well-kept hair was a mess.

"Oh, thank God." She was short of breath. "I thought for sure we were dead."

"Give it some time, we aren't out of here yet—" The word *we* registered late in his brain.

"I can't believe you're here. I'm so sorry. Frank made me—"

She stopped abruptly.

"You got my daughter already, right? That's why you're down here. Because you already got my daughter? Please tell me Erin is safe!"

"Frank has your daughter?"

Cassie would hate it, but the word *insurance* immediately came to mind. Of course taking Victoria's daughter, Erin, was the way he made her cooperate. It had been the very same way he tried to make Lawson cooperate. Lawson felt for Victoria. He knew all too well how she felt. And it just took the stakes of the entire situation to a whole other level.

"Oh God, he still has my baby? Please, you have to get her!"

Lawson already knew of course that she was right. He couldn't let something happen to Erin.

Lawson started unraveling the duct tape from her wrists and ankles. The gunshots upstairs continued.

"I'll get her."

The look in Victoria's eyes was enough to light a fire in Lawson. She was on another level of terrified. The worry in a situation like this can be crippling.

He felt he needed to say more. "I promise, I won't let Frank hurt her."

Lawson took the phone from his lapel pocket and stared into it.

"Claudia, how long till the police get here? It's a shoot-out upstairs."

Claudia came into view. "Two minutes, maybe less. Is everyone all right?"

"We're alive. Did you get all of that?"

"All of it."

"Any suggestions?"

"Just stay put. If they are shooting at each other upstairs, don't get in the middle of it."

Claudia was right. It would be easier to wait for the police to clear things above them, then come out. But he couldn't just sit down there with an innocent girl in danger. It wasn't how he was wired.

"Tell Lexi I'll be home soon."

He put the phone back in his pocket and helped Victoria out of her chair.

"Get under the stairs over there and don't move."

Immediately Victoria hurried over and huddled under the stairs, stacking nearby pieces of wood and drywall to give her something to hide behind. Lawson moved over to the stairs.

"Did I hear that correctly? Frank has her daughter?" Cassie said.

"He must have gone back for her when Victoria initially wouldn't help him."

"Damn it. I knew Frank was an asshole. Always was. But how did he slide this low?"

Lawson readied his gun.

"Not sure, but let's help him slide the rest of the way down."

47

THE GUNFIRE WAS STILL ACTIVE AS LAWSON MOVED UP THE stairs. He would hear a few rounds from inside, then a few rounds outside. A couple windows would break, then he would hear some bullets thudding into the shingle siding. It wasn't that he didn't hear Claudia when she suggested they wait in the basement until the cops could clean things up. He just couldn't let Frank hurt Erin; plus, when the police pulled up in front of the house, he didn't want Frank to be able to escape out the back before they cornered him.

Though he was technically not in the FBI, or a detective, Lawson was no average citizen either. And neither was Cassie. This is what they did, it's who they were, even if it had been a while. Last year in Vegas they made a damn good team again, and he hadn't held a gun in ten years. This time he'd only had a year off, and he'd been several times to the gun range to keep his skills sharp. With the two of them in there, it was like the police had experts planted inside. He couldn't just sit around. He knew the cops would be patient because technically there were four hostages and they wouldn't just come shooting their way in.

He crept up to the door at the top of the basement stairs, just to take a look. Cassie moved right in behind him. He knew she would have the same thoughts about their situation as he did. And she definitely didn't want Frank getting away either. He strained his ears and heard sirens. There had been a lot of hearing sirens all day it seemed. If Frank was going to run, he would do it as soon as he heard them too. Frank was an arrogant man, so it was possible he thought he could talk his way out of this one. But two kidnappings was enough to put you away for good. Somewhere along the line, Frank had completely lost his mind over Martin Sloan. So much so that he buried himself in the very crime he'd always fought against. The other thing burning in Lawson's subconscious, though, was that he knew firsthand the judicial system didn't always get it right, so there was a chance Frank actually could go free. Good lawyers find a lot of technicalities to get obvious criminals acquitted. So there was a part of Lawson that hoped Frank would run. It could give Lawson an excuse to make sure he never had a chance to do anything like this ever again.

Lawson motioned for Cassie to stay behind him. She nodded. He poked his head out around the door and looked left. There was a man shooting out the dining room window. He pulled his head back in, then looked to his right where he saw another man shooting out the living room window. There were two more men plus Frank. He could hear other gunshots that sounded like they were coming from upstairs. He and Cassie would be able to take down the two men at the windows without alerting anyone. There was so much shooting that Frank and his two men, wherever they were, would never be able to decipher whose guns were shooting. The problem was the sirens, so Lawson knew they had to hurry.

Lawson turned to Cassie and pointed to himself then the guy on the left, then directed her to take the guy on the right. Cassie nodded and put her hand on Lawson's shoulder as soon as he turned his back to her. He held up his left hand and counted down, three . . . two . . . one.

Lawson moved forward and aimed for the man at the dining room window; he gave a one count so Cassie had time to do the same to the other man in the living room. They both fired simultaneously, and both men took two shots to the body and fell to the ground. The sirens were getting closer. Close enough that the shooting outside stopped. Lawson heard the cars loading up and pulling away from the house.

Lawson heard a female scream and a door slam at the back of the kitchen. He knew it was Frank making a run for it. The coward was not only leaving his men to take the fall, he was taking Erin with him.

"That's Frank. Get downstairs and keep Victoria safe. The police are here so it shouldn't be long."

Cassie was dead serious. "Do not let that son of a bitch get away."

As he moved toward the kitchen, Lawson said, "No chance in hell."

Lawson bolted for the kitchen and threw open the back door just in time to see Frank's foot going over the privacy fence in the glow of the floodlights. Lawson ran around the pool, jumped to reach both hands on top of the fence, and pulled himself all the way over. He started running as soon as he landed, and he watched Frank and another of his men turning left across the street ahead of him into an alley. The house backed up to a commercial street, and when Lawson caught up to the same turn, he entered into the same alley Frank had. Now Lawson saw there were two men with

Frank, and Erin. He was relieved to see that all of them had stayed together; it meant that Cassie and Victoria were out of danger. It wasn't the case for Erin, but Lawson wasn't going to let her out of his sight.

Lawson knew that Frank would do his best to stay off the main road. Up ahead the alley was about to end, opening onto another main road. And just as Lawson began to worry he'd lose them if they made it there, an SUV screeched to a stop right in front of Frank and his men, guns hanging out the window.

Lawson couldn't help but freeze in surprise himself.

One of Frank's men was gunned down, but Frank pulled Erin down and they were able to duck behind a parked car with Frank's other man. The car took a hailstorm of bullets.

Lawson knew, when he figured out Jenny would track Clint's car on Sloan's behalf, that Sloan would only send his men to the house. Sloan wouldn't be involved in the shooting himself. But there was a small possibility he was in the SUV that had clearly waited at the back of the house for anyone who might try to make a run for it. Just as Lawson moved forward again, the gunfire stopped, and under a streetlight Lawson could see Frank holding up his hands.

Sloan's men were about to take him. And they were about to take Erin too. If Lawson lost them, there was a strong possibility something awful could happen to her.

Two gunshots rang out, followed by an awful scream. Sloan's men had just executed Frank's men, and now they were loading Frank and Erin into the truck. Lawson scanned the area; he needed transportation, and he needed it fast. The alley was full of cars, but no one in their right mind would ever leave one of them unlocked with keys in it. Not in Los Angeles. Erin was fighting the man, trying one last time to escape, but he took her by the arms and practically folded her inside the SUV.

Out of the corner of Lawson's eye to the right he saw the headlights of a car coming to a stop for street parking on the main road. Lawson sprinted over to the end of the building, and just as the man was hitting lock on his key fob, Lawson pulled his gun and demanded the keys.

"Sorry, but I've gotta do it."

The man's hands hit the sky as soon as he saw the gun. Lawson took the keys to the Lexus sedan and jumped in. As soon as he hit the push-button start, he wheeled the car right, then another right down the alley. The SUV was just pulling out onto the cross street.

Lawson was relieved. Though he had no idea where they were going, he knew exactly whom they were headed to see. And he knew one way or another, this thing was ending tonight.

48

"Lawson, are you there? Can you hear me?"

It was Claudia. Lawson had been tailing the SUV with Frank and Victoria's daughter inside for almost twenty minutes. They had been heading East and had just turned onto a street called Pico Boulevard. Lawson was completely unfamiliar with the area. There was a Lowe's just up ahead, which seemed really out of place in the middle of Holly-wood, or Beverly Hills, or wherever he was now.

Lawson took the phone out of his pocket. Claudia's face was waiting on the screen. "I hear you. How's Cassie?"

"Victoria was taken out of the house just a minute ago by police. No sign of Cassie. I'd hoped she was with you."

His first instinct was to worry, but as far as he knew, there weren't any more of Frank's men at the house.

"Did Victoria say if she saw Cassie again?"

"She told the police the last time she saw her was with you. That's why I assumed you were with her."

That was not what Lawson expected to hear, but Cassie could handle herself. Especially when she knew trouble could be near.

"Keep looking for her, okay?"

Claudia nodded. "Of course. We'll find her."

"Where am I, Claudia?"

"GPS says you're almost to Mid City. Listen, we have two units about a mile behind you. Just stay with the Yukon until they get to where they are going and then move on. You've gone above and beyond, but let us handle this from here. If that is Sloan's men like we think, there is no telling what you might be walking into, so we will take over."

Lawson didn't respond. He was doing his best not to be an obvious tail. This was not one of his stronger skills, and he knew it. The traffic had thinned considerably over the last several miles too, making it even more difficult to be discreet. He was trying to figure out a way to explain that there was no way he was going to leave the situation now. Not with an innocent girl's life at stake.

"Lawson?"

He couldn't think of a good way to put it, so he ended the FaceTime call. Then he held the button on the side of the phone until the screen prompted him to slide his finger to the right to power off. Then he shut it down. The battery had looked like it was pretty low; if questioned, he would blame the disconnection on that. He knew Claudia would still be able to track the phone, so it wasn't like he was keeping them from doing their job. He just knew this was the only way he could do his.

Now he could focus.

The Yukon turned left past the Lowe's onto a side street. He followed, keeping his distance. Then Lawson just continued to drive right on by when the SUV turned into the parking lot of a small office building. It wasn't Sloan's office, not the one he tracked Hector to earlier, but that didn't mean that it didn't belong to him. He turned into the adjacent strip mall, where a few people were dining at Subway, did a turnabout and killed his headlights as he pulled into a parking space. He could see the front of the office building, but the Yukon had gone around back. He would have to hoof it from there.

He got out of the car and walked to the back of the building behind the Subway. He peered around a dumpster just in time to see a man walk through a back entrance of the office building. The Yukon was parked beside two other vehicles in back. That's the entrance he would have to use too.

As he was making his way toward the building, in the dark, all by himself, he longed to have Cassie beside him. These men weren't the type to ask questions first, shoot later, so he was going to have to go in with an offensive mentality. This wouldn't be a problem for him, not when dealing with such high-level scumbags, but it would be a lot more comforting if he had her there to have his back.

Lawson was at the end of the small strip center, and only a small break in the concrete walkway separated him from the office building's parking lot. He could see that there were a couple lights on at the top of the building. Far right side. This would help give him direction. He also knew the place would be wired with cameras, so being stealthy would almost be no option at all. Once in the building, he was going to have to move fast. He would also need to pick up another weapon along the way. He only had two rounds left in his ten-round magazine.

Halfway across the opening between buildings, two cars pulled into the front of the parking lot: Claudia's team. Once he disconnected from her, she must have given the okay to move in. This meant a task force was close behind. Lawson kicked it into high gear and ran to the back of the building. For a brief moment, he thought about letting them handle it. It wasn't Lexi inside that building; he didn't even know Erin or her mother Victoria really, either. Most would question why he would be concerning himself with strangers in the first place, but Lawson didn't question it. He knew he had to go in after Erin, because if he were in Victoria's shoes, he would pray to have someone like Lawson fighting for his daughter amongst these savages. Someone who didn't have to play by the rules. Someone who was capable of being just as savage as the bad guys were.

He could hear the police in the distance. They weren't far. This thing was going to get ugly fast. He needed to get in there before anyone else did. He hoped he'd be able to protect Erin from the worst of it. He knew Sloan wouldn't go down without a fight. And with Frank in the building, Sloan might try to find a way to put it all on him. Lawson imagined, if worse came to worst, Sloan would put a gun in Frank's hand and make him shoot Erin, just to get rid of the evidence. That thought burned in Lawson's mind, and he moved for the glass door in the back of the building, his gun out and already in position.

49

With a quick peek through the door's window, he almost gave himself away. There was a man walking right for him, but luckily he was loading a magazine into his pistol. Lawson pulled his head back, waited a moment, and when the man came outside through the door, Lawson brought the butt of his Sig Sauer down like a hammer, creating a dense thud when it struck the man in the temple. He fell onto his side, and Lawson scavenged him like a vulture. First his gun, then his phone, then his keys so at least one of the vehicles wasn't going anywhere.

Tires squalled and sirens wailed from the front side of the building. That would draw Sloan's and his men's attention and perhaps make them act irrationally, possibly doing Erin harm. Just as Lawson stepped inside the building, he saw two police cruisers come racing around the corner outside. He hustled down a short hallway that opened to the elevators. Down the hall to his left were the stairs. He sprinted that way and flung open the door. When no one was there to greet him, he began his sprint up the stairs.

Outside he had counted four stories. He was at the top floor in a matter of seconds.

The door to the hallway had no window. If it was the same setup as four floors below, he would find rows of offices lining both sides. The lights he'd seen earlier were on the opposite end of the building. There was no time to wait. He pulled the handle on the door and swung a right hand at the man he knew would be waiting, but he miscalculated how short the stocky man would be. The guard was caught by surprise, but because Lawson had thrown the punch too high, he recovered and wrapped his arms around Lawson's waist, carrying him backward through the door and onto the landing in the stairwell. The trip ended in Lawson being slammed onto his back, the stout bulldog of a man heavy on top of him.

Lawson didn't know much offensive Brazilian jiujitsu, but he had been taught a few defensive moves in prison in exchange for some boxing lessons. He'd drilled them enough that instinct kicked in, and he wrapped his right leg around the outside of the man's leg, trapping it with his foot on the inside of the man's knee. When the man raised up to punch him, Lawson trapped the man's left arm, then bucked his hips, pushed forward with his left arm, and swept the man onto his back, Lawson now in top position. The man punched Lawson in the face, but he had no leverage for power from his back. Lawson dropped an anvil of an elbow down on his forehead, and the man's body went limp.

Lawson disengaged immediately and moved back into the hallway, jumping through the open door of the first office so the men at the end of the hallway wouldn't see him. The sound of their voices carried down the hallway. Lawson could hear every word.

"I told you we should never have picked him up. And then you brought them straight to me!"

Lawson then heard a gunshot. The man shouting sounded like Sloan, but it wasn't as if Lawson had known Sloan long enough to be certain.

"Listen, I can get us out of this. I speak their language. I have contacts."

The second man he heard was having a hard time talking. It was Frank and his broken jaw.

"Your contacts have brought me nothing but trouble. I gave you a million dollars to get this movie for me."

Sloan.

Sloan continued. "And I let you use my men. I told you that if it didn't work, or if this brought me trouble, I was going to kill you. Not let you off easy like I did last time. Now here we are. You've dug your own grave."

"If you kill me, you definitely don't have a way out of this. You see the lights, the building is surrounded. I'm the only shot you have left."

"You're the reason I'm trapped here!" Sloan shouted.

Lawson heard a thud, then what sounded like a body dropping to the floor. Then a man groaning. Tough day for Frank Shaw.

"What do you want me to do, Mr. Sloan?" a new voice asked.

"Kill the girl. Make it look like Frank did it, then killed himself," Sloan said.

"No, I can get you out of this!" Frank slurred.

He heard Victoria's daughter begin to sob from a nearby room.

Something was about to happen either way, and Lawson needed to be ready. The gun he took from the guard downstairs was a Glock. It had a round chambered and was ready to shoot. He crouched and put his back to the open door, ready to strike if he had to.

"Do it," Sloan said. "But do it downstairs. I'll call the police right now and tell them there is a madman in the lobby. Marcos, you erase the cameras. We'll play it like he cut them or wiped them. Just go do it, you know what to do. José, when you're finished in the lobby, get right back up here and let's lock off this floor like we were trying to keep him out. It isn't much, but it's all we've got. The DA will take care of us. She owes me. Now go get it done, they will be beating down the door any second."

"No! Wait! I can fix this!" Frank shouted.

Then the girl screamed. Lawson secured both hands on his gun. Ready.

"Yes, police? This is Martin Sloan. There is a madman, Frank Shaw, in my office lobby. There are police here already, but I didn't know what to do, so I called you. I think he has a girl and is going to kill her. It's the last thing we saw before our camera system went out. He must have someone else working with him. I think he's trying to frame me. Please help us. I'm afraid I'm next!"

Lawson wished he could have caught that performance on camera, but it wasn't meant to be. He could hear movement and muffled groans and cries getting closer to him. He was hoping they would use the stairs to take Frank and Erin down to the lobby, but he heard the elevator ding. He took a deep breath. It was time to move.

Lawson swung out into the middle of the hallway with his gun extended. When he saw a large man holding Frank, he squeezed the trigger three times, and the man dropped out of sight. Frank lunged forward into the elevator, and the man holding Erin raised his gun. It was too risky to try to adjust aim and shoot only him, so he dove to his left into a nearby office just as the man got a shot off.

Erin was screaming at the top of her lungs, and the men were shouting at each other trying to figure out what to do next. The air was filled with chaos.

"Stop," a man shouted. Probably Sloan. "Mack, get her downstairs and finish what I told José to do. You two, get whoever the hell that is who made it up here!"

Lawson couldn't let them take her downstairs. She was dead if they did. He rolled over on his stomach, pushed his torso out around the door, and fired low. If he happened to hit Erin, it's unlikely it would be fatal. He got several shots off before the return fire came. If nothing else, even if Lawson didn't make it out of there alive, he knew Sloan was done. The story he set up for Frank to take the fall wouldn't hold up. The police outside would see and hear the shots being fired on the top floor, which would nullify Sloan's made-up story of holing up in fear of what was happening downstairs with Frank acting crazy in the lobby.

Lawson knew he'd hit the man trying to get Erin on the elevator, but he couldn't tell if it was enough to stop him. The man he shot who was holding Frank had fallen forward, keeping the elevator door from closing. The gunshots in the hallway were getting closer. The men were moving toward him.

"Get her out of here, and get him!" Sloan shouted.

Lawson stood and went high out of the doorway this time, hoping the men would still be aiming low. They were, but he only got one shot off before the Glock locked back on him, the magazine empty. It must not have been a fully loaded. He missed with the one shot he took, and both men saw that his gun was empty. Just before Lawson ducked back inside the office, he saw one man shove Erin onto the elevator, and he saw Sloan following behind his men down the hallway, about ten feet back.

Lawson discarded the Glock and pulled his Sig from his belt line. He knew he had two shots left, and he knew it would surprise the men that he had any at all. He poked back out into the hallway, just his arm and the right side of his face visible to them. The men were within ten feet of him. He squeezed once aiming to the right and once to the left, taking both men down. The second shot was more right than he wanted, only hitting the man in the arm. He would be back. Sloan ducked, prepared for more, but he recognized that the Sig was now empty as well. He also got his first glance at Lawson, and the look of surprise on his face was priceless.

Sloan returned fire, and once again Lawson bounded back inside the office. But this time he was trapped. He heard the elevator ding; Erin was on her way downstairs. Sloan was on his way to take care of Lawson. Lawson searched the small office for anything he could use, but all that was there were office supplies. He picked up the chair and held it out in front of him. He would need a miracle to make it out of there. And he was going to need one fast.

50

In a last-ditch effort to buy some time, Lawson lowered the chair to the floor and picked up his empty Sig Sauer.

"You should have never gotten involved, Raines. You're like a leech, you have no idea when to let go."

Lawson made a production out of ejecting the magazine, then shoving it back in, and pulling back the slide. For a moment at least, it made Sloan hesitate. It was better than nothing.

"You walk inside this office, I'll shoot you."

"I call bullshit."

Lawson once again grabbed the chair and held it out in front of him. Sloan turned the corner ready to shoot, but when he saw the chair, he stopped and a smile grew across his face. Lawson was all out of tricks. He'd put it all on the line, and he wasn't even able to save Victoria's daughter. Of course he thought of Lexi. How devastated she would be. But there was nothing he could do about it. She was like her mother. Tough as nails. She would get through it. Eventually.

Sloan stood proud in the doorway and opened his mouth. Lawson was sure some smart-ass remark was coming, but he never heard it. Instead, there was a loud *bang bang*, and part of Sloan's beard went missing as a mist of blood carried it away. Lawson moved to the inside wall of the office, still holding the chair.

Bang! Bang! Bang!

Three more shots. Whoever had come in and saved him from Sloan must have seen the man Lawson shot in the arm still moving and took him out.

There was a moment of silence. The gunshots still ringing in his ears.

"Lawson?"

Cassie. Cassie?

How the hell was she there? The police had beat her there. How did—

He saw her gun swing into the office.

"It's me, don't shoot." He held the chair in front of his chest.

The look on her face when she saw him standing there with the chair was at first relief that he was alive. But it quickly turned into a mocking smirk. Lawson knew there was no time for games.

"Did you pass Frank? Did you see Victoria's daughter?"

Cassie's face went serious. "I didn't see anyone. I went right up the stairs. I had to. I was afraid the police would shoot me."

"You can explain later. We have to get down there!"

Lawson rushed past Cassie, turned right, stepping over Sloan, and ran for the stairwell. He nearly jumped every flight on the way down. He made it to the bottom and rushed for the door.

"Wait! Lawson!" Cassie shouted, she was more than a flight of stairs behind him. "My gun!"

Lawson slid to a stop on the slick tile floor. He took a step back, and when Cassie rounded the stairs, she tossed him down her gun. He caught it, stepped right, swung open the door, and walked forward with gun raised.

"I swear to God I'll shoot her! Move back!"

Sloan's man was holding a gun to Erin's head. The two of them were facing the back door. Lawson knew he was staring at a few guns from the officers who'd watched Cassie run in while they were awaiting orders.

"Put them down! I'm going to shoot!" Sloan's man threatened again.

The man was so focused on the police at the door that he didn't even see Lawson coming from the stairwell. Lawson stepped forward to make sure the shot was clean. Then he took it. Two taps on the trigger and the man was no longer holding Erin hostage. The police rushed in and Lawson immediately dropped the gun and held up his hands. He let out a huge sigh of relief. Several officers moved in fast, but to Lawson things were moving in slow motion. There was a real moment upstairs that he thought he would never get to see Lexi again. It shook him to his core. He knew that everything with the police would get sorted out, so all he could think about was holding her and letting her know once again that he would never leave her.

All of the officers pointed their guns at Lawson and Cassie, had them get on their knees while they cuffed them. Lawson didn't fight it. Neither did Cassie. He looked over and was able to catch her eye. She had saved his life, but more importantly to him, she had kept Lexi's father alive. The thought of her spending the rest of her life without either one of her parents was haunting. Cassie and Lawson usually had a very brother-sister relationship, one never letting the other go without giving them a hard time. But this moment was different. Lawson nodded to her and mouthed the words, "Thank you." She just sent back a loving smile.

Sloan had gotten what he deserved, and Lawson knew that Frank would too. Though it wasn't smooth, Lawson and Cassie had managed to get everyone out of trouble without losing someone they loved. The bruises would all heal, and though it would take much longer for some of the mental wounds, those would eventually heal too.

Happy endings don't come often when you get caught up with the kind of people in that building, but this time was the exception.

The police walked Lawson and Cassie out of the building and put them both in separate cars. The back of a police car was a rare place for a man to feel at peace, but after the last couple days, that is exactly what Lawson felt. And it was good.

51

Lawson took another sip of his bourbon. He was nothing if not predictable. He was sipping Angel's Envy, neat. He liked Angel's Envy because it was finished in port wine barrels, giving it a unique flavor without interfering with the essence of the spirit. Everyone else at the patio table was enjoying a margarita, even Lexi—hers was a virgin margarita of course. After all, they were at a Mexican restaurant. He was surprised they had any bourbon on the shelf at all.

The place was called Baja Sharkeez. The name was almost as cheesy as the swordfish they had hanging out of the outside wall. But they were only a stone's throw from the ocean, so one couldn't really fault them for playing to the crowd. It was a sunny day. No surprise there either. Most days were sunny in Southern California. Lawson, Cassie, and Lexi were still getting used to their new home in

Newport Beach. It was their first time at this restaurant. It was good, but what made it great was the company.

Lexi wanted to order her margarita, even though it had no alcohol, because she wanted to share in the toast. It was a special day. Taylor Lockhart had driven down from Hollywood to see them, and the four of them toasted to her health. She had made a full recovery.

After the toast Lawson had explained to Taylor everything that happened. They had been on the phone with each other a lot over the last six months, but they never talked about how everything went down the day she was shot. Their conversations had been more geared at getting to know each other. To Lawson's surprise, the famous actress had been just as interested in getting to know him as he was her. She often expressed her surprise at how she couldn't believe he would ever want to talk to her, seeing as how they met on such shaky ground.

On the sunny patio, he and Cassie explained how they rescued Victoria from Frank, and of course how she was actually innocent in the entire ordeal. They both continued to walk her through what happened with Sloan, then Victoria's daughter, skipping the gory details of course. Taylor made the joke that maybe she would make the whole thing into a movie. Cassie's only request was that she get to play herself. Of course that brought a roll of the eyes and a laugh from Lawson.

Lawson then explained that Frank had since been sentenced to thirty years in prison. The only reason he didn't get life was because he ratted on a few of the higher-ups in Sloan's operation. Lawson knew from his own time in prison that all that would do was get him killed in jail, so Frank was getting the death penalty either way. Taylor was relieved to hear that everyone involved got what was coming to them.

Taylor looked over at Lawson and gave him a smile. He knew what she meant. Taylor didn't only drive down to say hello; she also came down to deliver some special news to Lexi.

Taylor raised her margarita. "Now a toast to you, Lexi."

Lexi smiled. "Me? Why?"

"Because I spoke with Victoria Marshall yesterday, and you are going to be starring in the movie we're making. You're going to play my sister." Taylor's grin was ear to ear.

Lexi jumped up from her chair. "Shut. Up. Are you serious?" She jumped up and down. "Dad, did you know about this?"

Lawson smiled. "Maybe."

Taylor gave him a wink. She really needed to stop doing that.

Taylor said to the others at the table, "You mind if I steal the big guy for a few minutes?"

Cassie said, "You kidding? Take him for good. He's been grumpy 'cause it's been so sunny every day."

"Ha-ha." Lawson finished his bourbon and followed Taylor. She had to stop a few times on her way out of the restaurant to sign some autographs, but eventually they made it.

They walked the sidewalk toward the beach. The blue water stretched out infinitely just a block away from them now.

"Is it always that way? Everywhere you go?" Lawson said, referring to the attention she was getting.

"It is. I know it seems strange to someone like you, but you do eventually get used to it. Like anything else in life."

She couldn't be more right about that. Sometimes you

got so used to things that after it stopped, even though it was bad, you missed it. Lawson remembered the first night he spent outside of prison. He ended up sleeping in the closet because the room he was in felt too big after being used to an eight-by-eight cell.

"Is Lexi a lot like her mother?" Taylor said.

The question threw him off completely. She smiled at his silence. "You don't have to answer. I just want you to know that you can talk about her if you want to. I know she was special to you."

That helped Lawson relax. So did the genuine look in her beautiful green eyes. "She was special. And so is Lexi because, yes, they are so much alike. Even the trying side of her personality."

"That's sweet. Lexi is great. We talk all the time. I'm so excited to work with her."

"At least one good thing came out of this whole situation."

"Just one?"

The smile on Taylor's face struck like a lightning bolt.

Lawson gave her a small grin, then looked away. Taylor hooked her arm around his. The two of them walked up the ramp onto the pier.

By the grace of God, Taylor changed the subject. "So, how is the private investigation business coming along?"

After all that happened, Lawson wanted out of LA. Thankfully, Lexi was in agreement. When Lawson told Cassie he wanted to move the PI firm to Orange County, she was excited about it. He made good money on the sale of the house in the hills, and they were able to get a nice little place in Newport. Cassie and Lawson were just about ready to start taking cases. His paperwork had finally gone through, and his record was cleared so they could proceed.

"Going to start taking cases next week. So, we'll see."

"That's exciting!"

They walked to the edge of the pier just in front of the water, but neither of them enjoyed the view. They were facing each other.

"Any movies coming up?" Lawson said.

"Just wrapped on one, should be out in a few months. It was fun, so I'm excited. It felt good to get back to work." She glanced at the water, then looked back up at him. "I'm happy you all are settling in here, but I'm not going to lie, I'd hoped you would be staying in LA."

"Why? Were you going to try to hire me to be your bodyguard?"

She smiled. "Was that a joke? Cassie would be proud. And no. I was hoping to get to see Lexi more. And you too, I guess." She slapped him on the arm.

"Well, good thing you and Lexi are working together then. We'll be up your way a lot, I assume."

"Good." Taylor leaned in a little. "I know I've told you this before, but thank you."

"I didn't do anything, you're the one who saved Lexi's life."

"Yeah, after I put her in that position. And you. It takes a special person to forgive that, and I just want you to know how sorry I am. Truly. If there is anything I can do for you or Lexi. Just tell me and it's done."

"I'm just glad you were able to make a full recovery. I would have hated for your fans not to get any more of you on the big screen."

"Two jokes," Taylor smiled. "Maybe Newport Beach *is* just what you needed."

"Maybe it's just getting to see you."

Lawson thought two things. The first was that all he

wanted to do was kiss her. Immediately following that he thought of Lauren. As he stared at the beautiful woman in front of him, he wondered if thoughts of his wife would ever go away. Then he decided right there, as the breeze flirted with Taylor's hair, that maybe it just didn't matter. Maybe her memory would always be there, just like the urge to keep going after criminals. He had decided that he and Cassie were going to keep doing that, so maybe he should move forward in other ways too.

He felt a sense of calm wash over him. Maybe it was the ocean breeze, maybe it was Lauren telling him it was okay. Either way, he wrapped his right arm around Taylor's waist and pulled her close, tucked the blowing strands of hair behind her ear, and then he kissed her.

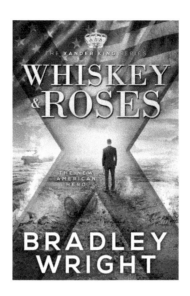

The Xander King Series
by
Bradley Wright

———————————————

WHISKEY & ROSES: Imagine James Bond meets
Mitch Rapp.

———————————————

The world knows him as a handsome, charismatic, and successful young businessman.
The CIA knows Xander as the US military's most legendary soldier, turned vigilante
assassin, who sharpens his skills in the shadows until he can exact revenge on the
monster who murdered his family. They have watched his double life go on long enough,
and now the government wants their weapon back.

SAMPLE: WHISKEY & ROSES

Chapter 1: The Legend of Xander King

"Some people don't deserve to live. One man is *exceptional* at making sure they don't," Director William Manning announced as he addressed the roomful of the CIA's finest. "The decision that lies before us is whether we make this man an ally or an enemy. And I'm afraid we can't afford the latter."

Just before Director Manning blasted into the room and uttered those chilling words, Sarah Gilbright sat alone trying desperately to keep from nervous-sweating through her blouse. She knew it wasn't all that unusual for the director of the CIA to call a top secret meeting of the seven highest-ranking officials in the agency. However, it was highly unusual for the eighth person involved in that meeting to be a comparatively low-ranked special agent like herself. Sarah knew there could only be one reason she had been invited to a meeting so far above her clearance level: they had decided to do something about Xander King.

Sarah fidgeted in her seat and shuffled through her prepared portfolios. She felt as if she were back in college. The plain white walls of the square room, the cheap collapsible faux-wood tables, and the metal folding chairs were almost enough to give her that familiar college hungover feeling.

That was when the heavy wooden door flung open, clanging against the painted cinder block wall with a loud crash, and Director Manning buzzed into the room. Though he didn't look anything like the TV character, his clumsy, hurried entry reminded Sarah of Kramer from *Seinfeld*. No, Director Manning couldn't have looked less like Cosmo Kramer. Manning's short, stout frame and his cloud-white hair made certain of that.

Director Manning finished his morbid opening remarks about Xander.

"Either way, enemy or ally, we've got to do something. Let's get through this as quickly as possible." His tone was more of a growl as he dropped his black leather briefcase onto the table. The button on his light-gray suit jacket seemed to be holding on by a mere thread.

Sarah imagined the button on his pants probably shared a similar stretch.

"All of you know each other, with the exception of Special Agent Sarah Gilbright here." Manning pointed to Sarah.

The palms of Sarah's hands filled with sweat at the sound of her name among all those important people. This was a big damn deal. She played it off as best she could, tucking her long blonde hair back behind her ear.

"Sarah, if you could please hand everyone a file and come up front with me."

She did as Manning asked and began passing around Xander's file. She worried that her slim-fitting black skirt and tight royal-blue silk blouse might be inappropriate. She had decided to button one more button on her blouse in the bathroom just moments ago. It was hard for her to contain her mother's gift of large breasts, but she wanted the men in this meeting to take her seriously. The women too. She wanted them all to listen because of her merit, not because of her curves and slender waist, as had all too often been the case since she joined the agency.

Director Manning continued. "Six months ago I gave Sarah an assignment to keep an eye on a man named Alexander King. I'm sure that all of you have heard the name at one time or another due to the legend of his time in our military, but his service to our country has taken on a much different role these days. Sarah is going to fill us in, and then we are going to figure out just what in the hell we are going to do about him. Sarah?"

Sarah handed off her last file and took the podium in front of the deputy and executive directors, the head of admin, the head of espionage, and the head of public affairs for the Central *freaking* Intelligence Agency of the United States of *freaking* America.

Wow.

Her voice was shaky. "Good afternoon, everyone. It's an honor to—"

"Sarah . . . all due respect, spare us," Director Manning broke in. "We have other things to worry about so please keep this short."

"Yes, sir, Mr. Manning. Alexander King." She did as she was told and got right to it, swallowing the growing nerves and digging in. "All of you are familiar with the name?"

The roomful of stuffy higher-ups all nodded in unison.

Sarah continued. "The Alexander—Xander—King of today is known to the world as the billionaire son of Martin King, of King Oil. After his parents were brutally murdered in front of him, Xander decided not to follow in his father's footsteps. Instead, he sold King Oil and, as you well know by his *legend*, as Director Manning put it, he joined the navy. If you will, please open to the first page of the portfolio."

"And he's handsome," Mary Hartsfield, Director of Espionage, remarked when she opened the folder and saw a picture of Xander holding a bottle of bourbon.

"Mary, please. Could you wait till you get the portfolio home before you start drooling over it?" Director Manning scolded.

The group laughed at Mary's outburst, and Sarah, for the first time since entering the room, let the tension fall from her shoulders. She looked again, for probably the thousandth time, at the blue eyes staring at her in that picture and wholeheartedly agreed with Mary.

"I'm with you, Mary, he is quite handsome."

Director Manning rolled his eyes and motioned for Sarah to move on.

"That bottle in his hand is from his own bourbon company—King's Ransom—that he launched recently, and as some of you may or may not have heard, he has a horse by the same name running in the Kentucky Derby this coming Saturday. Those are the things he's known for to the outside world. However, the reason we are here today is because of what the public doesn't know, what Xander King doesn't know we know, and the reason Director Manning has had me monitoring Xander for the last six months. Xander King is an *assassin*."

The air in the room changed, shifting with the dark word Sarah uttered, surprising them all.

"Now, before you get the wrong idea about Xander, let me brief you on exactly what I mean."

Sarah turned the page, and the picture this time was of a beautiful dark-haired woman whose stern demeanor suggested she had seen her share of cruelty in the world.

"If you'll turn the page, you'll find Samantha Harrison, or Sam, as Xander calls her. Sam had quite the reputation at

MI6 in the UK for being what used to be an unparalleled agent. We aren't exactly sure how she and Xander initially connected, but together they have formed quite a team. Sam is in charge of finding and coordinating the targets, and Xander goes about eliminating them. She is the coach, and he is the talent, if you will."

"Targets, Ms. Gilbright?" Mary asked.

"Yes, targets. The scum of the earth. The most evil and vile human beings on the planet."

Deputy Director Richards, a silver-haired, tall, and lanky man, spoke up. "And he just kills them? No justice system? Vigilante style, he's the judge and jury? I see now why we are here. This is a problem."

Sarah felt the mood in the room shift again, and she wanted to make sure she gave the rest of the facts in such a manner to show that what Xander was doing, though not legal, was just about the most noble and honorable thing a man with his particular set of skills could do. She had been watching him for months. All of the charity events he had hosted, all of the people he had saved by taking out these miserable targets. She didn't want this audience to get the wrong impression of him.

"Well, I understand your skepticism, Mr. Richards, but I assure you this isn't some amateur running around killing random people he thinks *might* be doing bad things. Sam painstakingly researches each and every target, and if you will turn the page, I'll introduce you to some of these evil people."

They all turned the page. There was a picture of a forty-something man with an emptiness to his stare.

"The first man you see was killed by Xander three months ago. Jerrold Connors. Jerrold was—"

"Hey, I remember this guy," Deputy Director Richards

interjected. "We were building a case against him when he was suddenly killed. Horrible, the things he was doing. Didn't we find the bodies of more than seven male teenagers out in his shed?"

"Yes, that's the guy."

"Awful. I remember, they were all drugged and tortured over a span of months, if I'm not mistaken."

"You are not mistaken. I'm glad you remember, Mr. Richards."

Director Manning cleared his throat. "Move along, Sarah."

"Right. The second target on the list, Mitch Boyle, was eliminated last month—"

"Oh God." Mary winced. "I remember him. He was the guy—the nurse—who was going around stealing newborn babies from the hospital nursery, then taking them home, killing them, and stuffing them like dolls."

"Good God," the Head of Public Affairs blurted.

Sarah could already feel that they were coming to understand Xander like she did. She had been skeptical at first too. She had thought there was no way this could be right, a man exacting vigilante justice; then she spent time getting to know him from afar. "I know. It's terrible. Mitch Boyle was a monster."

Director Manning cut in again. "Look, I think we get the point. The other six *monsters* on this page all deserve what Xander gave them, but that isn't what we need to focus on. Get to that please, Sarah."

Director Manning paused, then held up his hand. "You know what, actually . . . let me just take it from here." He stood up and shuffled Sarah to the side.

"But Director Manning—"

"Thank you, Sarah," he said, dismissing her. Sarah took

a seat by the podium. She wanted to give them a better sense of things. She wasn't sure they understood Xander yet. She didn't want them to stop the good things he was doing to right the wrongs the judicial system couldn't manage to take care of. There was nothing more she could do now, though; it was Manning's show. She had assumed he was thinking the same way she was, but he had called this meeting for a reason.

Manning took the podium. "Now, the way I see it, we have three options here. One, we could shut Xander down and bring him up on charges . . ."

Sarah's stomach dropped.

"Two, we could let Mr. King continue to go about this, what I think we all would agree is noble work and just continue to monitor him—"

"What, and just let him play like he's Batman?" Richards interjected.

"Deputy Richards, I understand that concern, and that's why I think my third option is the only way to go. We will just have to be careful how we go about it."

"Which is?" Richards said.

"Which is, we get him to go to work for us."

Sarah tried to hold her tongue, but she couldn't. "Xander will never work for the government, Director Manning. You're wasting your time on that notion."

"Now hold on, Sarah. I just told you we would have to be careful how we went about it."

"I don't understand, why wouldn't we just *make* him work for us?" Mary asked. "We do have evidence that he has killed these people."

Again Sarah couldn't help herself. "He just simply won't do it—"

Director Manning gave Sarah an "I'm warning you"

glare and continued to explain. "What Ms. Gilbright is so passionately stating is that Xander doesn't agree with how the United States government goes about some of its business. He made this very clear when he abruptly left our Special Ops team. He loves his country, but not its governing body."

"Xander was Special Ops?" Mary said.

"Xander King was everything you could be in our military. After his parents died, his sole mission was revenge and he wanted to be trained by the best. He joined the navy, quickly becoming a Navy SEAL; then in record time he was running Special Ops missions. I'm not sure what you have or have not heard, but he just might be the best damn soldier this military has *ever* known."

"So what happened?" Mary asked.

"Well, like a lot of our soldiers, he didn't agree with the missions he was sent on and frankly, as you all know, some of the innocent casualties that go along with keeping this country safe. So he'd had enough. To be honest with you, I'm not so sure this wasn't his plan all along."

"What do you mean?" Richards asked.

"I mean, I think he used our military."

"Used us?"

"Don't get me wrong, he laid his life on the line every single day for his country, but yes, I think ultimately he used us. I think the only thing Xander ever wanted was to find the people responsible for the murder of his parents."

"And he used the military to train him to do so," Mary Hartsfield said as she let that sink in.

"That's right. But we *need* a man like this. A man with his skills. Sometimes a surgical strike works far better than bringing in the entire army. Saves a lot of lives too. As you know, things are getting downright scary on the terrorist front and we could use a silent weapon like King."

Mary stood up. "So what then? What are we supposed to do?"

"The only thing we can do. Use our resources to find what he wants before he finds it. Then we give it to him . . . at a price."

"We find out who killed his parents and force him to do jobs for us for the information." Richards recognized the direction Manning was suggesting.

"It's the only way it will work." Manning hiked up his pants. "He will go to prison before he stops hunting their killer, and we can't have that happen. We can't lose him. He wouldn't go to prison anyway; he has too many resources. If he really wanted to, he could just disappear. That is why we have to take our time and get this right, and that is why Sarah is going to head up a team that will monitor Xander and Sam while finding the information that King desires."

Sarah couldn't contain the joy she found in that news, and a smile grew across her face.

"When we find that information—who killed Xander's family—we will approach him. But . . ."

Manning paused and looked over to Sarah.

"We have to be careful. If something goes wrong, if Xander were to kill the wrong person and it gets out that we knew what he was doing and we let it happen, we kiss all of our jobs good-bye."

Richards stood and gathered his things. "If you don't mind me asking, sir, why take the risk? You ask me, we should shut him down and find a soldier who *wants* to work for us. There has to be a hundred guys in our great military who can do the jobs we need done, the jobs he can do—"

"I assure you there is not."

Director Manning's expression was dead serious.

"There isn't one. Not in our military, or any other military. That's the only reason I would even call this meeting. If it was someone besides King doing this, we *would* just shut it down. But this soldier is special. We just have to make him an offer he can't refuse, and we need to do it fast. As far as I'm concerned, this is of the highest priority. The United States needs Xander King."

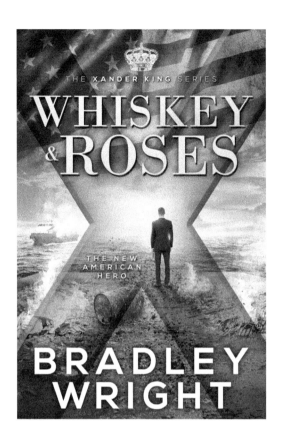

GET YOUR COPY TODAY
Only at Amazon.com
Free on Kindle Unlimited

ACKNOWLEDGMENTS

First and foremost, I want to thank you, the reader. I love what I do, and no matter how many people help me along the way, none of it would be possible if you weren't turning the pages.

To my family and friends. Every creative person is neurotic as hell about their creations, and I just want to thank you for always helping to keep my head on straight. And for indulging all of my ridiculous ideas.

To my editor, Deb Hall. Thank you for continuing to turn my poorly constructed sentences into a readable story. You are great at what you do, and my work is better for it.

To my advanced reader team. You are my megaphone in helping spread the word about each new novel I release. You all have become friends, and I thank you for catching those last few sneaky typos, and always letting me know when something isn't good enough. Lawson Raines appreciates you, and so do I.

ABOUT THE AUTHOR

Bradley Wright is the bestselling author of seven novels. He lives with his family in Lexington, Kentucky. He has always been a fan of great stories, whether it be a song, a movie, a novel, or a binge-worthy television series. Bradley loves interacting with readers on Facebook, Twitter, and via email.

Join the online family:
www.bradleywrightauthor.com
info@bradleywrightauthor.com